# MY INDIA, LONGING AND BELONGING

**Ruskin Bond** is known for his signature simplistic and witty writing style. He is the author of several bestselling short stories, novellas, collections, essays and children's books; and has contributed a number of poems and articles to various magazines and anthologies. At the age of twenty-three, he won the prestigious John Llewellyn Rhys Prize for his first novel, *The Room on the Roof*. He was also the recipient of the Padma Shri in 1999, Lifetime Achievement Award by the Delhi Government in 2012 and the Padma Bhushan in 2014.

Born in 1934, Ruskin Bond grew up in Jamnagar, Shimla, New Delhi and Dehradun. Apart from three years in the UK, he has spent all his life in India, and now lives in Landour, Mussoorie, with his adopted family.

# RUSKIN BOND

**MY INDIA, LONGING AND BELONGING**

Published by
Rupa Publications India Pvt. Ltd 2023
7/16, Ansari Road, Daryaganj
New Delhi 110002

*Sales centres:*
Prayagraj Bengaluru Chennai
Hyderabad Jaipur Kathmandu
Kolkata Mumbai

Copyright © Ruskin Bond 2023

This is a work of fiction. Names, characters, places and incidents are either the product of the author's imagination or are used fictitiously and any resemblance to any actual person, living or dead, events or locales is entirely coincidental.

All rights reserved.
No part of this publication may be reproduced, transmitted, or stored in a retrieval system, in any form or by any means, electronic, mechanical, photocopying, recording or otherwise, without the prior permission of the publisher.

P-ISBN: 978-93-5702-456-3
E-ISBN: 978-93-5702-489-1

First impression 2023

10 9 8 7 6 5 4 3 2 1

Moral right of the author has been asserted.

This book is sold subject to the condition that it shall not, by way of trade or otherwise, be lent, resold, hired out, or otherwise circulated, without the publisher's prior consent, in any form of binding or cover other than that in which it is published.

# Contents

*Introduction* ix

## PEOPLE OF INDIA
The Lady of Sardhana 3
Bhabiji's House 11
Rani of the Doon 24
Untouchable 28
The Bar that Time Forgot 33
The Homeless 46
The Woman on Platform No. 8 56
The Kitemaker 62
The Lafunga 67
Rum and Curry 81
A Case for Inspector Lal 89
Strychnine in the Cognac 97
Sher Singh and the Hot-water Bottle 107
An English Jester at the Mughal Court 112
Children of India 115

## PLACES OF INDIA

| | |
|---|---:|
| Rainy Day in June | 123 |
| Landour Bazaar | 125 |
| Voting at Fosterganj | 133 |
| Shahjahanpur | 142 |
| The Dehra I Know | 145 |
| Desert Rhapsody | 150 |
| Belting around Mumbai | 155 |
| Pistols at Twenty Paces: A Duel at Poona | 158 |
| The Last Time I Saw Delhi | 161 |
| Street of the Red Well | 166 |
| Mathura's Hallowed Haunts | 170 |
| Jaipur | 173 |
| Footloose in Agra | 177 |
| Rishikesh | 186 |

## ON THE ROAD IN INDIA

| | |
|---|---:|
| The India I Carried with Me | 195 |
| The Road to Badrinath | 206 |
| The Grand Trunk Road | 214 |
| On the Road to Delhi | 220 |
| The Great Indian Rope Trick | 227 |
| The Last Days of the Tonga | 230 |
| The Open Road | 233 |
| A Wayside Tea Shop | 236 |

## RIVERS OF INDIA

| | |
|---|---:|
| A Song of Many Rivers | 243 |
| Of Rivers and Pilgrims | 260 |
| Flowers on the Ganga | 265 |
| Sita and the River | 271 |

## TREES OF INDIA

| | |
|---|---:|
| My Trees in Himalayas | 301 |
| Gentle Shade by Day | 304 |
| Music in the Trees | 306 |
| The Cherry Tree | 310 |
| Death of the Trees | 316 |

# Introduction

India means different things to each of us. It may be a refuge one longs for or simply just a home—the place one belongs to. Although our experiences of this ancient land differ vastly, some of its unique charms transcend its many differences. We have all experienced the camaraderie of a train bogey full of people who do not speak each other's languages but who are united by their journey; the gaiety of celebrating a festival with your mohalla; the kindness of a stranger helping you find your way in a new town; the delight of eating particularly scrumptious, piping hot roti and dal at a quaint roadside dhaba; the sweltering dreariness of India's relentless summers, made bearable by its deliciously juicy mangoes; or the spectacular relief of its first monsoon shower.

Over the years, so much of my writing has been inspired by these fascinating aspects of the country I call home. Travelling across India, I have met some of the most unusual people; come across the most majestic natural beauty; and visited some of the most stunning and bizarre places. This collection is homage to those experiences.

In *My India, Longing and Belonging*, I have brought together some of my favourite things about India: its diverse but consistently interesting people, bustling cities, quaint towns and, above all, awe-inspiring natural bounty. The book is divided into five, rather self-explanatory, sections: 'People of India', 'Places of India', 'On the Road in India', 'Rivers of India' and 'Trees of India'. Through a selection of stories and essays, each section explores an aspect of the country I find particularly endearing.

I hope that this omnibus of stories resonates with your unique experience of our beloved nation. Come, celebrate this land of paradoxes we call home with me!

Ruskin Bond

PEOPLE OF INDIA

# The Lady of Sardhana

The bus that took us to Sardhana was prehistoric. I do believe it was kept from falling apart by a liberal use of sellotape. The noise and rattle made by its nuts and bolts and shaky chassis reminded me of Kipling's story 'The Ship That Found Herself'. Every part seemed alive and complaining. The bus conductor found the crank handle under somebody's seat, and, panting and sweating in the sun, kept turning it until, reluctantly, the engine spluttered to life. The bus moved off of its own volition, and the conductor just had time to get on and collect our tickets. Most of the passengers were rural folk, descendants of those Jats and Rohillas who made this fertile Doab region (the Doab is the area between the Ganges and the Jamuna) one of the richest granaries of India, only to have it plundered by marauding Marathas, Sikhs and Afghans. They smoked bidis or chewed paan, shooting the coloured spittle out of the open windows; and, seeing my watch, asked me the time every few minutes.

The Sardhana bus stop, when we got to it, was the usual unexciting swamp of churned-up mud, with a tea stall, and several stray dogs and pigs nosing about in a garbage heap. We hailed a cycle rickshaw and told the man to take us to the church.

The Sardhana church was built at the expense of

Begum Samru by an Italian architect. Upon her husband's death, she had become a devout Catholic, and earned from the Pope the title of 'Joanna Nobilis'. The Emperor at Delhi, grateful to her for services rendered in the battlefield, gave her another title: Zeb-un-Nissa, the 'Ornament of Her Sex'. Her life, until she reached old age, was a succession of love affairs, intrigue and petty warfare. It was never a dull life. She had certain admirable qualities which made her attractive to men. As a young girl, she was beautiful; in middle age, rather plump. She was a courageous woman, and rode into battle at the head of her troops, something which few women have done before or since. But we must begin at the beginning, and in the beginning was Sombre, alias Samru, alias Walter Reinhardt…

Sombre's real name was Walter Reinhardt, but due to a dusky complexion he acquired the name of Sombre, which in Hindustani was soon corrupted to Samru. He was perhaps the most notorious of foreign adventurers, and this notoriety was acquired when he was in the service of the Nawab of Bengal, Kassim Ali, who, warring with the English, had attacked and captured a large number of English residents at Patna, and ordered them to be executed.

None of Kassim's own native officers came forward to undertake this, but Sombre, wishing to ingratiate himself with his new employer, agreed to carry out the execution. Details of the murders are given in the Annual Register:

'Somers [sic] invited about forty officers and other gentlemen, who were among these unfortunate prisoners, to sup with him on the day he had fixed for the execution, and when his guests were in full security, protected as they imagined by the laws of hospitality, as well as by the right of prisoners, he ordered the Indians under his command to fall upon them and cut their throats. Even these barbarous soldiers revolted at the orders of this savage European. They refused to obey, and desired that arms should be given to the English, and that they would then engage them. Somers, fixed in his villainy, compelled them with blows and threats to the accomplishment of that odious service. The unfortunate victims, though thus suddenly attacked and wholly unarmed, made a long and brave defence, and with their plates and bottles even killed some of their assailants, but in the end they were all slaughtered... Proceeding then, with a file of sepoys, to the prison where a number of prisoners then remained, he directed the massacre, and with his own hands assisted in the inhuman slaughter of 148 defenceless Europeans confined within its walls—an appalling act of atrocity that has stamped his name with infamy for ever.'

Sombre left Kassim Ali's service before an avenging British army could catch up with him, and by the end of his subsequent career he had served twelve to fourteen masters. He finally tendered his services to Shah Alam, the Emperor of Delhi, who agreed to pay him ₹65,000 for his services and those of his two battalions. He remained in the service of the Delhi Court and was assigned a rich jagir, or estate, at Sardhana, a district forty miles north of the capital, where he built and fortified his headquarters and settled down. He had adopted native dress, and the custom of keeping a harem.

At Sardhana, he fell in love with a very beautiful woman. One historian asserts that she was the daughter of a decadent Moghul nobleman, another that she was a Kashmiri dancing girl, and a third that she was a lineal descendant of the Prophet. In due course, she became Sombre's Begum. He died at Agra on the fourth of May 1778, aged fifty-eight years; infamous, unloved even by his own followers, but successful to the end.

After his death, the command of his troops, their pay and the jagir of Sardhana became the property of his Begum, who, on being baptized and received into the Roman Catholic faith, was christened 'Joanna Nobilis'. By means of rare ability and force of character, she proved equal to her responsibilities; but she was unfortunate in her officers. Only the most dissolute had cared to join Sombre, and their conduct often incited the troops to mutiny. She gave the command to a German named Pauly 'perhaps because he was a countryman of her husband, but, it has been suggested, for more tender reasons'; Pauly was murdered 'by a bloody process' in 1783; and those who succeeded him did not remain long in command.

It was at this time that George Thomas, the Irish freelance, rose to a position of some importance in the army of Begum Samru.

When the Begum saw Thomas, it did not take her long to decide to give him a command. He had the pleasing, honeyed speech of the Irishman; he was tall, handsome, virile; far more attractive physically than most of the Europeans in her service. How could the Begum resist him? For months he would remain her most trusted officer, her lover, and then, seeking some other novelty, she would transfer her affections to another, only appealing to Thomas for help in time of distress.

This arrangement suited Thomas. He was willing to make love to the Begum without making the mistake of falling in love with her. He used her as she used him; but he never betrayed her, as she was often to betray him.

Several years after Thomas had left her service and had established himself at Panipat and Karnal, Begum Samru, faced with a mutiny, appealed to him for help. She must have known Thomas's character well, for she had only recently raided his territory; any other person would have shown retaliation instead of succour; but when beauty was in distress Thomas always forsook his own interests to become the gallant knight-errant.

The Begum was now forty-five, inclined to plumpness, but her skin was still very smooth and fair, and her eyes black, large and animated. The trouble at Sardhana had arisen from her having taken a new husband, a Frenchman named Le Vassoult.

Le Vassoult was no friend of Thomas's and had in fact proposed marriage to the Begum earlier, in order to gain an advantage over the Irishman who was then in her service. He was well educated and from an aristocratic family, but aloof by nature and unpopular with his men. A free and easy roisterer like Thomas got more from his troops than the conventional disciplinarian. Both officers and troops resented the fact that Le Vassoult, after his marriage to the Begum, refused to eat with them or treat them as equals; they planned on deposing the Begum and transferring their allegiance to Balthazar Sombre, a debauched son of Sombre by his first wife. This first wife was still alive, and when she died in 1838, she must have been over a hundred years old. (The Sardhana cemetery contains the remains of many centenarians.)

Another officer named Legois, a friend of George Thomas, had tried to dissuade the Begum from raiding Thomas's territory in Hariana, and for this had been badly treated by Le Vassoult. The troops, who had served Legois for a long time, and obviously liked him, broke into mutiny, and the Begum and her husband had no alternative but to try and reach Anupshahr, then the last outpost of British territory in northern India.

The troops had sent for Balthazar Sombre from Delhi. Le Vassoult and the Begum slipped away, but were soon pursued and overtaken. The lovers had agreed that rather than fall into the hands of the mutineers they would first kill themselves. While Le Vassoult, an unimaginative man of honour, was quite serious about this pact, the Begum treated it lightly. On being surrounded, she drew a dagger and made a half-hearted attempt at stabbing herself; but all she did was nick her breast and spatter her blouse with blood. Le Vassoult was more thorough. On hearing that the Begum was bleeding to death, he drew his pistol, put the muzzle to his mouth, and pulled the trigger.

'The ball passed through his brain, and he sprang from the saddle a full foot in the air, before he fell dead to the ground. His corpse was subjected to every indignity and insult that the gross and bestial imagination of his officers and men could conceive, and left to rot, unburied, on the ground.'

However, the Begum did not get off too lightly. She was taken back to Sardhana and chained between two guns, occasionally being placed astride one of them at midday, when it was nearly red hot. The only food she received was smuggled to her by her maidservants. This was the Begum's plight when Thomas, by forced marches, reached Sardhana and quelled the mutiny.

The command of the Begum's force was now given to Colonel Saleur (the only European who could write) and he and the others signed or affixed their seals to a document in which they swore allegiance to their mistress. This was drawn up by a Mohammedan scribe in Persian, and as his religion prevented him from acknowledging Christ as God, the document was superscribed: 'In the name of God, and of His Majesty Christ!'

In 1803, after the British had defeated the Marathas, and established themselves in Hindustan (then the name for most of northern India) the Begum submitted to General Lake near Agra. James Skinner, the famous Eurasian adventurer, left a description of her meeting with the General: 'When the Begum came in person to pay her respects to General Lake, an incident occurred of a curious and characteristic description. She arrived at headquarters just after dinner, and being carried in her palanquin at once to the reception tent, the General came out to meet and receive her. As the adhesion of every petty chieftain was, in those days, of consequence, Lord Lake was not a little pleased at the early demonstration of the Begum's loyalty, and being a little elevated by the wine which had just been drunk, he forgot the novel circumstance of its being a native female, instead of some well-bearded chief, so he gallantly advanced, and, to the utter dismay of her attendants, took her in his arms and kissed her. The mistake might have been awkward, but the lady's presence of mind put all right. Receiving courteously the proferred attention, she turned calmly around to her astonished attendants and observed, "It is the salute of a priest to his daughter."'

When the Begum accepted British protection, her income increased, and she disbanded most of her troops. Bishop Heber saw her in 1825 and described her as a 'very queer-looking old woman, with brilliant but wicked eyes, and the remains of beauty in her features'.

She became very rich and philanthropic. She sent the Pope at Rome ₹150,000, the Archbishop of Canterbury ₹50,000. She built a church at Meerut—less pretentious but more handsome than the one at Sardhana—where the Roman Catholic bishop was an Italian named Julius Caesar. At Meerut, she often entertained governors-general and commanders-in-chief, and when she died in 1836, at the age of ninety, she left behind a fortune of £700,000 and an immense army of pensioners.

The Sardhana church hasn't changed much over the years. The dome is nobly proportioned, but the twin spires on either side somehow spoil the effect. They are not spires actually, but pyramidal structures that serve no purpose, aesthetic or practical. The interior of the church is handsome, and has several new additions; but the centre of interest are the eleven life-size statues and three panels in bas-relief. This marble monument is the work of an Italian sculptor, Adamo Tadolini of Bologna. The Begum in her rich dress is seated on a chair of state holding in her right hand a folded scroll, the Emperor's firman conferring on her the jagir of Sardhana. On her right stands Dyce Sombre, her stepson, and on her left Dewan Rae Singh, her minister. Immediately behind are Bishop Julius Caesar and Innayat Ullah, her commandant of cavalry.

Of the three panels one represents an incident in the consecration of the church when she presented rich vestments to the Bishop (these are still in existence). The other panel shows the Begum holding a durbar, surrounded by European officers; and the third shows the Begum mounted on an elephant in triumphant procession.

We felt like intruders, our footsteps resounding in the silent church, and we did not stay long. There was nothing else to see except the Begum's palace, now a school, and a few old houses and graves. The spirit of the Begum's time has left Sardhana, and it is just another district town, hot and dusty and malarious. It is difficult to believe that there were drama, intrigue, battle and romance here once. The place is a backwater, cut off somehow from the mainstream of life. A few nuns pass through the church cloisters, and a bullock cart trundles along the road. The fields are waterlogged.

We went away before sunset, afraid that if we stayed too long we might meet the ghost of a queer-looking old woman with brilliant and wicked eyes, lurking in the mango grove near the church.

# Bhabiji's House

*(My neighbours in Rajouri Garden back in the 1960s were the Kamal family. This entry from my journal, which I wrote on one of my later visits, describes a typical day in that household.)*

At first light there is a tremendous burst of birdsong from the guava tree in the little garden. Over a hundred sparrows wake up all at once and give tongue to whatever it is that sparrows have to say to each other at five o'clock on a foggy winter's morning in Delhi.

In the small house, people sleep on; that is, everyone except Bhabiji—Granny—the head of the lively Punjabi middle-class family with whom I nearly always stay when I am in Delhi.

She coughs, stirs, groans, grumbles and gets out of bed. The fire has to be lit, and food prepared for two of her sons to take to work. There is a daughter-in-law, Shobha, to help her; but the girl is not very bright at getting up in the morning. Actually, it is this way: Bhabiji wants to show up her daughter-in-law; so, no matter how hard Shobha tries to be up first, Bhabiji forestalls her. The old lady does not sleep well, anyway; her eyes are open long before the first sparrow chirps, and as soon as she sees her daughter-in-law stirring, she scrambles out of bed and hurries to the kitchen. This gives her the opportunity to say: 'What good is a daughter-in-law when I have to get up to prepare her husband's food?'

The truth is that Bhabiji does not like anyone else preparing her sons' food. She looks no older than when I first saw her ten years ago. She still has complete control over a large family and, with tremendous confidence and enthusiasm, presides over the lives of three sons, a daughter, two daughters-in-law and fourteen grandchildren. This is a joint family (there are not many left in a big city like Delhi), in which the sons and their families all live together as one unit under their mother's benevolent (and sometimes slightly malevolent) autocracy. Even when her husband was alive, Bhabiji dominated the household.

The eldest son, Shiv, has a separate kitchen, but his wife and children participate in all the family celebrations and quarrels. It is a small miracle how everyone (including myself when I visit) manages to fit into the house; and a stranger might be forgiven for wondering where everyone sleeps, for no beds are visible during the day. That is because the beds—light wooden frames with rough strings across—are brought in only at night, and are taken out first thing in the morning and kept in the garden shed.

As Bhabiji lights the kitchen fire, the household begins to stir, and Shobha joins her mother-in-law in the kitchen. As a guest I am privileged and may get up last. But my bed soon becomes an island battered by waves of scurrying, shouting children, eager to bathe, dress, eat and find their school books. Before I can get up, someone brings me a tumbler of hot sweet tea. It is a brass tumbler and burns my fingers; I have yet to learn how to hold one properly. Punjabis like their tea with lots of milk and sugar—so much so that I often wonder why they bother to add any tea.

Ten years ago, 'bed tea' was unheard of in Bhabiji's house.

Then, the first time I came to stay, Kamal, the youngest son, told Bhabiji: 'My friend is Angrez. He must have tea in bed.' He forgot to mention that I usually took my morning cup at seven; they gave it to me at five. I gulped it down and went to sleep again. Then, slowly, others in the household began indulging in morning cups of tea. Now everyone, including the older children, has 'bed tea'. They bless my English forebears for instituting the custom; I bless the Punjabis for perpetuating it.

Breakfast is by rota, in the kitchen. It is a tiny room and accommodates only four adults at a time. The children have eaten first; but the smallest children, Shobha's toddlers, keep coming in and climbing over us. Says Bhabiji of the youngest and most mischievous: 'He lives only because God keeps a special eye on him.'

Kamal, his elder brother Arun and I sit cross-legged and barefooted on the floor while Bhabiji serves us hot parathas stuffed with potatoes and onions, along with omelettes, an excellent dish. Arun then goes to work on his scooter, while Kamal catches a bus for the city, where he attends an art college. After they have gone, Bhabiji and Shobha have their breakfast.

By nine o'clock everyone who is still in the house is busy doing something. Shobha is washing clothes. Bhabiji has settled down on a cot with a huge pile of spinach, which she methodically cleans and chops up. Madhu, her fourteen-year-old granddaughter, who attends school only in the afternoons, is washing down the sitting-room floor. Madhu's mother is a teacher in a primary school in Delhi, and earns a pittance of ₹150 a month. Her husband went to England ten years ago, and never returned; he does not send any money home.

Madhu is made attractive by the gravity of her countenance. She is always thoughtful, reflective; seldom speaks, smiles rarely (but looks very pretty when she does). I wonder what she thinks about as she scrubs floors, prepares meals with Bhabiji, washes dishes and even finds a few hard-pressed moments for her school work. She is the Cinderella of the house. Not that she has to put up with anything like a cruel stepmother. Madhu is Bhabiji's favourite. She has made herself so useful that she is above all reproach. Apart from that, there is a certain measure of aloofness about her—she does not get involved in domestic squabbles—and this is foreign to a household in which everyone has something to say for himself or herself. Her two young brothers are constantly being reprimanded; but no one says anything to Madhu. Only yesterday morning, when clothes were being washed and Madhu was scrubbing the floor, the following dialogue took place.

Madhu's mother (picking up a school book left in the courtyard): Where's that boy Popat? See how careless he is with his books! Popat! He's run off. Just wait till he gets back. I'll give him a good beating.

Vinod's mother: It's not Popat's book. It's Vinod's. Where's Vinod?

Vinod (grumpily): It's Madhu's book.

Silence for a minute or two. Madhu continued scrubbing the floor; she did not bother to look up. Vinod picked up the book and took it indoors. The women returned to their chores.

Manju, daughter of Shiv and sister of Vinod, is averse to housework and, as a result, is always being scolded—by her parents, grandmother, uncles and aunts.

Now, she is engaged in the unwelcome chore of sweeping the front yard. She does this with a sulky look, ignoring my cheerful remarks. I have been sitting under the guava tree, but Manju soon sweeps me away from this spot. She creates a drifting cloud of dust, and seems satisfied only when the dust settles on the clothes that have just been hung up to dry. Manju is a sensuous creature and, like most sensuous people, is lazy by nature. She does not like sweeping because the boy next door can see her at it, and she wants to appear before him in a more glamorous light. Her first action every morning is to turn to the cinema advertisements in the newspaper. Bombay's movie moguls cater for girls like Manju who long to be tragic heroines. Life is so very dull for middle-class teenagers in Delhi that it is only natural that they should lean so heavily on escapist entertainment. Every residential area has a cinema. But there is not a single bookshop in this particular suburb, although it has a population of over 20,000 literate people. Few children read books; but they are adept at swotting up examination 'guides'; and students of, say, Hardy or Dickens read the guides and not the novels.

Bhabiji is now grinding onions and chillies in a mortar. Her eyes are watering but she is in a good mood. Shobha sits quietly in the kitchen. A little while ago she was complaining to me of a backache. I am the only one who lends a sympathetic ear to complaints of aches and pains. But since last night, my sympathies have been under severe strain. When I got into bed at about ten o'clock, I found the sheets wet. Apparently Shobha had put her baby to sleep in my bed during the afternoon.

While the housework is still in progress, cousin Kishore arrives. He is an itinerant musician who makes a living by arranging performances at marriages. He visits Bhabiji's house frequently and at odd hours, often a little tipsy, always brimming over with goodwill and grandiose plans for the future. It was once his ambition to be a film producer, and some years back he lost a lot of Bhabiji's money in producing a film that was never completed. He still talks of finishing it.

'Brother,' he says, taking me into his confidence for the hundredth time, 'do you know anyone who has a movie camera?'

'No,' I say, knowing only too well how these admissions can lead me into a morass of complicated manoeuvres. But Kishore is not easily put off, especially when he has been fortified with country liquor.

'But you *knew* someone with a movie camera?' he asks.

'That was long ago.'

'How long ago?' (I have got him going now.)

'About five years back.'

'Only five years? Find him, find him!'

'It's no use. He doesn't have the movie camera anymore. He sold it.'

'Sold it!' Kishore looks at me as though I have done him an injury. 'But why didn't you buy it? All we need is a movie camera, and our fortune is made. I will produce the film, I will direct it, I will write the music. Two in one, Charlie Chaplin and Raj Kapoor. Why didn't you buy the camera?'

'Because I didn't have the money.'

'But we could have borrowed the money.'

'If you are in a position to borrow money, you can go out and buy another movie camera.'

'We could have borrowed the camera. Do you know anyone else who has one?'

'Not a soul.' I am firm this time; I will not be led into another maze.

'Very sad, very sad,' mutters Kishore. And with a dejected, hangdog expression designed to make me feel that I am responsible for all his failures, he moves off.

Bhabiji had expressed some annoyance at his arrival, but he softens her up by leaving behind an invitation to a marriage party this evening. No one in the house knows the bride's or bridegroom's family, but that does not matter; knowing one of the musicians is just as good. Almost everyone will go.

While Bhabiji, Shobha and Madhu are preparing lunch, Bhabiji engages in one of her favourite subjects of conversation, Kamal's marriage, which she hopes she will be able to arrange in the near future. She freely acknowledges that she made grave blunders in selecting wives for her other sons—this is meant to be heard by Shobha—and promises not to repeat her mistakes. According to Bhabiji, Kamal's bride should be both educated and domesticated; and of course she must be fair.

'What if he likes a dark girl?' I ask teasingly.

Bhabiji looks horrified. 'He cannot marry a dark girl,' she declares.

'But dark girls are beautiful,' I tell her.

'Impossible!'

'Do you want him to marry a European girl?'

'No foreigners! I know them, they'll take my son away. He shall have a good Punjabi girl, with a complexion the colour of wheat.'

Noon. The shadows shift and cross the road. I sit beneath the guava tree and watch the women at work. They will not let me do anything, but they like talking to me and they love to hear my broken Punjabi. Sparrows flit about at their feet, snapping up the grain that runs away from their busy fingers. A crow looks speculatively at the empty kitchen, sidles towards the open door; but Bhabiji has only to glance up and the experienced crow flies away. He knows he will not be able to make off with anything from this house.

One by one the children come home, demanding food. Now it is Madhu's turn to go to school. Her younger brother

Popat, an intelligent but undersized boy of thirteen, appears in the doorway and asks for lunch.

'Be off!' says Bhabiji. 'It isn't ready yet.'

Actually the food is ready and only the chapattis remain to be made. Shobha will attend to them. Bhabiji lies down on her cot in the sun, complaining of a pain in her back and ringing noises in her ears.

'I'll press your back,' says Popat. He has been out of Bhabiji's favour lately, and is looking for an opportunity to be rehabilitated.

Barefooted he stands on Bhabiji's back and treads her weary flesh and bones with a gentle walking-in-one-spot movement. Bhabiji grunts with relief. Every day she has new pains in new places. Her age and the daily business of feeding the family and running everyone's affairs are beginning to tell on her. But she would sooner die than give up her position of dominance in the house. Her working sons still hand over their pay to her, and she dispenses the money as she sees fit.

The pummelling she gets from Popat puts her in a better mood, and she holds forth on another favourite subject, the respective merits of various dowries. Shiv's wife (according to Bhabiji) brought nothing with her but a string cot; Kishore's wife brought only a sharp and clever tongue; Shobha brought a wonderful steel cupboard, fully expecting that it would do all the housework for her.

This last observation upsets Shobha, and a little later I find her under the guava tree, weeping profusely. I give her the comforting words she obviously expects; but it is her husband Arun who will have to bear the brunt of her outraged feelings when he comes home this evening. He is rather nervous of his wife. Last night he wanted to eat out, at a restaurant, but did not want to be accused of wasting money; so he stuffed fifteen rupees into my pocket and asked me to invite both him and Shobha to dinner, which I did.

We had a good dinner. Such unexpected hospitality on my part has further improved my standing with Shobha. Now, in spite of other chores, she sees that I get cups of tea and coffee at odd hours of the day.

Bhabiji knows Arun is soft with his wife, and taunts him about it. She was saying this morning that whenever there is any work to be done Shobha retires to bed with a headache (partly true). She says even Manju does more housework (not true). Bhabiji has certain talents as an actress, and does a good take-off of Shobha sulking and grumbling at having too much to do.

While Bhabiji talks, Popat sneaks off and goes for a ride on the bicycle. It is a very old bicycle and is constantly undergoing repairs. 'The soul has gone out of it,' says Vinod philosophically and makes his way on to the roof, where he keeps a store of pornographic literature. Up there, he cannot be seen and cannot be remembered, and so avoids being sent out on errands.

One of the boys is bathing at the hand-pump. Manju, who should have gone to school with Madhu, is stretched out on a cot, complaining of fever. But she will be up in time to attend the marriage party...

Towards evening, as the birds return to roost in the guava tree, their chatter is challenged by the tumult of people in the house getting ready for the marriage party.

Manju presses her tight pyjamas but neglects to darn them. She wears a loose-fitting, diaphanous shirt. She keeps flitting in and out of the front room so that I can admire the way she glitters. Shobha has used too much powder and lipstick in an effort to look like the femme fatale which she indubitably is not. Shiv's more conservative wife floats around in loose, old-fashioned pyjamas. Bhabiji is sober and austere in a white sari. Madhu looks neat. The men wear their suits.

Popat is holding up a mirror for his Uncle Kishore, who is combing his long hair. (Kishore kept his hair long, like a court musician at the time of Akbar, before the hippies had been heard of.) He is nodding benevolently, having fortified himself from a bottle labelled 'Som Ras' ('Nectar of the Gods'), obtained cheaply from an illicit still.

Kishore: Don't shake the mirror, boy!

Popat: Uncle, it's your head that's shaking.

Shobha is happy. She loves going out, especially to marriages, and she always takes her two small boys with her, although they invariably spoil the carpets.

Only Kamal, Popat and I remain behind. I have had more than my share of marriage parties.

The house is strangely quiet. It does not seem so small now, with only three people left in it. The kitchen has been locked (Bhabiji will not leave it open while Popat is still in the house), so we visit the dhaba, the wayside restaurant near the main road, and this time I pay the bill with my own money. We have kebabs and chicken curry.

Yesterday Kamal and I took our lunch on the grass of the Buddha Jayanti Gardens (Buddha's Birthday Gardens). There was no college for Kamal, as the majority of Delhi's students had hijacked a number of corporation buses and headed for the Pakistan High Commission, with every intention of levelling it to the ground if possible, as a protest against the hijacking of an Indian plane from Srinagar to Lahore. The students were met by the Delhi police in full strength, and a pitched battle took place, in which stones from the students and tear gas shells from the police were the favoured missiles. There were two shells fired every minute, according to a newspaper report. And this went on all day. A number of students and policemen were injured, but by some miracle no one was killed. The police held their ground, and the Pakistan High Commission remained inviolate. But the Australian High Commission, situated to the rear of the student brigade, received most of the tear gas shells, and had to close down for the day.

Kamal and I attended the siege for about an hour, before retiring to the Gardens with our ham sandwiches. A couple of friendly squirrels came up to investigate, and were soon taking bread from our hands. We could hear the chanting of the students in the distance. I lay back on the grass and opened my copy of *Barchester Towers*. Whenever life in Delhi, or in Bhabiji's house (or anywhere, for that matter), becomes too tumultuous, I turn to Trollope. Nothing could be further removed from the turmoil of our times than an English cathedral town in the nineteenth century. But I think Jane Austen would have appreciated life in Bhabiji's house.

By ten o'clock, everyone is back from the marriage. (They had gone for the feast, and not for the ceremonies, which continue into the early hours of the morning.) Shobha is full of praise for the bridegroom's good looks and fair complexion. She describes him as being 'gora-chitta'—very white! She does not have a high opinion of the bride.

Shiv, in a happy and reflective mood, extols the qualities of his own wife, referring to her as The Barrel. He tells us how, shortly after their marriage, she had threatened to throw a brick at the next-door girl. This little incident remains fresh in Shiv's mind, after eighteen years of marriage.

He says, 'When the neighbours came and complained, I

told them, "It is quite possible that my wife will throw a brick at your daughter. She is in the habit of throwing bricks." The neighbours held their peace.'

I think Shiv is rather proud of his wife's militancy when it comes to taking on neighbours; recently, she vanquished the woman next door (a formidable Sikh lady) after a verbal battle that lasted three hours. But in arguments or quarrels with Bhabiji, Shiv's wife always loses, because Shiv takes his mother's side. Arun, on the other hand, is afraid of both wife and mother, and simply makes himself scarce when a quarrel develops. Or he tells his mother she is right, and then, to placate Shobha, takes her to the pictures.

Kishore turns up just as everyone is about to go to bed. Bhabiji is annoyed at first, because he has been drinking too much; but when he produces a bunch of cinema tickets, she is mollified and asks him to stay the night. Not even Bhabiji likes missing a new picture.

Kishore is urging me to write his life story.

'Your life would make a most interesting story,' I tell him. 'But it will be interesting only if I put in everything—your successes *and* your failures.'

'No, no, only successes,' exhorts Kishore. 'I want you to describe me as a popular music director.'

'But you have yet to become popular.'

'I will be popular if you write about me.'

Fortunately we are interrupted by the cots being brought in. Then Bhabiji and Shiv go into a huddle, discussing plans for building an extra room. After all, Kamal may be married soon.

One by one, the children get under their quilts. Popat starts massaging Bhabiji's back. She gives him her favourite blessing: 'God protect you and give you lots of children.' If God listens to all Bhabiji's prayers and blessings, there will never be a fall in the population.

The lights are off and Bhabiji settles down for the night. She is almost asleep when a small voice pipes up: 'Bhabiji, tell us a story.'

At first Bhabiji pretends not to hear; then, when the request is repeated, she says: 'You'll keep Aunty Shobha awake, and then she'll have an excuse for getting up late in the morning.' But the children know Bhabiji's one great weakness, and they renew their demand.

'Your grandmother is tired,' says Arun. 'Let her sleep.'

But Bhabiji's eyes are open. Her mind is going back over the crowded years, and she remembers something very interesting that happened when her younger brother's wife's sister married the eldest son of her third cousin…

Before long, the children are asleep, and I am wondering if I will ever sleep, for Bhabiji's voice drones on, into the darker reaches of the night.

# Rani of the Doon

Remembering the Dehradun of my boyhood in the 1940s, with its modest population of about forty thousand souls, and contemplating it now, with a population of roughly five lakh persons, I cannot help tossing a question into the void and asking the Creator, 'God, what will it be twenty years from now?'

To this God, as enigmatic as ever, replies, 'A computer should be able to tell you. Find out for yourself.'

All the same, for one who presumably created our earth and all that moves upon it, it must be a little daunting to observe the growth of mankind (in sheer numbers), often at the expense of other creatures and the forest and plant life that has sustained us. God may be forgiving, but Nature is not, and we upset the ecological balance at our own peril.

To take this one small corner of the world, this particular valley, it is fascinating to realize that just four hundred years ago the only habitations were a few scattered villages.

It is possible to identify them, although they have long since been swallowed up in urban Dehradun. In the late sixteenth and early seventeenth centuries, the Doon was governed by a woman, Rani Karnavati, who apparently administered the territory on behalf of the Garhwal rajas. Her consort, a certain Abju Kanwar, was content to remain in the background. Early records mention that her palace was at a place called Nawada, on Nagsidh Hill, a few miles south-east of the present city.

Included in her domain were the villages of Kaulagarh, Karnapur, Rajpur and Kyarkuli. Karnapur and Kaulagarh have long since been absorbed into the city. Guru Ram Rai's settlement at Khurbura in the late seventeenth century started the process. Rajpur remained a separate hamlet until it became a staging post on the way to Mussoorie, when that hill station was founded by the British in the 1820s.

Only Kyarkuli has remained more or less aloof from both Dehra and Mussoorie. You can see it straddling its own ridge as you drive up to Mussoorie; almost, but not quite, swallowed up by the limestone quarries that had until recently spread like a cancer over the hills.

Rani Karnavati must have been an outstanding woman in her time. She is credited with having built the original Rajpur Canal, which was later restored by the British to water their tea-estates and lichi gardens. Atkinson, in his *Gazetteer*, tells us that on a peak in the Dudatoli range there is a temple of Shiva at Binsar; a temple celebrated throughout the lower foothills for its sanctity and power of working miracles. It was here that Rani Karnavati was saved from her enemies by god, who destroyed them in a hailstorm. Out of gratitude, she built a new tower for the temple.

One of the many legends concerning Binsar states that should anyone remove anything belonging to god or his worshippers from the temple precincts, an avenging spirit pursues the culprit and compels him to restore it twenty-fold. Even the faithless and dishonest are reformed by a visit to Binsar. Hence the proverb : *Bhai, Binsar ka loha janlo samajhlo.*

It is said that although the forests in the neighbourhood

abounded with tigers, not one attacked a pilgrim, owing to the protecting influence of god. Indeed, it was considered propitious to see a tiger on the way to Binsar. This belief is still held, although tigers now being less numerous, the chances of seeing one are not as good as in those days of yore.

Unusual though it was for a woman to have ruled over a large tract of hill country, there were women rulers before Karnavati in parts of western Garhwal. Huien Tsang, the seventh century traveller, in his sub-Himalayan travels, speaks of a kingdom called Barhampura, later identified with Barahat in Rawain Garhwal (now Uttarkashi), which 'produced gold and where for ages a woman has been the ruler and so it is called the kingdom of a woman. The husband of the reigning woman is called king, but he knows nothing of the affairs of state. This man manages the wars and sows the land....'

There is little or no recorded history for that period, but it would appear that for a woman to have governed large tracts of land was not unusual. The sociology of the area has always been unique.

Nearer in time, I can imagine the Doon of Rani Karnavati's reign—scattered villages, a little cultivation here and there, and large tracts of forest reaching up to the foothills and beyond. Tigers and elephants roamed these forests, and so did many wild animals now extinct in the area.

Inevitably, immigration took place from other parts of the country, but even as late as 1817, when the British wrested the Doon from the Gurkhas, a population count (Walton's *Gazetteer*) showed Dehradun to have a population of two thousand and one hundred, with five hundred dwelling-places; hardly a town by today's standards.

Compare this with today's five lakh and you have a classic

example of urbanization and population growth on an impressive scale, most of it during the last fifty years.

And yet, parts of the Doon are still lovely. Almost any tree or flower will grow in this fertile valley. Hopefully, when we go into the twenty-first century, there will still be a few gardens and open spaces for our children to enjoy.

And now that Dehradun is the capital of the state of Uttarakhand, all statistics need an upward revision. Never having been any good at maths, I can safely leave all calculations to the computers.

# Untouchable

The sweeper boy splashed water over the khus matting that hung in the doorway and for a while the air was cooled.

I sat on the edge of my bed, staring out of the open window, brooding upon the dusty road shimmering in the noonday heat. A car passed and the dust rose in billowing clouds.

Across the road lived the people who were supposed to look after me while my father lay in hospital with malaria. I was supposed to stay with them, sleep with them. But except for meals, I kept away. I did not like them and they did not like me.

For a week, longer probably, I was going to live alone in the red-brick bungalow on the outskirts of the town, on the fringe of the jungle. At night, the sweeper boy would keep guard, sleeping in the kitchen. Apart from him, I had no company; only the neighbours' children, and I did not like them and they did not like me.

Their mother said, 'Don't play with the sweeper boy, he is unclean. Don't touch him. Remember, he is a servant. You must come and play with my boys.'

Well, I did not intend playing with the sweeper boy; but neither did I intend playing with her children. I was going to sit on my bed all week and wait for my father to come home.

Sweeper boy...all day he pattered up and down between

the house and the water tank, with the bucket clanging against his knees.

Back and forth, with a wide, friendly smile.

I frowned at him.

He was about my age, ten. He had short-cropped hair, very white teeth, and muddy feet, hands, and face. All he wore was an old pair of khaki shorts; the rest of his body was bare, burnt a deep brown.

At every trip to the water tank he bathed, and returned dripping and glistening from head to toe.

I dripped with sweat.

It was supposedly below my station to bathe at the tank, where the gardener, water-carrier, cooks, ayahs, sweepers, and their children all collected. I was the son of a 'sahib' and convention ruled that I did not play with servant children.

But I was just as determined not to play with the other sahibs' children, for I did not like them and they did not like me.

I watched the flies buzzing against the windowpane, the lizards scuttling across the rafters, the wind scattering petals of scorched, long-dead flowers.

The sweeper boy smiled and saluted in play. I avoided his eyes and said, 'Go away.'

He went into the kitchen.

I rose and crossed the room, and lifted my sun helmet off the hatstand.

A centipede ran down the wall, across the floor.

I screamed and jumped on the bed, shouting for help.

The sweeper boy darted in. He saw me on the bed, the centipede on the floor; and picking a large book off the shelf, slammed it down on the repulsive insect.

I remained standing on my bed, trembling with fear and revulsion.

He laughed at me, showing his teeth, and I blushed and said, 'Get out!'

I would not, could hot, touch or approach the hat or hatstand. I sat on the bed and longed for my father to come home.

A mosquito passed close by me and sang in my ear. Half-heartedly, I clutched at it and missed; and it disappeared behind the dressing table.

That mosquito, I reasoned, gave the malaria to my father. And now it was trying to give it to me!

The next-door lady walked through the compound and smiled thinly from outside the window. I glared back at her.

The sweeper boy passed with the bucket, and grinned. I turned away.

In bed at night, with the lights on, I tried reading. But even books could not quell my anxiety.

The sweeper boy moved about the house, bolting doors, fastening windows. He asked me if I had any orders.

I shook my head.

He skipped across to the electric switch, turned off the light, and slipped into his quarters. Outside, inside, all was dark; only one shaft of light squeezed in through a crack in the sweeper boy's door, and then that too went out.

I began to wish I had stayed with the neighbours. The darkness worried me—silent and close—silent, as if in suspense.

Once a bat flew flat against the window, falling to the ground outside; once an owl hooted. Sometimes a dog barked. And I tautened as a jackal howled hideously in the jungle behind the bungalow. But nothing could break the overall stillness, the night's silence…

Only a dry puff of wind...

It rustled in the trees, and put me in mind of a snake slithering over dry leaves and twigs. I remembered a tale I had been told not long ago, of a sleeping boy who had been bitten by a cobra.

I would not, could not, sleep. I longed for my father...

The shutters rattled, the doors creaked. It was a night for ghosts.

Ghosts!

God, why did I have to think of them?

My God! There, standing by the bathroom door...

My father! My father dead from the malaria, and come to see me!

I threw myself at the switch. The room lit up. I sank down on the bed in complete exhaustion, the sweat soaking my nightclothes.

It was not my father I had seen. It was his dressing gown hanging on the bathroom door. It had not been taken with him to the hospital.

I turned off the light.

The hush outside seemed deeper, nearer. I remembered the centipede, the bat, thought of the cobra and the sleeping boy; pulled the sheet tight over my head. If I could see nothing, well then, nothing could see me.

A thunderclap shattered the brooding stillness.

A streak of lightning forked across the sky, so close that even through the sheet I saw a tree and the opposite house silhouetted against the flashing canvas of gold.

I dived deeper beneath the bedclothes, gathered the pillow about my ears.

But at the next thunderclap, louder this time, louder than

I had ever heard, I leapt from my bed. I could not stand it. I fled, blundering into the sweeper boy's room.

The boy sat on the bare floor.

'What is happening?' he asked.

The lightning flashed, and his teeth and eyes flashed with it. Then he was a blur in the darkness.

'I am afraid,' I said.

I moved towards him and my hand touched a cold shoulder.

'Stay here,' he said. 'I too am afraid.'

I sat down, my back against the wall; beside the untouchable, the outcaste…and the thunder and lightning ceased, and the rain came down, swishing and drumming on the corrugated roof.

'The rainy season has started,' observed the sweeper boy, turning to me. His smile played with the darkness, and then he laughed. And I laughed too, but feebly.

But I was happy and safe. The scent of the wet earth blew in through the skylight and the rain fell harder.

*(This was my first short story, written when I was sixteen.)*

# The Bar that Time Forgot

'Cockroaches!' exclaimed Her Highness the Maharani. 'Cockroaches everywhere! Can't put down my glass without finding a cockroach beneath it!'

'Cockroaches have a special liking for this room,' observed Colonel Wilkie, from his corner by the disused fireplace. 'For one thing, our Melaram there,' and he indicated the bartender with a tilt of his double chin, 'never washes the glasses properly. And there are sandwich remains all over the place. Last week's sandwiches, I might add. From that party of yours, Krishan.'

Krishan, former Test cricketer, now forty and with a forty-three-inch waist, turned to the Colonel. 'You should see the kitchen. A pigsty. The cook is seldom sober.'

'*We* are seldom sober,' said Suresh Mathur, income-tax lawyer, from his favourite bar stool.

'Speak for yourself,' snapped H.H. 'Simon, fetch me another whisky.'

Simon Lee, secretary-companion to Her Highness, rose dutifully from his chair and took her glass over to the bar counter.

'Indian whisky or scotch, sir?' asked the bartender in a loud voice, knowing the Maharani was too mean to buy scotch.

'Whisky will do,' said Simon, 'and a beer for me.' Just then he felt like spiking the Maharani's whisky with something really lethal, and being free of her for the rest of his days. Years of loyalty and companionship had given way to abject slavery, and there was nothing he could do about it. Nearing seventy, unqualified and unworldly, he could hardly set about creating any sort of career for himself.

'And what are *you* having?' he asked Suresh Mathur, who had just put away his first drink.

'I am never vague, I ask for Haig!' Suresh replied, chuckling at his clever rhyme. None of the others thought it amusing, but this was usual. 'When they stop giving me credit, I'll try the local stuff.'

'Good on you!' called Colonel Wilkie from his corner. 'But there's nothing to beat Solan No. 1. Don't trust these single malts—they always give one gout!'

'I've never seen you move from that chair,' said Krishan. 'No wonder you suffer from gout.'

'Played cricket once, like you,' said the Colonel. 'Made a few runs. But they always made me twelfth man. Got fed up of carrying out the drinks, or fielding when the star batsman felt indisposed. Gave up cricket. Indoor games are better. Why don't we have a dartboard in here? In England, every respectable pub has a dartboard.'

I'd been listening to the conversation from a small table behind a potted palm. I was sixteen, just out of school, and I wasn't supposed to be in the bar, even if I wasn't drinking. The large potted palm separated the bar-room from the outer lounge; it was neutral territory.

'I have a dartboard!' I piped up, and every head turned towards me. Most of them had been unaware of my presence. They knew, of course, that I was the son of the lady who managed the hotel.

Suresh Mathur, the most literary-inclined of the lot, said:

'Young Copperfield has a dartboard!'

'I'll go and fetch it,' I said, only too ready to justify my presence in the bar.

I dashed down the corridor to my room and collided with my mother who was doing her nightly round of the hotel.

'What are you doing here? You mustn't hang around the bar,' she said sharply. 'You have a radio in your room, apart from all your books.'

The radio had been given to me the previous year by a guest who was now wanted by the police (on suspicion of being a serial killer), but I did not feel in any way guilty about possessing it; the guest had been very friendly and generous.

'Darts,' I told my mother. 'They want to play darts. That's what a pub is for, isn't it?' And I charged into my room, picked up my old dartboard and set of darts, and returned breathless to the bar-room.

My arrival was greeted by cheers, and Krishan helped me find a place for the dartboard, just below a framed picture of winged cherubs sporting about on some unlikely clouds.

'Whoever gets the highest score gets a free drink,' announced Krishan.

'Who pays for it?' asked Suresh Mathur.

'We all do—income-tax lawyers included.'

'He never saved anyone a rupee of tax,' declared the Maharani. 'But come on, let's have a game.'

'Would you like to start the proceedings, H.H.?'

'No, I'll wait till everyone's finished. You can start with Colonel Wilkie.'

'Age before beauty,' said Krishan. 'Come on, Colonel, we know you have a steady hand.'

Colonel Wilkie's hand was far from steady. His hands were

always trembling. But he struggled out of his chair and took up his position at a point indicated by Krishan. Only one of his darts struck the board, earning him fifteen points. The others were near misses. Two darts bounced off the picture on the wall.

'The old fool's aiming at those naked cherubs,' crowed H.H. 'Go on, Simon, see if you can win a free drink for me.'

Simon did his best, but scored a meagre thirty points.

'Idiot!' cried H.H. 'And you always said you were a good darts player.'

'Out of practice,' Simon mumbled.

Meanwhile, someone had opened up the old radiogram and placed a record on the turntable. The cheeky voice of Maurice Chevalier filled the room:

> All I want is just one girl,
> But I have to have one girl
> All I want is one
> For a start!

The evening was livening up. Suresh Mathur scored a few points, but it was Krishan who hit the bullseye and claimed a drink on the house.

'Not until I've had my turn,' shouted H.H., and made a grab for the darts.

She flung them at the board at random, missing wildly—so much so that one dart lodged itself in Colonel Wilkie's old felt hat which was hanging from a peg, while another streaked across the room and narrowly missed the Roman nose of Reggie Bhowmik, ex-actor, who had just entered the room accompanied by his demure little wife.

Between ex-actor Reggie and former cricketer Krishan, there was no love lost. Both middle aged and no longer in demand, they were rivals in failure. One spoke of the prejudice and incompetence of the cricket selectors, the other of jealousy in the film industry and his subsequent neglect. Both lived in the past—Krishan recalling the one outstanding innings he had played for the country (before being dropped after a series of failures), Reggie living on memories of his one great romantic role before a sagging waistline and alcohol-coarsened features had led to a rapid decline in his popularity. Somehow they had drifted into the backwater that was Dehra in 1950.

There are some places, no matter how dull or lacking in opportunity, which nevertheless take a grip on the individual, especially the more easy-going types, and hold him in thrall, rendering him unfit for life in a larger, more competitive milieu. Dehra was one such place.

The bar at Green's Hotel was their refuge and their strength. Here they could reminisce, hark back to glory days, even speak optimistically of the future. Colonel Wilkie, Suresh Mathur, Krishan Kapoor, Reggie Bhowmik, H.H.—the Maharani—and Simon Lee, were all dropouts, failures in their own way. Had they been busy and successful, they would not have found their way to Green's every evening.

Reggie Bhowmik liked making dramatic entrances, but the Maharani was just as fond of being the centre of attention, and wasn't about to give up centre stage to a fading actor.

'A double whisky for Krishan!' she declared. 'He's the only one here who still has a steady hand.'

'You haven't felt *my* hand,' said Reggie, bearing down on her. 'You missed my nose by a whisker.'

'You'd look better with a scar running down your face,' said H.H. 'Then you might get a role as Frankenstein or the phantom of the opera.'

This touched a raw nerve, as Reggie had been having some difficulty in getting a decent role in recent months. But he snapped back: 'I'll play the phantom on condition that you're cast as the fat soprano—then I shall take great pleasure in strangling you.'

'Let's change the subject,' said his wife Ruby, always ready to pour oil on troubled waters. She moved over to Colonel Wilkie's table and asked: 'How have you been, Colonel?'

'Like an old bus just about moving, and badly in need of spare parts.'

'Well, have a beer with us—and some French fries if we can get any.'

'Cook's on strike,' said Krishan. 'Only liquid diet today.' I saw my opportunity, and piped up again from behind the potted palm. 'I can boil some eggs for you if you like!' There was a stunned silence, broken by Suresh Mathur who said, sounding a little incredulous, 'Young Master Copperfield can boil an egg!'

Everyone clapped, and Krishan said, 'Copperfield has certainly saved the day for us. First he produces a dartboard, and now he's about to save us from starvation. Go to it, Copperfield!'

Off I went, then, not to boil eggs—there weren't any in the kitchen—but to find Sitaram, the room-boy, who was the only person of my age in the hotel. I found him in my room, listening to 'Binaca Geetmala', the popular musical request programme, on my radio.

'We need some eggs,' I told him. 'Boiled.'

'Egg-man comes tomorrow,' he said. 'Cook finished the rest. Made himself an omelette, got drunk, and took off!'

'Well, let's go down to the bazaar and buy some eggs. I've got enough money on me.'

So off we went, and near the clock tower found a street

vendor selling boiled eggs. We bought a dozen and hurried back to the bar-room, where Krishan and Reggie were having a heated argument on the relative merits of cricket and football. Reggie didn't think much of cricket, and Krishan didn't think much of football.

'And what's *your* favourite game?' asked Ruby of Suresh Mathur.

'Snakes and ladders,' he said, chuckling, and returned to his drink.

'Boiled eggs!' I announced. 'On the house!'

Sitaram produced saucers, and distributed the eggs among the guests—two each, exactly.

'Do I have to peel my own egg?' asked the Maharani querulously, staring down at the two eggs rolling about on her plate. 'Peel them for me, Simon!'

Simon dutifully cracked one of the eggs and began peeling it for her. 'Not that way, you fool. You're leaving all the skin on it.' And seizing the half-peeled egg from her companion, she flung it across the room, narrowly missing the bartender.

'Good throw!' exclaimed Krishan. 'You'd be great fielding on the boundary.'

'Better at baseball,' said Reggie.

'Snakes and ladders,' said Suresh again, now quite drunk.

Colonel Wilkie, equally drunk, gave a loud belch.

The Maharani got up to leave. 'Well, I'm not going to sit here to be insulted by everyone. Come on, Simon, drive me home!' And she marched out of the room with an attempt at majesty, but tripped over the hotel cat, an ugly, striped creature who had sensed that there was food around and had come looking for it. The cat caterwauled, H.H. screamed and cursed, Reggie cheered, and Suresh Mather pronounced, 'When two cats are fighting they make a hideous sound.'

Not to be outdone in nastiness, the Maharani went up to Suresh, looked him up and down, and said, 'It's easy to tell you're a single man.'

'I'm not homosexual,' said Suresh defensively. (The word 'gay' had yet to be used in any sense other than 'happy' in those days.)

'No,' the Maharani smiled wickedly. 'You're single because you are so damn ugly!'

And on that triumphant note she left the room, followed by the obedient Simon.

'Pay no attention to her, Suresh,' said Krishan generously. 'You're better-looking than that old lapdog who follows her around.'

'I understand she's leaving him her fortunes,' said Reggie. 'I could do with some of it myself. Perhaps I could interest her in producing a film.'

'She's tight-fisted,' said Krishan. 'If you look closely at Simon you'll notice he's wearing the late Maharaja's smoking jacket and deerstalker cap. The old Maharaja loved dressing up like Sherlock Holmes.'

Colonel Wilkie came out of his reverie. 'When I was in Jamnagar—' he began.

'We've heard that a hundred times,' said Krishan.

'*I* haven't,' said Ruby.

'When I was in Jamnagar,' continued Colonel Wilkie, 'I saw Duleep Singh ji make a hundred. That was against Lord Tennyson's team.'

'Yesterday you said Ranjit Singh ji,' remarked Krishan.

'I'm not that old,' said Colonel Wilkie, struggling to his feet. 'But old enough to want to go to bed. I'll toddle off now.' Locating his walking-stick, he found his way to the door, wishing everyone goodnight as he passed them. They heard the tap of his walking stick as he walked away down the corridor.

'Shouldn't someone go with him?' asked Ruby. 'It's very late and he isn't too steady on his feet.'

'Oh, he'll find his way home,' said Suresh nonchalantly. 'Lives just around the corner, in rented rooms near the Club.'

'Why doesn't he join the Club?'

'Can't afford it. Neither can I.'

'Neither can I,' said Krishan.

'Neither can we,' added Ruby, sadly. 'And anyway, it's more homely here. Even when the Maharani is around.'

'*She* can afford the Club,' said Suresh. 'But they won't let her in. Created a disturbance once too often. Insulted the secretary and emptied a dish of chicken biryani on his head.'

'Not done,' said Krishan. 'Not cricket.'

'I don't believe it,' said Reggie. 'Can't be true.'

'Calling me a liar?' asked Suresh, bristling.

Ruby poured oil on troubled waters again. 'Interesting if true,' she said. 'And if not true, still interesting.'

'Mark Twain.'

My mother came along the corridor just as Krishan had shown off his knowledge of literature, and found me behind the palms listening to all this fascinating talk.

'Time you went to your room, young man,' she said.

'I'm waiting for everyone to go home,' I said. 'Then I'll help Sitaram tidy up. There's no cook, as you know.'

'Let him stay,' called Suresh from his bar stool. 'It's all part of his education. And he's old enough for a glass of beer. How old are you, sonny?'

'Sixteen,' I said.

'Well, enjoy yourself. It's later than you think.'

But I wasn't thinking of beer just then. I knew there were sausages in the fridge, and I had every intention of polishing them off as soon as all the guests had gone. I wanted to be a writer, but I had no intention of starving in a garret. However, all thoughts of food vanished when I looked across the room and saw Colonel Wilkie framed in the opposite doorway. He was staring at us through the glass. The glass door then opened of its own volition, and Colonel Wilkie stepped into the room. We all looked up, and Reggie said, 'Back again, Colonel? Still feeling thirsty?' But Colonel Wilkie ignored the jibe, and walked slowly across the room to the table where he had been sitting. This was close to where I was standing. He bent down and picked up his pipe from the table. He'd forgotten it when he'd left the bar-room. Shoving the pipe into his pocket, he turned and retraced his steps, leaving the room by the door from which he had entered.

'Well, I'm blowed,' said Krishan. 'I thought he was sleepwalking.'

'Never goes anywhere without his pipe,' said Suresh. 'A perfect example of single-mindedness.'

'Didn't say a word.'

'The pipe was all that mattered.'

'Like a favourite cricket bat,' said Krishan.

'Maybe I'll come back for mine when I'm dead.'

A silence fell upon the room. The mention of death had a sobering effect upon the small group. And come to think of it, Colonel Wilkie on his return to the bar-room had something of the zombie about him—the walking dead.

There was a commotion in the passageway, and my mother burst into the room, followed by the night-watchman.

'Colonel Wilkie's dead,' said my mother. 'He collapsed on his steps about half an hour ago.'

'But he was here five minutes ago,' said Krishan.

'No, sir,' said Gopal the watchman. 'I went home with him when he left here some time back. Madam said to keep an eye on him. When we got to his place, he began climbing his steps with some difficulty. I helped him to the top step, and then he collapsed. I dragged him into his room and then ran for Dr Bhist. He is there now.'

There was silence for a couple of minutes, and then Ruby said, 'We all saw him. Colonel Wilkie.'

'We saw his ghost,' Krishan murmured.

'He came for his pipe,' said Suresh quietly. 'I told you he wouldn't go anywhere without it.'

Colonel Wilkie was buried the next day, and we made sure his pipe was buried with him. We did not want him turning up from time to time, looking for it. It could be a bit unnerving for the customers.

In all the excitement I'd forgotten about the sausages, but decided they would keep until after the funeral.

All the regular barflies turned up for the funeral. H.H. was quite sloshed when she arrived and had to be extricated from an open grave into which she had slipped, the ground being soft and yielding after recent rain. She blamed secretary Simon for the mishap and called him an *ullu ka patha*—son of an owl—but he was quite used to such broadsides and took them in his stride. Was it love or loyalty or dependence that kept him in abeyance? Or was it, as some said, the prospect of becoming her heir? If so, he was paying a heavy price well in advance of such a prospect. Not everyone relishes being abused and kicked around in public by a half-crazed maharani.

When Colonel Wilkie's coffin was lowered into the grave, we all said 'Cheers!' He would have liked that. We then returned to Green's for an early opening of the bar. Alcoholics Unanimous held a subdued but not too melancholy meeting.

But bad news was in store for everyone. A day or two later, I heard the owner, our Sardarji, inform my mother that the hotel had been sold and that she'd have to leave at the end of the month. She'd been expecting something like this, and had already accepted a matron's job at one of the schools in the valley. As for me, I was to be packed off to England to my aunt's home in Jersey. The prospect did not thrill me, but I was more or less resigned to it. And there did not appear to be much future for me in Dehra.

Even before the month was out, workers had begun pulling down parts of the building. It was to be rebuilt as a cinema hall, and would show the latest hits from Bombay. It was even rumoured that Dilip Kumar, the biggest star of that era, would inaugurate the new cinema when it was ready to open.

The spirit and character of a building lasts only while the building lasts. Remove the roof-beams, pull down the walls, smash the stairways, and you are left with nothing but memories. Even the ghosts have nowhere to go.

An old hotel that once had a personality of its own was now dismantled with startling rapidity. It had gone up slowly, brick by brick; it came down like a house of cards. No treasures cascaded from its walls; no skeletons were discovered. In two or three days the demolishers had wiped out the past, removed Green's Hotel from the face of the earth so effectively that it might never have existed.

Searching through the ruins one day, I found a bottle-opener lying in the dust, and kept it as a souvenir.

The bar had been the only common factor in the lives of those disparate individuals who had come there so regularly—drawn to the place rather than to each other.

Now they went their different ways—Suresh Mathur to the Club, the Maharani to her card table and private bar, Krishan to a public school as a cricket coach, Reggie Bhowmik and Ruby to Darjeeling to make a documentary... Sitaram continued to work for my mother, so I had his company whenever he was free.

The cinema came up quite rapidly, but I had left for England before it opened. When I returned five years later, it was showing Madhubala and Guru Dutt in a romantic comedy, *Mr & Mrs 55*.

Then I moved to Delhi.

In recent years, some of the old single cinemas have been closing down, giving way to multiplexes. The other day, passing through Dehra, I saw that 'our' cinema hall was being pulled down. 'What now?' I asked my taxi driver. 'A multiplex?' 'No, sir. A shopping mall!'

And such is progress.

I think I'm the only one around who is old enough to remember the old Green's Hotel, its dusty corridors, shabby bar-room, and oddball customers. All have gone. All forgotten! Not even footprints in the sands of time. But by putting down this memoir of an evening or two at that forgotten watering place, I think I have cheated Time just a little.

# The Homeless

On the road to Dehra, a boy played a flute as he drove his flock of sheep down the road. He was barefooted and his clothes were old. A faded red shawl was thrown across his shoulders. It was December and the sun was up, pouring into the banyan tree at the side of the road, where two boys were sitting on the great tree's gnarled, protruding roots.

The flute-player passed the banyan tree and glanced at the boys but did not stop playing. Presently, he was only a speck on the dusty road, and the flute music was thin and distant, subdued by the tinkle of sheep-bells.

The boys left the shelter of the banyan tree and began walking in the direction of the distant hills.

The road stretched ahead, lonely and endless, towards the low ranges of the Siwalik Hills. The dust was in their clothes and in their eyes and in their mouths. The sun rose higher in the sky and, as they walked, the sweat trickled down their armpits and legs.

The older boy, Rusty, was seventeen. He walked with his hands in the pockets of his thin cotton trousers, and he gazed at the ground. His fair hair was matted with dust, and his cheeks and arms were scorched red by the fierce sun. His eyes were blue and thoughtful.

'We will be in Raiwala soon,' he said. 'Would you like to rest, Bhaiyya?'

Kishen shrugged his thin shoulders. 'We'll rest when we get to Raiwala. If I sit down now, I'll never be able to get up. I suppose we have walked about ten miles this morning.'

He was a slim boy, almost as tall as Rusty though he was two years younger. He had dark, rebellious eyes, bushy eyebrows and thick black hair. His dusty white pyjamas were rolled up above his ankles, and he wore loose Peshawari chappals. An unbuttoned khaki shirt hung over his pyjamas.

Like Rusty, he was without a home. Rusty had run away from an indifferent guardian a little over a year ago. Kishen had run away from a drunken father. He possessed distant relatives, but he preferred the risks and pleasures of vagrancy to the security of living with people he did not know. He had been with Rusty for a year, and his home was by his friend's side. He was Punjabi; Rusty was Anglo-Indian.

'From Raiwala we'll take the train,' said Rusty. 'It will cost us about five rupees.'

'Never mind,' said Kishen. 'We've done enough walking. And we've still got twelve rupees. Is there anything in our old rooms in Dehra that we can sell?'

'Let me see... The table, the bed and the chair are not mine. There's an old tiger-skin, a bit eaten by rats, which no one will buy. There are one or two shirts and trousers.'

'Which we will need. These are all torn.'

'And some of my books—'

'Which no one will buy.'

'I would not sell them. Well, those were the only things I got out of my guardian's house, before I ran away—'

'Somi!' interrupted Kishen. 'Somi will be in Dehra—he'll help us! He got you a job once, he can do it again.'

Rusty was silent, remembering his friend Somi, who had

won him with a smile, and altered the course of his life. Somi, with his turban at an angle, a song on his lips...

Kishen had left Dehra in a hurry and had been taken to Haridwar, a town on the banks of the sacred Ganges, by his aunt, and Rusty had followed him and his aunt. Only priests, beggars and shopkeepers could make a living in Haridwar, and the boys were soon back on the road to Dehra.

Now a cool breeze came across the plain, blowing down from the hills. In the fields, there was a gentle swaying movement as the wind stirred the wheat. Then, the breeze hit the road, and the dust began to swirl and eddy about the footpath. The boys moved into the middle of the road, holding their hands to their eyes and stumbling forward. Out of the dust behind them came the rumbling of bullock-cart wheels.

'Ho, there! Out of my way!' shouted the driver of the cart. The bullocks snorted and came lumbering through the dust. The boys moved to the side of the road.

'Are you going to Raiwala?' called Rusty. 'Can you take us with you?'

'Climb up!' said the man, and the boys ran through the dust and clambered on to the back of the moving cart.

The cart lurched and rattled and bumped, and they had to cling to its sides to avoid falling off. It smelt of dry grass and cow-dung cakes. The driver had a red cloth tied around his head, and wore a tight vest and a dhoti around his waist. His feet and legs were bare, scorched black by the burning sun over the plains. He was smoking a bidi and shouting to his bullocks, cursing them at times, but sometimes speaking to them in endearing terms. He seemed to have forgotten the presence of the boys at the back, had dismissed them from his mind the moment they had climbed up. Rusty and Kishen were too busy clinging to the lopsided cart to bother about making conversation with the driver.

'I'd rather walk,' complained Kishen. 'Rusty, who suggested that we get into this silly old contraption? I am full of bumps and bruises already.'

'Beggars can't be choosers,' said Rusty.

'Please, we are not beggars—not yet, anyway. And if we were, we'd be much better off financially, I can assure you! As far as the rest of the world is concerned, you are still the son of an English sahib, and I am still the distant relative of a distant maharaja.'

'A prince,' said Rusty derisively, 'and riding in a bullock-cart!'

'Well, not every prince can boast of the experience.'

A little later the bullock-cart rumbled across a canal and became involved in the traffic of Raiwala, a busy little market town. The boys jumped off and walked beside the cart.

'Should we give him something?' asked Rusty. 'We ought to offer him some money.'

'How can we? said Kishen. 'Why didn't you think of that before we jumped on?'

'All right, we'll just thank him. Thank you, Bhaiji!' he called as the cart moved off.

'Thank you, Bhaiji!' shouted Kishen.

But either the driver did not hear or did not bother to look around; he continued smoking his bidi and talking to his animals. To all appearances had not even noticed that the boys had got down. He drove his bullock-cart away, leaving Rusty and Kishen standing on the road.

'I'm hungry,' said Kishen. 'We haven't eaten since last night.'

'Then we must eat,' said Rusty. 'Come on, Bhaiyya, we will eat,'

They walked through the narrow Raiwala bazaar, looking in at the tea and sweet shops until they found a place that looked dirty enough to be cheap. A servant-boy brought them chapatis and dal and Kishen ordered an ounce of butter; this was melted and poured over the dal. The meal cost them a rupee, and for this amount, they could eat as much as they liked. The butter was an extra and cost six annas. They were left with a little over ten rupees.

When they came out, the sun was low in the sky and the day was cooler.

'We can't walk tonight,' said Rusty. 'We'll have to sleep at the railway station. Maybe we can get on the train without a ticket.'

'And if we are caught, we'll spend a month in jail. Free board and lodging.'

'And then, the social workers will get you or they'll put you in a remand home and teach you to make mattresses.'

'I think it's better to buy tickets,' said Kishen.

'I know what we'll do,' said Rusty. 'We won't get the train till past midnight, so let's not buy tickets. We'll get to Harrawala early in the morning. Then, it's only about eight miles by road to Dehra.'

Kishen agreed, and they found their way to the railway station, where they made themselves comfortable in a first class waiting-room.

'We don't have tickets,' said Kishen.

'But we are first class, aren't we?'

Kishen settled down in an armchair and covered his face with a handkerchief. 'Wake me when the train comes in,' he said drowsily.

Rusty went into the bathroom. He put his head under a

tap and allowed cold water to play over his neck. He washed his face, drying it with a handkerchief, before returning to the waiting room.

A man entered, setting out his belongings on the big table in the centre of the room. Rusty judged him to be in his thirties. The man was white, but he was too restless to be a European. He looked virile but tired; he had a lean, sallow face and pouches under the eyes. Rusty sat down on the edge of Kishen's armchair.

'Going to Delhi?' asked the stranger. His accent, though not very pronounced, was American.

'No, the other way,' replied Rusty. 'We live in Dehra.'

'I've often been there,' said the man. 'I've been trying to popularize a new steel plough in northern India but without much success. Are you a student?'

'Not now. I finished with school two years ago.'

'And your friend?' He inclined his head towards the sleeping boy.

'He's with me,' said Rusty vaguely. 'We're travelling together.'

'Buddies.'

'Yes.'

The American took a flask from his bag and looked enquiringly at Rusty. 'Will you join me in a drink while we're waiting? There's almost an hour left for my train to arrive.'

'Well, I don't drink,' said Rusty, hesitating.

'A small one won't harm you. Just to keep me company.'

He took two small glasses from his bag, wiped them with a clean white handkerchief, and set them down on the table. Then, he poured some dark brown stuff from his flask into them.

'Brandy,' said Rusty, sniffing.

'So you recognize it. Yes, it's brandy.'

Rusty reached across the table and took the glass.

'Here's luck!' said the stranger.

'Thank you,' said Rusty, and gulped down a mouthful of neat liquor. He coughed and the tears came to his eyes. He put his head between his hands, but he was feeling better.

'You've come a long way,' said the American looking at the boy's clothes.

'On foot,' said Rusty, 'from Haridwar. Since morning.'

'Haridwar! That's a long walk. What made you do that?'

Rusty emptied his glass and set it down. The friendly stranger poured out more brandy. *This is the way they do things in America*, thought Rusty. When you meet a stranger, offer him a drink. He must go there one day.

'What made you walk?' asked the stranger again.

'Tomorrow we'll walk some more,' said Rusty.

'But why?'

'Because we have the time. We have all the time in the world.'

'How come?'

'Because we have no money. You can't have both time and money.'

'Oh, I agree. You are quite a philosopher. But what happened?' asked the American, looking at the sleeping boy. 'What is he to you?'

'He's with me,' said Rusty, ignoring the question. He was beginning to feel sleepy. The friendly stranger seemed to be getting further and further away and his voice was coming from a great distance.

'Tell me what happened.'

'I'll tell you,' said Rusty, leaning unsteadily across the table to see the other better, speaking slowly. 'I ran away. I ran away from home, nearly a year ago. I had a guardian, an Englishman—my parents died when I was very small—and I lived in his house, in his own community, and it was a world of our own and I never went outside it. Then, one day in the rain, I met Somi. I became his friend and he took me to his home and to the bazaar and he showed me India and the world and life itself. My guardian beat me when I came back from the bazaar, and he beat me when I played Holi and came home drenched in colour. I returned the beating, though, and ran away.'

Rusty paused in order to finish the drink and to see if the man was interested.

'Go on,' said the stranger.

'Somi was my good friend, he did a lot for me. He found a boy—Kishen over there—who needed English lessons, and his family took a liking to me and gave me a place to stay. She spent time with me often—I mean the boy's mother: Kishen's mother—and she was sweet and kind to me. She was beautiful. There will never be a woman as beautiful…'

He lapsed into silence for about a minute, gazed into the glass as though he sought something there other than brandy, and continued: 'But then they went away. Somi went away, everyone went away. What could I do, but go away too? What could I do, when Kishen's mother died, but go away? And if it wasn't for Kishen, I would never have come back. I tell you that straight, Sir—I would never have come back. I wouldn't be here now, talking to you, if it wasn't for Kishen.

'But I didn't know Kishen was alone. He had run away from his father, who was too drunk to care, and he had been living on his wits for weeks—he is good at that. But when I found him, I had to come back, we both had to come back. We have only got each other, you see.'

'I follow you a little,' said the stranger, and he filled Rusty's glass again. 'What are you going to do in Dehra, both of you? Do you have jobs to go to? I guess not. Well, if ever you find yourself in Delhi, look me up. Here's my card.'

A bell clanged on the station platform, and the stranger looked at his watch and said it was almost time for his train to arrive. He wiped the glasses with his handkerchief and returned them to his bag, then went outside and stood on the platform, waiting for the Delhi train.

Rusty leant against the waiting room door, staring across the railway tracks. He heard the shriek of the whistle as the front light of an engine played over the rails. The train came in slowly, the hissing engine sending out waves of steam. At the same time, the carriage doors opened and people started pouring out.

There was a jam on the platform while men, women and children pushed and struggled, and it was several minutes before anyone could get in or out of the carriage doors. The American had been swallowed up by the crowd. Bundles of belongings were passed through windows, over the heads of bystanders. Several young men climbed in from the windows, heads first, assisted by pushes from behind. Rusty assumed that there was another religious fair at Haridwar, for the rush was even greater than usual.

When the train left, calm descended on the platform. A few people waiting for the morning train to Dehra still slept near their bundles. Vendors selling soda water, lemons and curds, and cups of tea pushed their barrows down the platform, still calling their wares in desultory, sleepy voices. A baby cried, and the mother took the child to her bosom, but the baby kept on crying.

Rusty returned to the waiting room. Kishen was still sound asleep in the armchair.

Rusty went to the light switch and turned it off, but the light from the platform streamed in through the gauze-covered doors. He did not think anyone would be coming in again that night. He sat down beside Kishen.

'Kishen, Kishen,' he whispered, touching the boy's shoulder. Kishen stirred. 'What is it?' he mumbled drowsily. 'Why is it dark?'

'I put the light off,' said Rusty. 'You can sleep now.'

'I was sleeping,' said Kishen. 'But thank you all the same.'

# The Woman on Platform No. 8

It was my second year at boarding school, and I was sitting on platform no. 8 at Ambala station, waiting for the northern-bound train. I think I was about twelve at the time. My parents considered me old enough to travel alone, and I had arrived by bus at Ambala early in the evening; now there was a wait till midnight before my train arrived. Most of the time I had been pacing up and down the platform, browsing through the bookstall, or feeding broken biscuits to stray dogs; trains came and went, the platform would be quiet for a while and then, when a train arrived, it would be an inferno of heaving, shouting, agitated human bodies. As the carriage doors opened, a tide of people would sweep down upon the nervous little ticket collector at the gate; and every time this happened I would be caught in the rush and swept outside the station. Now tired of this game and of ambling about the platform, I sat down on my suitcase and gazed dismally across the railway tracks.

Trolleys rolled past me, and I was conscious of the cries of the various vendors—the men who sold curds and lemon, the sweetmeat seller, the newspaper boy—but I had lost interest in all that was going on along the busy platform, and continued to stare across the railway tracks, feeling bored and a little lonely.

'Are you all alone, my son?' asked a soft voice close behind me.

I looked up and saw a woman standing near me. She was leaning over, and I saw a pale face and dark, kind eyes. She wore no jewels, and was dressed very simply in a white sari.

'Yes, I am going to school,' I said, and stood up respectfully. She seemed poor, but there was a dignity about her that commanded respect.

'I have been watching you for some time,' she said. 'Didn't your parents come to see you off?'

'I don't live here,' I said. 'I had to change trains. Anyway, I can travel alone.'

'I am sure you can,' she said, and I liked her for saying that, and I also liked her for the simplicity of her dress, and for her deep, soft voice and the serenity of her face.

'Tell me, what is your name?' she asked.

'Arun,' I said.

'And how long do you have to wait for your train?'

'About an hour, I think. It comes at twelve o'clock.'

'Then come with me and have something to eat.'

I was going to refuse, out of shyness and suspicion, but she took me by the hand, and then I felt it would be silly to pull my hand away. She told a coolie to look after my suitcase, and then she led me away down the platform. Her hand was gentle, and she held mine neither too firmly nor too lightly. I looked up at her again. She was not young. And she was not old. She must have been over thirty, but had she been fifty, I think she would have looked much the same.

She took me into the station dining room, ordered tea and samosas and jalebis, and at once I began to thaw and take a new interest in this kind woman. The strange encounter had little effect on my appetite. I was a hungry schoolboy, and I ate as much as I could in as polite a manner as possible. She took obvious pleasure in watching me eat, and I think it was the food that strengthened the bond between us and cemented our friendship, for under the influence of the tea and sweets I began to talk quite freely, and told her about my school, my friends, my likes and dislikes. She questioned me quietly from time to time, but preferred listening; she drew me out very well, and I had soon forgotten that we were strangers. But she did not ask me about my family or where I lived, and I did not ask her where she lived. I accepted her for what she had been to me—a quiet, kind and gentle woman who gave sweets to a lonely boy on a railway platform...

After about half an hour we left the dining room and began walking back along the platform. An engine was shunting up and down beside platform no. 8, and as it approached, a boy leapt off the platform and ran across the rails, taking a shortcut to the next platform. He was at a safe distance from the engine, but as he leapt across the rails, the woman clutched my arm. Her fingers dug into my flesh, and I winced with pain. I caught her fingers and looked up at her, and I saw a spasm of pain and fear and sadness pass across her face. She watched the boy as he climbed the platform, and it was not until he had disappeared in the crowd that she relaxed her hold on my arm. She smiled at me reassuringly and took my hand again, but her fingers trembled against mine.

'He was all right,' I said, feeling that it was she who needed reassurance.

She smiled gratefully at me and pressed my hand. We walked together in silence until we reached the place where I had left my suitcase. One of my school fellows, Satish, a boy of about my age, had turned up with his mother.

'Hello, Arun!' he called. 'The train's coming in late, as usual.

Did you know we have a new headmaster this year?'

We shook hands, and then he turned to his mother and said: 'This is Arun, Mother. He is one of my friends, and the best bowler in the class.'

'I am glad to know that,' said his mother, a large imposing woman who wore spectacles. She looked at the woman who held my hand and said: 'And I suppose you're Arun's mother?'

I opened my mouth to make some explanation, but before I could say anything the woman replied: 'Yes, I am Arun's mother.'

I was unable to speak a word. I looked quickly up at the woman, but she did not appear to be at all embarrassed, and was smiling at Satish's mother.

Satish's mother said, 'It's such a nuisance having to wait for the train right in the middle of the night. But one can't let the child wait here alone. Anything can happen to a boy at a big station like this—there are so many suspicious characters hanging about. These days one has to be very careful of strangers.'

'Arun can travel alone, though,' said the woman beside me, and somehow I felt grateful to her for saying that. I had already forgiven her for lying; and besides, I had taken an instinctive dislike to Satish's mother.

'Well, be very careful, Arun,' said Satish's mother looking sternly at me through her spectacles. 'Be very careful when your mother is not with you. And never talk to strangers!'

I looked from Satish's mother to the woman who had given me tea and sweets, and back at Satish's mother.

'I like strangers,' I said.

Satish's mother definitely staggered a little, as obviously she was not used to being contradicted by small boys. 'There you are, you see! If you don't watch over them all the time, they'll walk straight into trouble. Always listen to what your mother tells you,' she said, wagging a fat little finger at me. 'And never, never talk to strangers.'

I glared resentfully at her, and moved closer to the woman who had befriended me. Satish was standing behind his mother, grinning at me, and delighting in my clash with his mother. Apparently he was on my side.

The station bell clanged, and the people who had till now been squatting resignedly on the platform began bustling about.

'Here it comes!' shouted Satish, as the engine whistle shrieked and the front lights played over the rails.

The train moved slowly into the station, the engine hissing and sending out waves of steam. As it came to a stop, Satish jumped on the footboard of a lighted compartment and shouted, 'Come on, Arun, this one's empty!' and I picked up my suitcase and made a dash for the open door.

We placed ourselves at the open windows, and the two women stood outside on the platform, talking up to us. Satish's mother did most of the talking.

'Now don't jump on and off moving trains as you did just now,' she said. 'And don't stick your heads out of the windows, and don't eat any rubbish on the way.' She allowed me to share the benefit of her advice, as she probably didn't think my 'mother' a very capable person. She handed Satish a bag of fruit, a cricket bat and a big box of chocolates, and told him to share the food with me. Then she stood back from the window to watch how my 'mother' behaved.

I was smarting under the patronizing tone of Satish's mother, who obviously thought mine a very poor family; and I did not intend giving the other woman away. I let her take my hand in hers, but I could think of nothing to say. I was conscious of Satish's mother staring at us with hard, beady eyes, and I found myself hating her with a firm, unreasoning hate. The guard walked up the platform, blowing his whistle for the train to leave. I looked straight into the eyes of the woman who held my hand, and she smiled in a gentle, understanding way. I leaned out of the window then, and put my lips to her cheek and kissed her.

The carriage jolted forward, and she drew her hand away.

'Goodbye, Mother!' said Satish, as the train began to move slowly out of the station. Satish and his mother waved to each other.

'Goodbye,' I said to the other woman, 'goodbye—Mother…' I didn't wave or shout, but sat still in front of the window, gazing at the woman on the platform. Satish's mother was talking to her, but she didn't appear to be listening; she was looking at me as the train took me away. She stood there on the busy platform, a pale sweet woman in white, and I watched her until she was lost in the milling crowd.

# The Kitemaker

There was but one tree in the street known as Gali Ram Nath—an ancient banyan that had grown through the cracks of an abandoned mosque—and little Ali's kite was caught in its branches. The boy, barefoot and clad only in a torn shirt, ran along the cobbled stones of the narrow street to where his grandfather sat nodding dreamily in the sunshine in their back courtyard.

'Grandfather,' shouted the boy. 'My kite has gone!'

The old man woke from his daydream with a start and, raising his head, displayed a beard that would have been white had it not been dyed red with mehendi leaves.

'Did the twine break?' he asked. 'I know that kite twine is not what it used to be.'

'No, Grandfather, the kite is stuck in the banyan tree.'

The old man chuckled. 'You have yet to learn how to fly a kite properly, my child. And I am too old to teach you, that's the pity of it. But you shall have another.'

He had just finished making a new kite from bamboo, paper and thin silk, and it lay in the sun, firming up. It was a pale pink kite, with a small green tail. The old man handed it to Ali, and the boy raised himself on his toes and kissed his grandfather's hollowed-out cheek.

'I will not lose this one,' he said. 'This kite will fly like a bird.' And he turned on his heels and skipped out of the courtyard.

The old man remained dreaming in the sun. His kite shop was gone, the premises long since sold to a junk dealer; but he still made kites for his own amusement and for the benefit of his grandson, Ali. Not many people bought kites these days. Adults disdained them, and children preferred to spend their money at the cinema. Moreover, there were not many open spaces left for the flying of kites. The city had swallowed up the open grassland that had stretched from the old fort's walls to the river bank.

But the old man remembered a time when grown men flew kites, and great battles were fought, the kites swerving and swooping in the sky, tangling with each other until the string of one was severed. Then the defeated but liberated kite would float away into the blue unknown. There was a good deal of betting, and money frequently changed hands.

Kite flying was then the sport of kings, and the old man remembered how the Nawab himself would come down to the riverside with his retinue to participate in this noble pastime. There was time, then, to spend an idle hour with a gay, dancing strip of paper. Now everyone hurried, in a heat of hope, and delicate things like kites and daydreams were trampled underfoot.

He, Mehmood the kitemaker, had in the prime of his life been well known throughout the city. Some of his more elaborate kites once sold for as much as three or four rupees each.

At the request of the Nawab, he had once made a very special kind of kite, unlike any that had been seen in the district. It consisted of a series of small, very light paper disks trailing on a thin bamboo frame. To the end of each disk he fixed a sprig of grass, forming a balance on both sides. The surface of the foremost disk was slightly convex, and a fantastic face was painted on it, having two eyes made of small mirrors. The disks, decreasing in size from head to tail, assumed an undulatory form and gave the kite the appearance of a crawling serpent. It required great skill to raise this cumbersome device from the ground, and only Mehmood could manage it.

Everyone had heard of the 'Dragon Kite' that Mehmood had built, and word went round that it possessed supernatural powers. A large crowd assembled in the open to watch its first public launching in the presence of the Nawab.

At the first attempt it refused to leave the ground. The disks made a plaintive, protesting sound, and the sun was trapped in the little mirrors, making the kite a living, complaining creature. Then the wind came from the right direction, and the Dragon Kite soared into the sky, wriggling its way higher and higher, the sun still glinting in its devil eyes. And when it went very high, it pulled fiercely at the twine, and Mehmood's young sons had to help him with the reel. Still the kite pulled, determined to be free, to break loose, to live a life of its own. And eventually it did so.

The twine snapped, the kite leaped away towards the sun, sailing on heavenward until it was lost to view. It was never found again, and Mehmood wondered afterwards if he had made too vivid, too living a thing of the great kite. He did not make another like it. Instead he presented to the Nawab a musical kite, one that made a sound like a violin when it rose into the air.

Those were more leisurely, more spacious days. But the Nawab had died years ago, and his descendants were almost as poor as Mehmood himself. Kitemakers, like poets, once had their patrons; but now no one knew Mehmood, simply because there were too many people in the Gali, and they could not be bothered with their neighbours.

When Mehmood was younger and had fallen sick, everyone in the neighbourhood had come to ask after his health; but now, when his days were drawing to a close, no one visited him. Most of his old friends were dead and his sons had grown up: one was working in a local garage and the other, who was in Pakistan at the time of the Partition, had not been able to rejoin his relatives.

The children who had bought kites from him ten years ago were now grown men, struggling for a living; they did not have time for the old man and his memories. They had grown up in a swiftly changing and competitive world, and they looked at the old kitemaker and the banyan tree with the same indifference.

Both were taken for granted—permanent fixtures that were of no concern to the raucous, sweating mass of humanity that surrounded them. No longer did people gather under the banyan tree to discuss their problems and their plans; only in the summer months did a few seek shelter from the fierce sun.

But there was the boy, his grandson. It was good that Mehmood's son worked close by, for it gladdened the old man's heart to watch the small boy at play in the winter sunshine, growing under his eyes like a young and well-nourished sapling putting forth new leaves each day. There is a great affinity between trees and men. We grow at much the same pace, if we are not hurt or starved or cut down. In our youth we are resplendent creatures, and in our declining years we stoop a little, we remember, we stretch our brittle limbs in the sun, and then, with a sigh, we shed our last leaves.

Mehmood was like the banyan, his hands gnarled and twisted like the roots of the ancient tree. Ali was like the young mimosa planted at the end of the courtyard. In two years, both he and the tree would acquire the strength and confidence of their early youth.

The voices in the street grew fainter, and Mehmood wondered if he was going to fall asleep and dream, as he so often did, of a kite so beautiful and powerful that it would resemble the great white bird of the Hindus—Garuda, God Vishnu's famous steed. He would like to make a wonderful new kite for little Ali. He had nothing else to leave the boy.

He heard Ali's voice in the distance, but did not realize that the boy was calling him. The voice seemed to come from very far away.

Ali was at the courtyard door, asking if his mother had as yet returned from the bazaar. When Mehmood did not answer, the boy came forward repeating his question. The sunlight was slanting across the old man's head, and a small white butterfly rested on his flowing beard. Mehmood was silent; and when Ali put his small brown hand on the old man's shoulder, he met with no response. The boy heard a faint sound, like the rubbing of marbles in his pocket.

Suddenly afraid, Ali turned and moved to the door, and then ran down the street shouting for his mother. The butterfly left the old man's beard and flew to the mimosa tree, and a sudden gust of wind caught the torn kite and lifted it in the air, carrying it far above the struggling city into the blind blue sky.

# The Lafunga

'If you have nothing to do,' and Devinder, 'will you come with me on my rounds?'

'First, we will see Hathi. If he has not left yet, I can accompany him to Lansdowne.'

Rusty set out with Devinder in the direction of the bazaar. As it was early morning, the shops were just beginning to open. Vegetable vendors were busy freshening their stock with liberal sprinklings of water, calling their prices and their wares; children dawdled in the road on their way to school, playing hopscotch or marbles. Girls going to college chattered in groups like gay, noisy parrots. Men cycled to work, and bullock-carts came in from the villages, laden with produce. The dust, which had taken all night to settle, rose again like a mist.

Rusty and Devinder stopped at the tea-shop to eat thickly buttered buns and drink strong, sweet tea. Then they looked for Hathi's room and found it above a cloth shop, lying empty, with its doors open. The string bed was leaning against the wall. On shelves and window ledges, in corners and on the floor, lay little coloured toys made of clay—elephants, bulls, horses and peacocks, and images of Krishna and Ganesha; a blue Krishna, with a flute to his lips, a jolly Ganesha with a delightful little trunk. Most of the toys were rough and unfinished, more charming than the completed pieces. Most of the finished products would now be on sale in the bazaar.

It came as a surprise to Rusty to discover that Hathi, the big wrestler, made toys for a living. He had not imagined there would be delicacy and skill in his friend's huge hands. The pleasantness of the discovery offset his disappointment at finding that Hathi had gone.

'He has left already,' said Rusty. 'Never mind. I know he will welcome me, even if I arrive unexpectedly.'

He left the bazaar with Devinder, making for the residential part of the town. As he would be leaving Dehra soon, there was no point in his visiting the school again; later, though, he would see Mr Pettigrew.

When they reached the Clock Tower, someone whistled to them from across the street, and a tall young man came striding towards them.

He looked taller than Devinder, mainly because of his long legs. He wore a lose-fitting bush-shirt that hung open in front. His face was long and pale, but he had quick, devilish eyes, and he smiled disarmingly.

'Here comes Sudheer the Lafunga,' whispered Devinder. 'Lafunga means loafer. He probably wants some money. He is the most charming and the most dangerous person in town.' Aloud, he said, 'Sudheer, when are you going to return the twenty rupees you owe me?'

'Don't talk that way, Devinder,' said the Lafunga, looking offended. 'Don't hurt my feelings. You know your money is safer with me than it is in the bank. It will even bring you dividends, mark my words. I have a plan that will come off in a few days, and then you will get back double your money. Please tell me, who is your friend?'

'We stay together,' said Devinder, introducing Rusty. 'And

he is bankrupt too, so don't get any ideas.'

'Please don't believe what he says of me,' said the Lafunga with a captivating smile that showed his strong teeth. 'Really I am not very harmful.'

'Well, completely harmless people are usually dull,' said Rusty.

'How I agree with you! I think we have a lot in common.'

'No, he hasn't got anything,' put in Devinder.

'Well then, he must start from the beginning. It is the best way to make a fortune. You will come and see me, won't you, mister Rusty? We could make a terrific combination, I am sure. You are the kind of person people trust! They take only one look at me and then feel their pockets to see if anything is missing!'

Rusty instinctively put his hand to his own pocket, and all three of them laughed.

'Well, I must go,' said Sudheer the Lafunga, now certain that Devinder was not likely to produce any funds. 'I have a small matter to attend to. It may bring me a fee of twenty or thirty rupees.'

'Go,' said Devinder. 'Strike while the iron is hot.'

'Not I,' said the Lafunga, grinning and moving off. 'I make the iron hot by striking.'

⁂

'Sudheer is not too bad,' said Devinder as they walked away from the Clock Tower. 'He is a crook, of course—Shree 420—but he would not harm people like us. As he is quite well educated, he manages to gain the confidence of some well-to-do people and acts on their behalf in matters that are not always respectable. But he spends what he makes, and is too generous to be successful.'

They had reached a quiet, tree-lined road and were walking in the shade of neem, mango, jamun and eucalyptus trees. Clumps of tall bamboo grew between the trees. Nowhere but in Dehra had Rusty seen so many kinds of trees. Trees that had no names. Tall, straight trees and broad, shady trees. Trees that slept or brooded in the afternoon stillness. And trees that shimmered, moved and whispered even when the winds were asleep.

Some marigolds grew wild on the footpath, and Devinder picked two of them, giving one to Rusty.

'There is a girl who lives at the bottom of the road,' he said. 'She is a pretty girl. Come with me and see her.'

They walked to the house at the end of the road and, while Rusty stood at the gate, Devinder went up the path. Devinder stood at the bottom of the veranda steps, a little to one side, where he could be seen from a window and whistled softly.

Presently, a girl came out on the veranda. When she saw Devinder, she smiled. She had a round, fresh face and long black hair, and she was not wearing any shoes.

Devinder gave her the marigold. She took it in her hand and, not knowing what to say, ran indoors.

That morning, Devinder and Rusty walked about four miles. Devinder's customers ranged from decadent maharanis and the wives of government officials to gardeners and sweeper women. Though his merchandise was cheap, the well-to-do were more finicky about a price than the poor. And there were a few who bought things from Devinder because they knew his circumstances and liked what he was doing.

A small girl with flapping pigtails came skipping down the road. She stopped to stare at Rusty as though he were something quite out of the ordinary but not unpleasant.

Rusty took the other marigold from his pocket and gave

it to the girl. It had been a long time since he had been able to make anyone a gift.

․⚬․

After some time, they parted, Devinder going back to the town while Rusty crossed the riverbed. He walked through the tea gardens until he found Mr Pettigrew's bungalow.

The old man was not in the veranda, but a young servant salaamed Rusty and asked him to sit down. Apparently Mr Pettigrew was having his bath.

'Does he always bathe in the afternoon?' asked Rusty.

'Yes, the Sahib likes his water to be put in the sun to get warm. He does not like cold baths or hot baths. The afternoon sun gives his water the right temperature.'

Rusty walked into the drawing room and nearly fell over a small table. The room was full of furniture, pictures and bric-a-brac. Tiger heads, stuffed and mounted, snarled down at him from the walls. On the carpet lay several cheetal skins, a bit worn at the sides. There were several shelves filled with books bound in morocco or calf. Photographs adorned the walls—one of a much younger Mr Pettigrew standing over a supine leopard, another of Mr Pettigrew perched on top of an elephant, with his rifle resting on his knees... Remembering his own experiences, Rusty wondered how such an active shikari ever found time for reading. While he was gazing at the photographs, Pettigrew himself came in, a large bathrobe wrapped round his thin frame, his grizzly chest looking very raw and red from the scrubbing he had just given it.

'Ah, there you are!' he said. 'The bearer told me you were here. Glad to see you again. Sit down and have a drink.'

Mr Pettigrew found the whisky and poured out two stiff

drinks. Then, still in his bathrobe and slippers, he made himself comfortable in an armchair. Rusty said something complimentary about one of the mounted tiger heads.

'Bagged it in Assam,' he said. 'Back in 1928, that was. I spent three nights on a machan before I got a shot at it.'

'You have a lot of books,' observed Rusty.

'A good collection, mostly flora and fauna. Some of them are extremely rare. By the way,' he said, looking around at the wall, 'did you ever see a picture of your father?'

'Have you got one?' asked Rusty. 'I've only a faint memory of what he looked like.'

'He's in that group photograph over there,' said Mr Pettigrew, pointing to a picture on the wall.

Rusty went over to the picture and saw three men dressed in white shirts and flannels, holding tennis rackets and looking very self-conscious.

'He's in the middle,' and Pettigrew. 'I'm on his right.'

Rusty saw a young man with fair hair and a fresh face. He was the only player who was smiling. Mr Pettigrew, sporting a fierce moustache, looked as though he was about to tackle a tiger with his racket. The third person was bald and uninteresting.

'Of course, he's very young in that photo,' said Pettigrew. 'It was taken long before you were ever thought of—before your father married.'

Rusty did not reply. He was trying to imagine his father in action on a tennis court, and wondered if he had been a better player than Pettigrew.

'Who was the best player among you?' he asked.

'Ah, well, we were both pretty good, you know. Except for poor old Wilkie on the left. He got in the picture by mistake.'

'Did my father talk much?' asked Rusty.

'Well, we all talked a lot, you know, especially after a few drinks. He talked as much as any of us. He could sing, when he wanted to. His rendering of the "Kashmiri Love Song" was always popular at parties, but it wasn't often he sang because he didn't like parties... Do you remember it? "Pale hands I love, beside the Shalimar..."'

Pettigrew began singing in a cracked, wavering voice, and Rusty was forced to take his eyes off the photograph. Halfway through the melody, Pettigrew forgot the words, so he took another gulp of whisky and began singing "The Rose of Tralee". The sight of the old man singing love songs in his bathrobe, with a glass of whisky in his hand, made Rusty smile.

'Well,' said Pettigrew, breaking off in the middle of the song, 'I don't sing as well as I used to. Never mind. Now tell me, boy, when are you going to Garhwal?'

'Tomorrow, perhaps.'

'Have you any money?'

'Enough to travel with. I have a friend in the hills with whom I can stay for some time.'

'And what about money?'

'I have enough.'

'Well, I'm lending you twenty rupees,' he said, thrusting an envelope into the boy's hands. 'Come and see me when you return, even if you don't find what you're looking for.'

'I'll do that, Mr Pettigrew.'

The old man looked at the boy for some time, as though summing him up.

'You don't really have to find out much about your father,' he said. 'You're just like him, you know.'

Returning to the bazaar, Devinder found Sudheer at a paan shop, his lips red with betel juice. Devinder got straight to the point.

'Sudheer,' he said, 'you owe me twenty rupees. I need it, not for myself, but for Rusty, who had to leave Dehra very urgently. You must get me the money by tonight.'

The Lafunga scratched his head.

'It will be difficult,' he said, 'but perhaps it can be managed. He really needs the money? It is not just a trick to get your own money back?'

'He is going to the hills. There may be money for him there, if he finds the person he is looking for.'

'Well, that's different,' said the Lafunga, brightening up. 'That makes Rusty an investment. Meet me at the Clock Tower at six o'clock, and I will have the money for you. I am glad to find you making useful friends for a change.' He stuffed another roll of paan into his mouth, and taking leave of Devinder with a bright red smile, strolled leisurely down the bazaar road.

As far as appearances went, he had little to do but loll around in the afternoon sunshine, frequenting tea shops and gambling with cards in small back rooms. All this he did very well—but it did not make him a living.

To say that he lived on his wits would be an exaggeration. He lived a great deal on other people's wits. There was the *seth*, for instance—Rusty's former landlord who owned much property and dabbled in many shady transactions—who was often represented by the Lafunga in affairs of an unsavoury nature.

Sudheer came originally from the Frontier, where little value was placed on human life; and while still a boy, he had wandered, a homeless refugee, over the border into India. A smuggler had adopted him, taught him something of the trade and introduced him to some of the best hands in the profession; but in a border-foray with the police, Sudheer's foster-father had been shot dead, and the youth had once again been on his own. By this time, he had been old enough to look after himself. With the help of his foster-father's connections, he had soon attained the service and confidence of the seth.

Sudheer was no petty criminal. He practised crime as a fine art and believed that thieves, and even murderers, had to have certain principles. If he stole then he stole from a rich man, who could afford to be robbed, or from a greedy man, who deserved to be robbed. And if he did not rob poor men, it was not because of any altruistic motive—it was because poor men were not worth robbing.

He was good to those friends, like Devinder, who were good to him. Perhaps his most valuable friends, as sources of both money and information, were the dancing girls who followed their profession on an almost inaccessible little road in the heart of the bazaar. His best friends were Hastini and Mrinalini. He borrowed money from them very freely and seldom paid back more than half of it.

Hastini could twang the sitar and dance—with a rather heavy tread—among various other accomplishments.

Mrinalini, a much smaller woman, had grown up in the profession. She was looked after by her mother, a former entertainer, who kept most of the money that Mrinalini made.

Sudheer woke Hastini in the middle of her afternoon siesta by tickling her under the chin with a feather.

'And who were you with last night, little brother?' she asked running her fingers through his thick brown hair. 'You are smelling of some horrible perfume.'

'You know I do not spend my nights with anyone,' said Sudheer. 'The perfume is from yesterday.'

'Someone new?'

'No, my butterfly. I have known her for a week.'

'Too long a time,' said Hastini petulantly. 'A dangerously long time. How much have you spent on her?'

'Nothing so far. But that is not why I came to see you. Have you got twenty rupees?'

'Villain!' cried Hastini. 'Why do you always borrow from me when you want to entertain some stupid young thing? Are you so heartless?'

'My little lotus flower!' protested Sudheer, pinching her rosy cheeks. 'I am not borrowing for any such reason. A friend of mine has to leave Dehra urgently, and I must get the money for his train fare. I owe it to him.'

'Since when did you have a friend?'

'Never mind that. I have one. And I come to you for help because I love you more than anyone. Would you prefer that I borrow the money from Mrinalini?'

'You dare not,' said Hastini. 'I will kill you if you do.'

Between Hastini, of the broad hips, and Mrinalini, who was small and slender, there existed a healthy rivalry for the affections of Sudheer. Perhaps it was the great difference in their proportions that animated the rivalry. Mrinalini envied the luxuriousness of Hastini's soft body, while Hastini envied Mrinalini's delicacy, poise, slenderness of foot and graceful walk. Mrinalini was the colour of milk and honey; she had the daintiness of a deer while Hastini possessed the elegance of an elephant.

Sudheer could appreciate both these qualities.

He stood up, looking young even for his twenty-two years, and smiled a crooked smile. He might have looked effeminate had it not been for his hands—they were big, long-fingered, strong hands.

'Where is the money?' he asked.

'You are so impatient! Sit down, sit down. I have it here beneath the mattress.'

Sudheer's hand made its way beneath the mattress and probed about in search of the money.

'Ah, here it is! You have a fortune stacked away here. Yes, ten rupees, fifteen, twenty—and one for luck... Now, give me a kiss!'

***

About an hour later, Sudheer was in the street again, whistling cheerfully to himself. He walked with a long, loping stride, his shirt hanging open. Warm sunshine filled one side of the narrow street and crept up the walls of shops and houses.

Sudheer passed a fruit stand, where the owner was busy talking to a customer, and helped himself to a choice red Kashmiri apple. He continued on his way down the bazaar road, munching the apple.

The bazaar continued for a mile, from the Clock Tower to the railway station, and Sudheer could hear the whistle of a train. He turned off at a little alley, throwing his half-eaten apple to a stray dog. Then, he climbed a flight of stairs—wooden stairs that were loose and rickety, liable to collapse at any moment....

Mrinalini's half-deaf mother was squatting on the kitchen floor, making a fire in an earthen brazier. Sudheer poked his head round the door and shouted: 'Good morning, Mother, I hope you are making me some tea. You look fine today!' And then, in a lower tone so that she could not hear: 'You look like a dried-up mango.'

'So it's you again,' grumbled the old woman. 'What do you want now?'

'Your most respectable daughter is what I want,' said Sudheer.

'What's that?' She cupped her hand to her ear and leaned forward.

'Where's Mrinalini?' shouted Sudheer.

'Don't shout like that! She is not here.'

'That's all I wanted to know,' said Sudheer, and he walked through the kitchen, through the living room, and onto the veranda balcony, where he found Mrinalini sitting in the sun, combing out her long, silken hair.

'Let me do it for you,' said Sudheer, and he took the comb from her hand and ran it through the silky black hair. 'For one so little, so much hair. You could conceal yourself in it and not be seen, except for your dainty little feet.'

'What are you after, Sudheer? You are so full of compliments this morning. And watch out for Mother—if she sees you combing my hair, she will have a fit!'

'And I hope it kills her.'

'Sudheer!'

'Don't be so sentimental about your mother. You are her little gold mine, and she treats you as such—soon, I will be having to fill in application forms before I can see you! It is time you kept your earnings for yourself.'

'So that it will be easier for you to help yourself?'

'Well, it would be more convenient. By the way, I have come to you for twenty rupees.'

Mrinalini laughed delightedly, and took the comb from Sudheer. 'What were you saying about my little feet?' she asked slyly.

'I said they were the feet of a princess, and I would be very happy to kiss them.'

'Kiss them, then.'

She held one delicate golden foot in the air, and Sudheer took it in his hands (which were as large as her feet) and kissed her ankle.

'That will be twenty rupees,' he said.

She pushed him away with her foot. 'But, Sudheer, I gave you fifteen rupees only three days ago. What have you done with it?'

'I haven't the slightest idea. I only know that I must have more. It is most urgent, you can be sure of that. But if you cannot help me, I must try elsewhere.'

'Do that, Sudheer. And may I ask, whom do you propose to try?'

'Well, I was thinking of Hastini.'

'*Who?*'

'You know, Hastini, the girl with the wonderful figure—'

'I should think I do! Sudheer, if you so much as dare to take a rupee from her, I'll never speak to you again!'

'Well then, what shall I do?'

Mrinalini beat the arms of the chair with her little fists and cursed Sudheer under her breath. Then, she got up and went into the kitchen. A great deal of shouting went on in the kitchen before Mrinalini came back with flushed cheeks and fifteen rupees.

'You don't know the trouble I had getting it,' she said. 'Now, don't come asking for more until at least a week has passed.'

'After a week, I will be able to supply you with funds. I am engaged tonight on a mission of some importance. In a few days, I will place golden bangles on your golden feet.'

'What mission?' asked Mrinalini, looking at him with an anxious frown. 'If it is anything to do with the seth, please leave it alone. You know what happened to Satish Dayal. He was smuggling opium for the seth, and now he is sitting in jail while the seth continues as always.'

'Don't worry about me. I can deal with the seth.'

'Then be off! I have to entertain a foreign delegation this evening. You can come tomorrow morning, if you are free.'

'I may come. Meanwhile, goodbye!'

He walked backwards into the living room, pivoted into the kitchen and, bending over the old woman, kissed her on the forehead.

'You dried-up old mango,' he said. And went away, whistling.

# Rum and Curry

Sudheer and Rusty left Lansdowne early one morning, and by the time they reached the oak and deodar forests of Kotli, they were shivering with the cold.

'I am not used to this sort of travel,' complained Sudheer. 'If this is a wild goose chase, I will curse you, Rusty. At least we should have mules to sit on.'

'We are sure to find a village soon,' said Rusty.

'We can spend a night there. As for it being a wild goose chase, it was you who told me that my aunt lived somewhere here. If she is not in this direction, it is all your fault, Lafunga.'

There was little light in the Kotli forest, for the tall, crowded deodars and oaks kept out the moonlight. The road was damp and covered with snails.

They were relieved to find a few small huts clustered together in an open clearing. A light showed from only one of the houses. Rusty rapped on the hard oak door, and called out: 'Is anyone there? We want a place to spend the night.'

'Who is it?' asked a nervous, irritable voice.

'Travellers,' said Sudheer, 'tired, hungry and poor.'

'This is not a *dharamshala*,' grumbled the man inside. 'This is no place for pilgrims.'

'We are not pilgrims,' said Sudheer, trying a different approach. 'We are road inspectors, servants of the government—

so open up, my friend!'

They heard much ill-natured muttering before the door opened, revealing an old and dirty man, who had stubble on his chin, warts on his feet and grease on his old clothes.

'Where do you come from?' he asked suspiciously.

'Lansdowne,' said Rusty. 'We have walked twenty miles since morning. Can we sleep in your house?'

'How do I know you are not thieves?' asked the old man, who did not look very honest himself.

'If we were thieves,' said Sudheer impatiently, 'we would not stand here, talking to you. We would have cut your throat and thrown you to the vultures, and carried off your beautiful daughter'.

'I have no daughter here.'

'What a pity! Never mind. My friend and I will sleep in your house tonight. We are not going to sleep in the forest.'

Sudheer strode into the lighted room but backed out almost immediately, holding his fingers to his nose.

'What dead animal are you keeping here?' he cried.

'They are sheepskins for curing,' said the old man. 'What is wrong?'

'Nothing, nothing,' said Sudheer, not wishing to hurt their host's feelings so soon; but in an aside to Rusty, he whispered, 'There is such a stink, I doubt if we will wake up in the morning.'

They stumbled into the room, and Rusty dumped his bundle on the ground. The room was bare, except for dilapidated sheep and deer skins hanging on the walls. There was a small fire in a corner of the room. Sudheer and Rusty got as close to it as they could, stamping their feet and chafing their hands. The old man sat down on his haunches and glared suspiciously at the intruders.

Sudheer looked at him and then at Rusty, and shrugged eloquently.

'May we know your name?' asked Rusty.

'It is Ram Singh,' said the old man grudgingly.

'Well, Ram Singh, my host,' said Sudheer solicitously, 'have you had your meal as yet?'

'I take it in the morning,' said Ram Singh.

'And in the evening?' Sudheer's voice held a note of hope.

'It is not necessary to eat more than once a day.'

'For a rusty old fellow like you, perhaps,' said Sudheer, 'but we have got blood in our veins. Is there nothing here to eat? Surely you have some bread, some vegetables?'

'I have nothing,' said the old man.

'Well, we will have to wait till morning,' said Sudheer. 'Rusty, take out the blanket and the bottle of rum.'

Rusty took the blanket from their bag and a flask of rum slipped out from the folds. Ram Singh showed unmistakable signs of coming to life.

'Is that medicine you have?' asked the old man. 'I have been suffering from headaches for the last month.'

'Well, this will give you a worse headache,' said Sudheer, gulping down a mouthful of rum and licking his lips. 'Besides, for people who eat only once a day, it is dangerous stuff.'

'We could get something to eat,' said the old man eagerly.

'You said you had nothing,' said Rusty, taking the bottle from Sudheer and putting it to his lips.

'There are some pumpkins on the roof,' said the old man. 'And I have a few potatoes and some spices. Shall I make a curry?'

And an hour later, warmed by rum and curry, they sat round the fire in a most convivial fashion. Rusty and Sudheer had gathered their only blanket about their shoulders, and Ram Singh had covered himself in sheepskins. He had been asking them questions about life in the cities—a life that was utterly foreign to him.

'You are men of the world,' said Ram Singh. 'You have been in most of the cities of India, you have known all kinds of men and women. I have never travelled beyond Lansdowne, nor have I seen the trains and ships which I hear so much about. I am seventy and I have not seen these things, though I have sons who have been away many years, and one who has even been out of India with his regiment. I would like to ask your advice. It is lonely living alone, and though I have had three wives, they are all dead.'

'If you have had three wives,' said Sudheer, 'you are a man of the world!'

He had his back to the wall, his feet stuck out towards the fire. Rusty was half-asleep, his head resting on Sudheer's shoulder.

'My daughters are all married,' continued Ram Singh. 'I would like to get married again, but tell me, how should I go about it?'

Sudheer laughed out loud. The old man in his youth must have been as crafty a devil as the Lafunga himself.

'Well, you would have to pay for her, of course,' said Sudheer.

'Tell me of a suitable woman. She should be young, of course. Her nose—what kind of nose should she have?'

'A flat nose,' said Sudheer, without the ghost of a smile. 'The nostrils should not be turned up.'

'Ah! And the shape of her body?'

'Not too manly. She should not be crooked. Do not expect too much, old man!'

'Her head?' asked the old man eagerly. 'What should her head be like?'

Sudheer gave this a moment's consideration. 'The head

should not be bald,' he said.

Ram Singh nodded his approval; his opinion of Sudheer was going up by leaps and bounds.

'And her colour, should it be white?'

'No, not very white.'

'Black?'

'Not too black. But she would have to be evil-smelling, otherwise she would not stay with you.'

⚬∞⚬

A bear kept them awake during the early part of the night. It clambered up on the roof and made a meal of the old man's store of pumpkins.

'Can it get in?' asked Rusty.

'It comes every night,' said Ram Singh. 'But it is a vegetarian and eats only the pumpkins.'

There was a thud as a pumpkin rolled off the roof and landed on the ground. Then, the bear climbed down from the roof and shambled off into the forest.

The fire was glowing feebly, but Sudheer and Rusty were warm beneath their blanket and, being very tired, were soon asleep, despite the efforts of an army of bugs to keep them awake. But, at about midnight, they were woken by a loud cry and, starting up, found the lantern lit, and the old man throwing a fit.

Ram Singh was leaping about the room, waving his arms, going into contortions, and bringing up gurgling sounds from the back of his throat.

'What is the matter?' shouted Rusty, from under the blanket. 'Have you gone mad?'

In response, the old man gurgled and shrieked, and

continued his frenzied dance.

'A demon!' he shouted. 'A demon has entered me!'

Sudheer leapt to his feet. He had heard of the superstitions of some hill-people, of their belief in spirits, but he had never expected to witness such a performance.

'It's the medicine you gave me!' cried Ram Singh. 'The medicine was evil, it is all your doing!' And he continued dancing about the room. 'Should I throw the medicine away?' asked Sudheer.

'No, don't do that!' shouted Ram Singh, appearing normal for a moment. 'Throw yourself on the ground!'

Sudheer threw himself on the ground.

'On your back!' gasped the old man.

Sudheer turned over onto his back. Rusty had lifted a corner of the blanket and was watching, fascinated.

'Raise your left foot,' said the old man. 'Take it in your mouth. That will charm the demon away.'

'I will not put my foot in my mouth,' said Sudheer, getting to his feet, having lost faith in the genuineness of the old man's fit. 'I don't think there is any demon in you. It is probably your curry. Have something more to drink, and you will be all right.'

He produced the all but empty flask of rum, made the old man open his mouth, and poured the rest of the spirit down his throat.

Ram Singh choked, shook his head violently and grinned at Sudheer. 'The demon has gone now,' he said.

'I am glad to know it,' said Sudheer. 'But you have emptied the bottle. Now let us try to sleep again.'

The cold had come in through the blanket, and Rusty found sleep difficult. Instead, he began to think of the purpose of his journey and wondered if it would not have been wiser to stay in

Dehra. Outside, the air was still; the wind had stopped whistling through the pines. Only a jackal howled in the distance. The old man was tossing and turning on his sheepskins.

'Ram Singh,' whispered Rusty. 'Are you awake?'

Ram Singh groaned softly.

'Tell me,' said Rusty. 'Have you heard of a woman living alone in these parts?'

'There are many old women here.'

'No, I mean a well-to-do woman. She must be about forty. At one time, she was married to a white sahib.'

'Ah, I have heard of such a woman.... She was beautiful when she was young, they tell me.'

Rusty was silent. He was afraid to ask any further questions: afraid to know too much; afraid of finding out too soon that there was nothing for him and nowhere to go.

'Ram Singh,' he whispered. 'Where does this woman live?'

'She had her house on the road to Rishikesh...'

'And the woman, where is she? Is she dead?'

'I do not know, I have not heard of her recently,' said Ram Singh. 'Why do you ask of her? Are you related to the sahib?'

'No,' said Rusty. 'I have heard of her, that's all.'

Silence. The old man grumbled to himself, muttering quietly, and then began to snore. The jackal was silent, the wind was up again; the moon was lost in the clouds. Rusty felt Sudheer's hand slip into his own, and press his fingers. He was surprised to find him awake.

'Forget it,' whispered Sudheer. 'Forget the dead, forget the past. Trouble your heart no longer. I have enough for both of us, so let us live on it till it is finished, and let us be happy, Rusty, my friend, let us be happy...'

Rusty did not reply, but he held the Lafunga's hand and

returned the pressure of his fingers to let him know that he was listening.

'This is only the beginning,' said Sudheer. 'The world is waiting for us.'

⸺

Rusty woke first, scratching and rubbing his legs. Looking up at the skylight, he saw the first glimmer of dawn. He slipped on his clothes and torn socks and, without waking Sudheer or the old man, unlatched the door and stepped outside.

Before him lay a world of white.

It had snowed in the early hours of the morning while they had been sleeping. The snow lay thick on the ground, carpeting the hillside. There was not a breath of wind; the pine trees stood blanched and still, and a deep silence hung over the forest and the hills.

Rusty did not immediately wake the others. He wanted this all to himself—the snow and the silence and the coming of the sun...

Towards the horizon, the sky was red; and then the sun came over the hills and struck the snow; and Rusty ran to the top of the hill and stood in the dazzling sunlight, shading his eyes from the glare, taking in the range of mountains and the valley and the stream that cut its way through the snow like a dark trickle of oil. He ran down the hill and into the house.

'Wake up!' he shouted, shaking Sudheer. 'Get up, and come outside!' 'Why—have you found your treasure?' complained Sudheer sleepily. 'Or has the old man had another fit?'

'More than that—it has snowed!'

'Then I shall definitely not come outside,' said Sudheer. And turning over, he went to sleep again.

# A Case for Inspector Lal

I met Inspector Keemat Lal about two years ago, while I was living in the hot, dusty town of Shahpur in the plains of northern India.

Keemat Lal had charge of the local police station. He was a heavily built man, slow and rather ponderous, and inclined to be lazy; but, like most lazy people, he was intelligent. He was also a failure. He had remained an inspector for a number of years, and had given up all hope of further promotion. His luck was against him, he said. He should never have been a policeman. He had been born under the sign of Capricorn and should really have gone into the restaurant business, but now it was too late to do anything about it.

The inspector and I had little in common. He was nearing forty, and I was twenty-five. But both of us spoke English, and in Shahpur there were very few people who did. In addition, we were both fond of beer. There were no places of entertainment in Shahpur. The searing heat, the dust that came whirling up from the east, the mosquitoes (almost as numerous as the flies), and the general monotony gave one a thirst for something more substantial than stale lemonade.

My house was on the outskirts of the town, where we were not often disturbed. On two or three evenings in the week, just as the sun was going down and making it possible for one to emerge from the khas-cooled confines of a dark, high-ceilinged bedroom, Inspector Keemat Lal would appear on the veranda steps, mopping the sweat from his face with a small towel, which he used instead of a handkerchief. My only servant, excited at the prospect of serving an inspector of police, would hurry out with glasses, a bucket of ice and several bottles of the best Indian beer.

One evening, after we had overtaken our fourth bottle, I said, 'You must have had some interesting cases in your career, Inspector.'

'Most of them were rather dull,' he said. 'At least the successful ones were. The sensational cases usually went unsolved—otherwise I might have been a superintendent by now. I suppose you are talking of murder cases. Do you remember the shooting of the minister of the interior? I was on that one, but it was a political murder and we never solved it.'

'Tell me about a case you solved,' I said. 'An interesting one.' When I saw him looking uncomfortable, I added, 'You don't have to worry, Inspector. I'm a very discreet person, in spite of all the beer I consume.'

'But how can you be discreet? You are a writer.'

I protested, 'Writers are usually very discreet. They always change the names of people and places.'

He gave me one of his rare smiles. 'And how would you describe me, if you were to put me into a story?'

'Oh, I'd leave you as you are. No one would believe in you, anyway.'

He laughed indulgently and poured out more beer. 'I suppose I can change names, too… I will tell you of a very interesting case. The victim was an unusual person, and so was the killer. But you must promise not to write this story.'

'I promise,' I lied.

'Do you know Panauli?'

'In the hills? Yes, I have been there once or twice.'

'Good, then you will follow me without my having to be too descriptive. This happened about three years ago, shortly after I had been stationed at Panauli. Nothing much ever happened there. There were a few cases of theft and cheating, and an occasional fight during the summer. A murder took place about once every ten years. It was therefore quite an event when the Rani of —— was found dead in her sitting room, her head split open with an axe. I knew that I would have to solve the case if I wanted to stay in Panauli.

'The trouble was, anyone could have killed the Rani, and there were some who made no secret of their satisfaction that she was dead. She had been an unpopular woman. Her husband was dead, her children were scattered, and her money—for she had never been a very wealthy rani—had been dwindling away. She lived alone in an old house on the outskirts of the town, ruling the locality with the stern authority of a matriarch. She had a servant, and he was the man who found the body and came to the police, dithering and tongue-tied. I arrested him at once, of course. I knew he was probably innocent, but a basic rule is to grab the first man on the scene of crime, especially if he happens to be a servant. But we let him go after a beating. There was nothing much he could tell us, and he had a sound alibi.

'The axe with which the Rani had been killed must have been a small woodcutter's axe—so we deduced from the wound. We couldn't find the weapon. It might have been used by a man or a woman, and there were several of both sexes who had a grudge against the Rani. There were bazaar rumours that she had been supplementing her income by trafficking in young women: she had the necessary connections. There were also rumours that she possessed vast wealth, and that it was stored away in her godowns. We did not find any treasure. There were so many rumours darting about like battered shuttlecocks that I decided to stop wasting my time in trying to follow them up. Instead, I restricted my inquiries to those people who had been close to the Rani—either in their personal relationships or in actual physical proximity.

'To begin with, there was Mr Kapur, a wealthy businessman from Bombay who had a house in Panauli. He was supposed to be an old admirer of the Rani's. I discovered that he had occasionally lent her money, and that, in spite of his professed friendship for her, had charged a high rate of interest.

'Then there were her immediate neighbours—an American missionary and his wife, who had been trying to convert the Rani to Christianity; an English spinster of seventy, who made no secret of the fact that she and the Rani had hated each other with great enthusiasm; a local councillor and his family, who did not get on well with their aristocratic neighbour; and a tailor, who kept his shop close by. None of these people had any powerful motive for killing the Rani—or none that I could discover. But the tailor's daughter interested me.

'Her name was Kusum. She was twelve or thirteen years old—a thin, dark girl, with lovely black eyes and a swift, disarming smile. While I was making my routine inquiries in the vicinity of the Rani's house, I noticed that the girl always tried to avoid me. When I questioned her about the Rani, and about her own movements on the day of the crime, she pretended to be very vague and stupid.

'But I could see she was not stupid, and I became convinced that she knew something unusual about the Rani. She might even know something about the murder. She could have been protecting someone, and was afraid to tell me what she knew. Often, when I spoke to her of the violence of the Rani's death, I saw fear in her eyes. I began to think the girl's life might be in danger, and I had a close watch kept on her. I liked her. I liked her youth and freshness, and the innocence and wonder in her eyes. I spoke to her whenever I could, kindly and paternally, and though I knew she rather liked me and found me amusing—the ups and downs of Panauli always left me panting for breath—and though I could see that she *wanted* to tell me something, she always held back at the last moment.

'Then, one afternoon, while I was in the rani's house going through her effects, I saw something glistening in a narrow crack near the doorstep. I would not have noticed it if the sun had not been pouring through the window, glinting off the little object. I stooped and picked up a piece of glass. It was part of a broken bangle.

'I turned the fragment over in my hand. There was something familiar about its colour and design. Didn't Kusum wear similar glass bangles? I went to look for the girl but she was not in her father's shop. I was told that she had gone down the hill, to gather firewood.

'I decided to take the narrow path down the hill. It went round some rocks and cacti, and then disappeared into a forest of oak trees. I found Kusum sitting at the edge of the forest, a bundle of twigs beside her.

'"You are always wandering about alone," I said. "Don't you feel afraid?"

'"It is safer when I am alone," she replied. "Nobody comes here."

'I glanced quickly at the bangles on her wrist, and noticed

that their colour matched that of the broken piece. I held out the bit of broken glass and said, "I found it in the Rani's house. It must have fallen..."

'She did not wait for me to finish what I was saying. With a look of terror, she sprang up from the grass and fled into the forest.

'I was completely taken aback. I had not expected such a reaction. Of what significance was the broken bangle? I hurried after the girl, slipping on the smooth pine needles that covered the slopes. I was searching among the trees when I heard someone sobbing behind me. When I turned round, I saw the girl standing on a boulder, facing me with an axe in her hands.

'When Kusum saw me staring at her, she raised the axe and rushed down the slope towards me.

'I was too bewildered to be able to do anything but stare with open mouth as she rushed at me with the axe. The impetus of her run would have brought her right up against me, and the axe, coming down, would probably have crushed my skull, thick though it is. But while she was still six feet from me, the axe flew out of her hands. It sprang into the air as though it had a life of its own and came curving towards me.

'In spite of my weight, I moved swiftly aside. The axe grazed my shoulder and sank into the soft bark of the tree behind me. And Kusum dropped at my feet weeping hysterically.'

Inspector Keemat Lal paused in order to replenish his glass. He took a long pull at the beer, and the froth glistened on his moustache.

'And then what happened?' I prompted him.

'Perhaps it could only have happened in India—and to a person like me,' he said. 'This sudden compassion for the person you are supposed to destroy. Instead of being furious and outraged, instead of seizing the girl and marching her off to the police station, I stroked her head and said silly comforting things.'

'And she told you that she had killed the Rani?'

'She told me how the Rani had called her to her house and given her tea and sweets. Mr Kapur had been there. After some time he began stroking Kusum's arms and squeezing her knees. She had drawn away, but Kapur kept pawing her. The Rani was telling Kusum not to be afraid, that no harm would come to her. Kusum slipped away from the man and made a rush for the door. The Rani caught her by the shoulders and pushed her back into the room. The Rani was getting angry. Kusum saw the axe lying in a corner of the room. She seized it, raised it above her head and threatened Kapur. The man realized that he had gone too far, and valuing his neck, backed away. But the Rani, in a great rage, sprang at the girl. And Kusum, in desperation and panic, brought the axe down upon the Rani's head.

'The Rani fell to the ground. Without waiting to see what Kapur might do, Kusum fled from the house. Her bangle must have broken when she stumbled against the door. She ran into the forest, and after concealing the axe among some tall ferns, lay weeping on the grass until it grew dark. But such was her nature, and such the resilience of youth, that she recovered sufficiently to be able to return home looking her normal self. And during the following days, she managed to remain silent about the whole business.'

'What did you do about it?' I asked.

Keemat Lal looked me straight in my beery eye.

'Nothing,' he said. 'I did absolutely nothing. I couldn't have the girl put away in a remand home. It would have crushed her spirit.'

'And what about Kapur?'

'Oh, he had his own reasons for remaining quiet, as you may guess. No, the case was closed—or perhaps I should say the file was put in my pending tray. My promotion, too, went into the pending tray.'

'It didn't turn out very well for you,' I said.

'No. Here I am in Shahpur, and still an inspector. But, tell me, what would you have done if you had been in my place?'

I considered his question carefully for a moment or two, then said, 'I suppose it would have depended on how much sympathy the girl evoked in me. She had killed in innocence...'

'Then, you would have put your personal feeling above your duty to uphold the law?'

'Yes. But I would not have made a very good policeman.'

'Exactly.'

'Still, it's a pity that Kapur got off so easily.'

'There was no alternative if I was to let the girl go. But he didn't get off altogether. He found himself in trouble later on for swindling some manufacturing concern, and went to jail for a couple of years.'

'And the girl—did you see her again?'

'Well, before I was transferred from Panauli, I saw her occasionally on the road. She was usually on her way to school. She would greet me with folded hands, and call me uncle.'

The beer bottles were all empty, and Inspector Keemat Lal got up to leave. His final words to me were, 'I should never have been a policeman.'

# Strychnine in the Cognac

Sick was she on Thursday,
Dead was she on Friday,
Glad was Tom on Saturday night
To bury his wife on Sunday.

Miss Bean was reclining in a cane chair in a corner of the hotel's Beer Garden, reciting old nursery rhymes to herself, when Mr Lobo, the resident pianist, walked over and placed a glass of lemon juice beside her.

'Oranges and lemons,' he said, sitting down beside her. 'Which do you prefer?'

'Both,' she said. 'Oranges for the complexion, lemons for the digestion.'

'Words of wisdom. But that nursery rhyme sounded a bit wicked. I can only remember the innocent ones like Jack and Jill.'

'Not so innocent. "Jack fell down and broke his crown"—he wouldn't have survived a broken head. Maybe Jill pushed him over a cliff—and went tumbling after!'

'Like the judge who fell into the Kempty Waterfall. Was he pushed, or did he fall?'

'We shall never know. No witnesses. But here come the Roys—what a handsome couple!'

The Roys were, indeed, a handsome couple, as you would expect them to be. Dilip Roy was in his mid-forties, but still a name to be reckoned with in Bollywood. He was greying a little at the temples, just below the edges of his wig; but he remained lean and athletic looking, and the meaty romantic roles still came his way. His wife, Rosie Roy, was two or three years younger than him, but inclined to plumpness. When she was in her late twenties and early thirties she had starred in several very popular films—two of them opposite Dilip Roy, whom she had married while on location with him in Kashmir—but of late she had been having some difficulty in getting parts to her liking. She hadn't been feeling very well and had taken to sleeping late in the mornings. Her doctor had suspected diabetes and had advised a complete check-up, but she kept putting off the necessary tests.

'You need change,' said Dilip, always concerned about her health. 'A change from Bombay. A fortnight in the hills will do wonders for you. I'll spend a few days with you too, before I start shooting in Switzerland. Where would you like to go—Simla, Mussoorie, Darjeeling, Ooty?'

'Why not Switzerland?'

Dilip laughed uneasily. 'It wouldn't be much of a holiday. I'd be shooting all the time and you'd be pestered by hangers-on and loads of admirers.'

'Former admirers.'

'Well, better an old admirer than none at all. And I'm still jealous.'

They settled on Mussoorie—partly because Dilip Roy's father was an old friend of Nandu, the owner of the hotel, and partly because Rosie had spent an idyllic summer there as a girl, staying with an aunt in Barlowganj. When the couple arrived at the hotel, the first person they encountered was Miss Bean, watering the potted aspidistras on the porch of the hotel.

'Hello,' said Rosie, smiling curiously at Miss Bean. 'Are you the new gardener?'

'I'm the old gardener,' said Miss Bean. 'A long-time resident, actually. But the gardener never waters these aspidistras—he thinks they are hardy enough to go without. But plants are like humans—they need a little attention from time to time, otherwise they die of neglect. I've seen you somewhere, haven't I?'

'Only if you go to the movies,' said Rosie. And added, 'Old movies.'

'You're Rosie Roy,' said Miss Bean. 'I saw you in *Cobra Lady*.'

'Wasn't it terrible?'

'It was so bad that I enjoyed every moment of it. And this must be the great Dilip Roy,' observed Miss Bean, as the well-known actor joined them, followed by room boys loaded with luggage. 'The hero of *Love in Kathmandu*,' said Miss Bean, but the hero ignored her.

Dilip Roy did not stop to gossip, but continued up the steps to the lobby, followed by his wife and the room boys. Miss Bean gave her attention to the aspidistras.

'Friendly heroine but not so friendly hero,' she said to the nearest potted plant. The aspidistra appeared to agree.

The couple settled in, and over the next few days Miss Bean saw quite a lot of them although she took care not to intrude in any way, for it was obvious that the Roys were not looking for company.

In the evenings Dilip Roy would plant himself on a bar stool, and work his way through several whiskies, occasionally answering polite questions from the bartender or a casual customer, but always rather morosely, his mind obviously elsewhere. In the background, Mr Lobo, the hotel pianist, would play popular numbers but without receiving any encouragement or applause.

Rosie did not join her husband at the bar. But occasionally a martini was served to her in her room—sometimes two martinis—it was obvious that she liked a gin and vermouth cocktail now and then. Nandu presented her with a bottle of cognac, and she kept it on her dresser, intending to open it only when her husband was in the mood to drink with her.

They went out for quiet walks together, avoiding the Mall where they would quickly be recognized by both locals and tourists. Sometimes they passed Miss Bean, who was herself a great walker. As they were fellow residents of the hotel they would stop to exchange comments on the weather, the view, the hotel, the town, sometimes even the country and the rest of the world. But from the quiet of the mountains the rest of the world can seem very far away.

Rosie Roy liked the look of Miss Bean and was always ready to stop and talk. Dilip Roy was polite but brusque. The local gossip did not interest him, and he thought Miss Bean a rather quaint and rather foolish bit of flotsam surviving from the days of the British Raj. But then (as Rosie argued) the hotel, the cottages, the winding footpaths, the hill station itself, were all survivors of the Raj, and if their old-world atmosphere did not please you, it might have been better to holiday in Goa—and soak up the Portuguese atmosphere!

India would always be haunted by its history...

One day the Roys had a violent quarrel. Miss Bean was no eavesdropper but she couldn't help overhearing every word that was spoken. Her favourite place was a bench situated behind a tall hibiscus hedge. It looked out upon the snows, and Miss Bean liked to spend a half hour there with a book while Fluff, her little terrier, investigated the hillside, looking for rats' holes. You couldn't see the bench from the Beer Garden, and it was in the Beer Garden that Rosie and Dilip Roy were confronting each other.

'You're off because of that woman in Bandra.' Rosie's voice was quite shrill. 'A week away from her and you're beginning to look like a real Majnu—all pale and melancholy.'

'Don't make up things.' Dilip Roy sounded impatient rather than melancholy. 'You know they start shooting on the new film next week. And it's in Switzerland, not Bandra.'

'You're not the star. They can do without you. You've been getting too fat for leading roles. And you're drinking too much.'

'I'll end up an alcoholic if I stay here much longer. The doctors advised rest for you, not for me. You've given yourself ulcers and you won't get any better if you worry over trifles.'

Here the couple were interrupted by a group of youngsters seeking autographs, and Miss Bean took advantage of the diversion to slip away, taking a roundabout path to her room. Fluff enjoyed the extended walk.

That evening Dilip Roy opened the bottle of cognac. He was leaving the next morning, and he was in a mood to celebrate. But he was not particularly fond of cognac, and did most of his celebrating with his favourite scotch. Rosie poured herself a glass of cognac, then put the bottle away on the dresser in their room. There it remained all night.

Dilip Roy breakfasted alone in the dining room, then sent

for a taxi to take him down to Dehradun. Rosie did not see him off.

'She's sleeping late,' explained Dilip. 'She has a headache. Don't disturb her.'

'Enjoy yourself in Switzerland,' said Nandu, the affable proprietor.

'Look after Rosie,' said Dilip Roy. 'Let her get plenty of rest.'

And everyone did their best to make Rosie comfortable and welcome, because she was much the more gracious of the two. The manager and staff fussed over her, and Mr Lobo played her favourite tunes, especially the one she always requested:

> The future is hard to see,
> Whatever will be will be...

Even Miss Bean was drawn towards Rosie and joined her on an inspection of the garden, for they were both fond of flowers, and in late summer the grounds were awash with bright yellow marigolds, petunias, larkspur and climbing roses. They had coffee together and Rosie recalled her parents and happy childhood days spent in Mussoorie; she did not talk about her marriage.

As evening came on, Rosie would retire to her room and send for a martini; it would be followed by a second. She would have a light supper in her room—usually a chicken or mushroom soup with toast—followed by a few sips of cognac as a nightcap...and then to bed.

This routine continued for three or four days, and the cognac bottle was still half full because Rosie preferred martinis. Dilip Roy made a couple of calls from Bombay—the crew would be off to Switzerland any day, and meanwhile they were shooting some scenes in Lonavala.

He had been away for almost a week when Rosie suddenly

fell ill. At about ten o'clock after her dinner she rang her bell. A room boy answered her summons, found her on her bed, still dressed, and having a fit of sorts. He ran for the manager. The manager hurried to the room, followed by a concerned Mr Lobo. They found her still having convulsions.

'I'll go get Dr Bisht,' said Lobo, and hurried from the room. Minutes later they heard the splutter of his scooter as he took the winding driveway down to the Mall. Dr Bisht had a scooter too—it was the Age of the Scooter—and he arrived in time to give Rosie some basic first aid and arrange for her to be taken to the local hospital. He was cautious in his diagnosis. 'Looks like food poisoning,' he said, and then his eye fell on the open bottle of cognac, of which about half remained. There was still some liquor in a glass, and he sniffed at it and made a face. 'Or something else.... We'd better have this bottle examined.' But that would take time.

A call was put through to Dilip Roy's studio in Bombay; but the actor was in Switzerland, and air flights were not very frequent those days. It would be two or three days before he could return.

Miss Bean visited Rosie Roy every day, and so, occasionally, did Nandu and Mr Lobo. To everyone's relief and amazement, Rosie made a good recovery. There were crystals of strychnine at the bottom of that bottle, but they had only just begun to dissolve. Another evening's drinking and Rosie would have reached the fatal dose lying in wait for her. For it was obvious that someone had placed the poison in the bottle, and that someone could only have been Dilip Roy, before he had left Mussoorie. Far away at the time of his wife's expiry, he would have the perfect alibi.

Of course, nothing could be proven—all was surmise and

conjecture—but Rosie was certain in her own mind that her husband had intended to do away with her in absentia, so to speak—and had very nearly succeeded.

She and Miss Bean had become fast friends, and Rosie found herself confiding all her fears and suspicions to the older person, and turning to her for advice and guidance.

∞

They sat together on the lawns of the Savoy, Rosie reclining in an easy chair, Miss Bean quite at ease on a wooden bench. From indoors came the tinkle of a piano as Mr Lobo played 'September Song'. Miss Bean sang the words softly, almost to herself:

> But it's a long time from May to December,
> And the days grown short when we reach September.

'That's a pretty song,' said Rosie. 'A little sad, though.'

'September is a sad month,' said Miss Bean musingly. 'The end of summer, the end of all those lovely picnics. Holding hands and paddling in mountain streams. Hot sunny days. And then all that rain—weeks of endless rain and mist. September brings back the sunshine if only for a short time, and then those icy winds will start coming down from the snows.'

'How romantic!' exclaimed Rosie. 'You are lucky to have lived here most of your life. Well, perhaps I'll come and join you when I've finished with that wretched husband of mine in Bombay.'

'What do you intend to do, my dear? Put arsenic in his vodka?'

'Arsenic is too slow. But if he eats enough of those chocolate-coated hazelnuts of which he is so fond, he could well come to a sticky end.'

'What do you mean, dear?'

'This is only for your ears, Auntie May.'

She addressed Miss Bean by her first name whenever she became trustful and confiding. 'I know you won't give me away—just in case something happens.'

'What could happen now?'

'Well, during the last two years I've been so miserable that I've always kept a little cyanide pill with me, just so that I can put an end to my life if it becomes too unbearable.'

'Oh, dear. Do throw it away. Don't even think of doing away with yourself.'

'Well, actually I did throw it away—got rid of it. I took the pill and gave it a nice coating of chocolate and then mixed it up with all the little hazelnut chocolates in the tin that Dilip always carries around.'

'Oh, but that was wicked of you. Quite diabolical! Understandable though, when you think of what he tried to do to you. But he could get to that chocolate pill any day. Pop it into his mouth, and then—'

'Pop off?' added Rosie, a glint in her hazel eyes.

'But it's been some time, hasn't it? Almost three weeks since he left. Someone else might have helped himself or herself to a chocolate—'

Just then they saw Nandu advancing across the lawn. It wasn't his usual amble, he looked very purposeful.

'Bad news,' he said, when he reached their sunny corner. 'I've just had a call from Dilip's manager. Your husband died last night. Suicide, it appears. Cyanide. He must have been feeling very guilty about what happened to you. I'm sorry for your loss, Rosie...'

That evening Miss Bean dined with Rosie in the old ballroom. It was the end of the season, and only a few tables were occupied. Mr Lobo was at the piano, playing nostalgic numbers.

'What will you have, Auntie May? You're my special guest today. It's not that I want to celebrate or anything like that—'

'I quite understand, my dear.'

'So you must have a decent wine, instead of that dreadful crème-de-menthe you make in your room. Here's the wine list.'

Miss Bean ran her eye down the wine list. She was no blackmailer, but she couldn't help feeling a little surge of power as she made her choice. And it was such a long time since she'd enjoyed a really good wine. So she plumped for the most expensive wine on the list, and sat back in anticipation.

# Sher Singh and the
# Hot-water Bottle

It's been many years since Sher Singh, of village Solti, came to my rescue.

At the time I was living right at the top of the Landour Hill, in a rented cottage that leaked badly. It was cold that winter and I was short of funds and in need of sustenance. And to make matters worse, our new Prime Minister, a strict moralist who knew what was good for everyone, had imposed prohibition on the country, and I was suffering from the non-availability of Solan No. 1 (a cheap but good whisky) and a certain XXX Rum that had been distilled at Rosa in UP since before the 1857 revolt. The distillery had changed hands more than once during the fighting, and both oppressors and oppressed had raided it until it was emptied of its energizing grog. It had recovered from those traumatic events; but now, in more peaceful times, it was to suffer again, along with those, such as this writer, who thirsted after the mellowed and matured juices of our all-purpose sugarcane.

Sher Singh was my milkman. Early every morning he trudged up the hill from his village, three miles distant, to deliver his milk to two or three homes on the hillside. On the way he watered it a little at a roadside hydrant; but it was good milk, once you had removed some of the grass that floated around in the can.

One morning, when Sher Singh found me sitting in the sun looking rather depressed, he offered condolences, well knowing the reason for my dejection.

'Not to worry, sir,' he said, 'When one door closes, another door opens. Every problem has its solution. In three days' time I will have solved your problem.'

Three dry and thirsty days passed. Sher Singh came and went. On the fourth morning he asked me for my hot-water bottle—one of those rubber bags which keep you warm for half the night, allowing you to freeze during the second half.

Anyway, I gave him my hot-water bottle. His need, I felt sure, was greater than mine.

'Do you have another?' he asked.

This was testing my generosity, but I was in a don't-care mood, and I said, 'To hell with it,' and gave him the second bottle.

Next morning he turned up with both bottles. They were full of something; certainly not milk.

'Don't you want them?' I asked.

'See if you like my home-made brandy,' he said, and unscrewing one of the bottles, he poured a vile-looking liquid into an empty jug.

'Go on, taste it,' he said.

I did as I was told. It tasted awful—a combination of turnips and castor oil—but it lit a small fire in my stomach, and I came to life immediately.

Sher Singh had created his own still and was busy producing a potent and heady liquor for all his friends—and customers.

The hillside came to life. A somnolent Landour became

a merry mountain. Strengthened and uplifted, the more adventurous residents of Landour—missionaries, retired colonels and brigadiers, school teachers, shopkeepers and the odd hippie (left over from the sixties)—found themselves immune to the mists of February and sharp winds of March.

We flung aside restraint. Mischief abounded. A respectable headmistress fell in love with a muleteer, and rode off with him to his village near Harsil. A retired vice-admiral drank too much one evening and performed a sailor's jig in the middle of the Upper Mall. A judge had an affair with the dhobi's sister, and the local padre developed acute peritonitis and perished from a burst appendix. Not all was merriment in the spring of 1980.

A posse of policemen was sent down to Solti village to find out what was going on down there. They were not seen for several days. After being entertained by Sher Singh and his friends, they had lost their way coming back, and had emerged near the Yamuna bridge, happy to be alive in spite of severe hangovers.

I spent most of my evening in the company of a famous shikari, who was paying me to write his memoirs. He made up most of his exploits, but it was fun anyway, and after consuming a hot-water bottle of firewater, we saw pink elephants and purple tigers.

Then suddenly this orgy of wine, women and song came to an end. Sher Singh's supply system had broken down. Our hot-water bottles were dry and empty.

There was no sign of Sher Singh, either.

I decided to go down to his village. Landour was in suspense.

I was in my forties then, still quite agile on a mountain slope, and it took me a little over an hour to scramble down the steep footpath to Solti village.

I found Sher Singh on his cot, his arm in a sling, his head

bandaged, strips of plaster on his hands and feet. He had just been carried home, piggyback on a neighbour's shoulder, from the mission hospital.

'The bear attacked me,' he explained. 'It had been raiding my still every evening, and it was becoming a nuisance—getting drunk and chasing the women as they returned from the fields.'

Armed with a lathi, Sher Singh had attempted to chase away the bear, but it had turned on him, using its claws to good effect before taking off into the forest. Lucky to be alive, Sher Singh would carry the scars for the rest of his life.

I was reluctant to trudge back to Landour on my own. I had no desire to encounter an alcoholic bear on the way. Deprived of Sher Singh's magic potion, it would be in a bad mood. Fortunately, several of the young men of the village offered to escort me home, and we went uphill in style, making a lot of noise to keep the bear away. One youth beat a drum, another blew a bugle, and a third shouted imprecations against bears in general.

The flow of high-spirited spirits having come to a halt, Landour returned to its sober and sombre self. The headmistress returned from Harsil as though nothing unusual had happened, the retired judge fell out of love with the dhobi's sister, and a new padre moved into the parson's house.

Fortunately for some of us, the government in Delhi changed around that time, and the prohibition law was repealed. 'Foreign liquor' (as made in India) appeared again in the stores, and the vendors of home-made spirits went out of business. My hot-water bottles were put to their legitimate use.

When Sher Singh recovered from his wounds he continued to deliver my milk, and did so for many years, always watering it down a little at the tap near Sisters' Bazaar. Then he grew too old to climb up to Landour, and I grew too old to scramble down to his village. But his grandson now delivers the milk on his way to school, and being a good boy, he doesn't water it down.

The other day he told me that his grandfather was feeling the cold. It has been a harsh winter. So I sent the old man one of my hot-water bottles. And for old times' sake, I filled it with the better part of a bottle of rum.

# An English Jester at the Mughal Court

In the diaries and correspondence of Sir Thomas Roe, the English ambassador to the Court of Jehangir, there are frequent references to a number of Englishmen who, for a few colourful years, strutted about the Indian scene, and then were heard of no more. The strangest of this group of fortune hunters and eccentrics was Thomas Corryat, known at home as the 'Odcombe legstretcher', a man of many parts who had earned a certain literary reputation as the author of *Corryat's Crudities*, a whimsical book on continental travel.

Corryat, the son of a Somerset clergyman, gained early distinction as a sort of buffoon at the court of James I. His physical peculiarities—a peaked 'sugar-loaf formation of head' perched on an ungainly frame—added to a ready wit, made him a favourite with the English king who later came to be called 'the wisest fool in Christendom'. Encouraged by his sovereign, he began, in 1608, a long series of wanderings which took him into almost every corner of Europe and resulted in his travel book, the *Crudities*, which was published by patrons whose help he obtained by 'unwearied pertinacity and unblushing opportunity'. The volume was foreworded with some mock-heroic verses by Ben Jonson, but the ridicule was lost on Tom Corryat, whose sense of humour lacked subtlety, thus rendering him immune to the barbs of satire.

In 1612 Corryat again started on his travels, this time in the direction of the East. He tramped through the Holy Land, on to Nineveh and Babylon, down the Euphrates Valley to Baghdad, through Persia to Kandahar and down into India. He turned up at Agra in 1615, and presented himself before Ambassador Roe, who had known the wanderer at King James's court. Sir Thomas was by no means pleased to see Corryat, who was far from being the ideal image of the Englishman which Roe wished to project for the benefit of Jehangir; but he felt it was his duty to help the traveller before speeding him on his way. Tom Corryat, however, was in no hurry to move on. He boasted that he had made his way through Asia on little more than two pence a day, having in fact lived off the generosity of various benefactors. At Agra, the Mughal capital, he soon made himself at home. A natural linguist, he acquired such proficiency in Hindustani that it was said of him that, in a quarrel with the Ambassador's troublesome washerwoman, he reduced the lady to silence within an hour...

He made more dangerous use of his knowledge of the language one evening at the time of Mohammedan prayer when, in response to the muezzin's cry, 'There is no God but Allah, and Mohammed is his prophet', he shouted in Hindustani that the true prophet was Christ. It says a great deal for the tolerance which then prevailed at the Mughal capital that this insult was overlooked as the indiscretion of the half-witted 'English fakir'. Corryat, however, made up for this blunder when, having somehow managed to obtain an audience with Jehangir, he recited a flattering eulogy of the Emperor, in Persian. Jehangir was both amused and pleased by this barefaced flattery, and dismissed Corryat with some kind words and a gift of a hundred rupees.

When Sir Thomas Roe heard of the goings-on of his itinerant guest, he was furious, and raved at Corryat for an hour, accusing him of degrading the good name of England.

'But,' said Corryat, in describing the encounter, 'I answered our ambassador in such a stout and resolute manner that he ceased nibbling at me.'

A time came when Tom Corryat, having exhausted the financial possibilities of the Mughal capital, decided to return home. Roe, only too happy to be rid of so embarrassing a guest, gave him a letter of introduction to the English consul at Alleppo, requesting the consul to receive Corryat with courtesy, 'for you shall find him a very honest poor wretch', and asking him to pay the bearer ten pounds. Corryat was hurt by the expression 'honest poor wretch', but he accepted the letter.

Leaving Agra, Corryat made for Surat, where he was hospitably received by the members of the English factory. In the course of a conversation mention was made of a shipment of sack which had just arrived from England. The wanderer's eyes glistened at this mention of his favourite drink, which he had long been without.

'Sack! Sack!' he exclaimed. 'Is there any such thing as sack? I pray you, give me some sack!' The factors obliged him, and Corryat, drinking to excess, collapsed dramatically. A few days later he was dead.

Tom Corryat was laid to rest near Surat. Time has obliterated all traces of his grave; but local tradition has identified it with a monument in the Muslim style at Rajgari, a village near Swally, the old seaport of Surat. The memory of this strange individual's eruption into seventeenth-century India will always fascinate those who follow the lesser-known paths of history.

# Children of India

They pass ME every day, on their way to school—boys and girls from the surrounding villages and the outskirts of the hill station. There are no school buses plying for these children: they walk.

For many of them, it's a very long walk to school.

Ranbir, who is ten, has to climb the mountain from his village, four miles distant and 2,000 feet below the town level. He comes in all weathers, wearing the same pair of cheap shoes until they have almost fallen apart.

Ranbir is a cheerful soul. He waves to me whenever he sees me at my window. Sometimes he brings me cucumbers from his father's field. I pay him for the cucumbers; he uses the money for books or for small things needed at home.

Many of the children are like Ranbir—poor, but slightly better off than what their parents were at the same age. They cannot attend the expensive residential and private schools that abound here, but must go to the government-aided schools with only basic facilities. Not many of their parents managed to go to school. They spent their lives working in the fields or delivering milk in the hill station. The lucky ones got into the army. Perhaps Ranbir will do something different when he grows up.

He has yet to see a train but he sees planes flying over the mountains almost every day.

'How far can a plane go?' he asks.

'All over the world,' I tell him. 'Thousands of miles in a day. You can go almost anywhere.'

'I'll go round the world one day,' he vows. 'I'll buy a plane and go everywhere!'

And maybe he will. He has a determined chin and a defiant look in his eye.

The following lines in my journal were put down for my own inspiration or encouragement, but they will do for any determined young person:

> We get out of life what we bring to it. There is not a dream which may not come true if we have the energy which determines our own fate. We can always get what we want if we will it intensely enough…So few people succeed greatly because so few people conceive a great end, working towards it without giving up. We all know that the man who works steadily for money gets rich; the man who works day and night for fame or power reaches his goal. And those who work for deeper, more spiritual achievements will find them too. It may come when we no longer have any use for it, but if we have been willing it long enough, it will come!

Up to a few years ago, very few girls in the hills or in the villages of India went to school. They helped in the home until they were old enough to be married, which wasn't very old. But there are now just as many girls as there are boys going to school.

Bindra is something of an extrovert—a confident fourteen-year-old who chatters away as she hurries down the road with her companions. Her father is a forest guard and knows me quite well: I meet him on my walks through the deodar woods behind Landour. And I had grown used to seeing Bindra almost every day. When she did not put in an appearance for a week, I asked her brother if anything was wrong.

'Oh, nothing,' he says, 'she is helping my mother cut grass. Soon the monsoon will end and the grass will dry up. So we cut it now and store it for the cows for winter.'

'And why aren't you cutting grass, too?'

'Oh, I have a cricket match today,' he says, and hurries away to join his team-mates. Unlike his sister, he puts pleasure before work!

Cricket, once the game of the elite, has become the game of the masses. On any holiday, in any part of this vast country, groups of boys can be seen making their way to the nearest field, or open patch of land, with bat, ball and any other cricketing gear that they can cobble together. Watching some of them play, I am amazed at the quality of talent, at the finesse with which they bat or bowl. Some of the local teams are as good, if not better, than any from the private schools, where there are better facilities. But the boys from these poor or lower-middle-class families will never get the exposure that is necessary to bring them to the attention of those who select state or national teams. They will never get near enough to the men of influence and power. They must continue to play for the love of the game, or watch their more fortunate heroes' exploits on television.

∞

As winter approaches and the days grow shorter, those children who live far away must quicken their pace in order to get home before dark. Ranbir and his friends find that darkness has fallen before they are halfway home.

'What is the time, Uncle?' he asks, as he trudges up the steep road past Ivy Cottage.

One gets used to being called 'Uncle' by almost every boy or girl one meets. I wonder how the custom began. Perhaps it has its origins in the folk tale about the tiger who refrained from pouncing on you if you called him 'uncle'. Tigers don't eat their relatives! Or do they? The ploy may not work if the tiger happens to be a tigress. Would you call her 'Aunty' as she (or your teacher!) descends on you?

It's dark at six and by then, Ranbir likes to be out of the deodar forest and on the open road to the village. The moon and the stars and the village lights are sufficient, but not in the forest, where it is dark even during the day. And the silent flitting of bats and flying foxes, and the eerie hoot of an owl, can be a little disconcerting for the hardiest of children. Once Ranbir and the other boys were chased by a bear.

When he told me about it, I said, 'Well, now we know you can run faster then a bear!'

'Yes, but you have to run downhill when chased by a bear.' He spoke as one having long experience of escaping from bears. 'They run much faster uphill!'

'I'll remember that,' I said, 'thanks for the advice.' And I don't suppose calling a bear 'Uncle' would help.

Usually Ranbir has the company of other boys, and they sing most of the way, for loud singing by small boys will silence owls and frighten away the forest demons. One of them plays a flute, and flute music in the mountains is always enchanting.

Not only in the hills, but all over India, children are constantly making their way to and from school, in conditions that range from dust storms in the Rajasthan desert to blizzards in Ladakh and Kashmir. In the larger towns and cities, there are school buses, but in remote rural areas getting to school can pose a problem.

Most children are more than equal to any obstacles that may arise. Like those youngsters in the Ganjam district of Orissa. In the absence of a bridge, they swim or wade across the Dhanei River every day in order to reach their school. I have a picture of them in my scrapbook. Holding books or satchels aloft in one hand, they do the breast stroke or dog-paddle with the other; or form a chain and help each other across.

Wherever you go in India, you will find children helping out with the family's source of livelihood, whether it be drying fish on the Malabar coast, or gathering saffron buds in Kashmir, or grazing camels or cattle in a village in Rajasthan or Gujarat.

Only the more fortunate can afford to send their children to English-medium private or 'public' schools, and those children really are fortunate, for some of these institutions are excellent schools, as good, and often better, than their counterparts in Britain or the US. Whether it's in Ajmer or Bangalore, New Delhi or Chandigarh, Kanpur or Calcutta, the best schools set very high standards. The growth of a prosperous middle class has led to an ever-increasing demand for quality education. But as private schools proliferate, standards suffer too, and many parents must settle for the second-rate.

The great majority of our children still attend schools run by the state or municipality. These vary from the good to the bad to the ugly, depending on how they are run and where they are situated. A classroom without windows, or with a roof that lets in the monsoon rain, is not uncommon. Even so, children from different communities learn to live and grow together. Hardship makes brothers of us all.

The census tells us that two in every five of the population is in the age group of five to fifteen. Almost half our population is on the way to school!

And here I stand at my window, watching some of them pass by—boys and girls, big and small, some scruffy, some smart, some mischievous, some serious, but all *going* somewhere—hopefully towards a better future.

# PLACES OF INDIA

# Rainy Day in June

A thunderstorm, followed by strong winds, brought down the temperature. That was yesterday. And today it is cloudy, cool, drizzling a little, almost monsoon weather; but it is still too early for the real monsoon.

The birds are enjoying the cool weather. The green-backed tits cool their bottoms in the rainwater pool. A king crow flashes past, winging through the air like an arrow. On the wing, it snaps up a hovering dragonfly. The mynahs fetch crow feathers to line their nests in the eaves of the house. I am lying so still on the window seat that a tit alights on the sill, within a few inches of my head. It snaps up a small dead moth before flying away.

At dusk I sit at the window and watch the trees and listen to the wind as it makes light conversation in the leafy tops of the maples. There is a whirr of wings as the king-crows fly into the trees to roost for the night. But for one large bat it is time to get busy, and he flits in and out of the trees. The sky is just light enough to enable me to see the bat and the outlines of the taller trees.

Up on Landour Hill, the lights are just beginning to come on. It is deliciously cool, eight o'clock, a perfect summer's evening. Prem is singing to himself in the kitchen. His wife and sister are chattering beneath the walnut tree. Down the hill, a kakar is barking, alarmed perhaps by the presence of a leopard.

The wind grows stronger and the tall maples bow before it: the maple moves its slender branches slowly from side to side, the oak moves its branches up and down. It is darker now; more lights on Landour. The cry of the barking deer has grown fainter, more distant, and now I hear a cricket singing in the bushes. The stars are out, the wind grows chilly, it is time to close the window.

# Landour Bazaar

In most North Indian bazaars, there is a clock tower. And like most clocks in clock towers, this one works in fits and starts: listless in summer, sluggish during the monsoon, stopping altogether when it snows in January. Almost every year the tall brick structure gets a coat of paint. It was pink last year. Now it's a livid purple.

From the clock tower at one end to the mule sheds at the other, this old Mussoorie bazaar is a mile long. The tall, shaky three-storey buildings cling to the mountainside, shutting out the sunlight. They are even shakier now that heavy trucks have started rumbling down the narrow street, originally made for nothing heavier than a rickshaw. The street is narrow and damp, retaining all the bazaar smells—sweetmeats frying, smoke from wood or charcoal fires, the sweat and urine of mules, petrol fumes, all these mingle with the smell of mist and old buildings and distant pines.

The bazaar sprang up about 150 years ago to serve the needs of British soldiers who were sent to the Landour convalescent depot to recover from sickness or wounds. The old military hospital, built in 1827, now houses the Defence Institute of Work Study.* One old resident of the bazaar, a ninety-year-old

---

*The Defence Institute of Work Study has been renamed the Institute of Technologic Management.

tailor, can remember the time, in the early years of the century, when the Redcoats marched through the small bazaar on their way to the cantonment church. And they always carried their rifles into church, remembering how many had been surprised in churches during the 1857 uprising.

Today, the Landour bazaar serves the local population, Mussoorie itself being more geared to the needs and interest of tourists. There are a number of silversmiths in Landour. They fashion silver nose-rings, earrings, bracelets and anklets, which are bought by the women from the surrounding Jaunpuri villages. One silversmith had a chest full of old silver rupees. These rupees are sometimes hung on thin silver chains and worn as pendants. I have often seen women in Garhwal wearing pendants or necklaces of rupees embossed with the profiles of Queen Victoria or King Edward VII.

At the other extreme there are the kabari shops, where you can pick up almost everything—a tape recorder discarded by a Woodstock student, or a piece of furniture from grandmother's time in the hill station. Old clothes, Victorian bric-a-brac, and bits of modern gadgetry vie for your attention.

The old clothes are often more reliable than the new. Last winter I bought a new pullover marked 'Made in Nepal' from a Tibetan pavement vendor. I was wearing it on the way home when it began to rain. By the time I reached my cottage, the pullover had shrunk inches and I had some difficulty getting out of it! It was now just the right size for Bijju, the milkman's twelve-year-old son, and I gave it to the boy. But it continued to shrink at every wash, and it is now being worn by Teju, Bijju's younger brother, who is eight.

At the dark windy corner in the bazaar, one always found an old man hunched up over his charcoal fire, roasting peanuts.

He'd been there for as long as I could remember, and he could be seen at almost any hour of the day or night, in all weathers.

He was probably quite tall, but I never saw him standing up. One judged his height from his long, loose limbs. He was very thin, probably tubercular, and the high cheekbones added to the tautness of his tightly stretched skin.

His peanuts were always fresh, crisp and hot. They were popular with small boys, who had a few coins to spend on their way to and from school. On cold winter evenings, there was always a demand for peanuts from people of all ages.

No one seemed to know the old man's name. No one had ever thought of asking. One just took his presence for granted. He was as fixed a landmark as the clock tower or the old cherry tree that grew crookedly from the hillside. He seemed less perishable than the tree, more dependable than the clock. He had no family, but in a way all the world was his family because he was in continuous contact with people. And yet he was a remote sort of being; always polite, even to children, but never familiar. He was seldom alone, but he must have been lonely.

Summer nights he rolled himself up in a thin blanket and slept on the ground beside the dying embers of his fire. During winter he waited until the last cinema show was over, before retiring to the rickshaw coolies' shelter where there was protection from the freezing wind.

Did he enjoy being alive? I often wondered. He was not a joyful person; but then neither was he miserable. Perhaps he was one of those who do not attach overmuch importance to themselves, who are emotionally uninvolved in the life around them, content with their limitations, their dark corners; people on whom cares rest lightly, simply because they do not care at all.

I wanted to get to know the old man better, to sound him

out on the immense questions involved in roasting peanuts all one's life; but it's too late now. He died last summer.

That corner remained very empty, very dark, and every time I passed it, I was haunted by visions of the old peanut vendor, troubled by the questions I did not ask; and I wondered if he was really as indifferent to life as he appeared to be.

Then, a few weeks ago, there was a new occupant of the corner, a new seller of peanuts. No relative of the old man, but a boy of thirteen or fourteen. The human personality can impose its own nature on its surroundings. In the old man's time it seemed a dark, gloomy corner. Now it's lit up by sunshine—a sunny personality, smiling, chattering. Old age gives way to youth; and I'm glad I won't be alive when the new peanut vendor grows old. One shouldn't see too many people grow old.

Leaving the main bazaar behind, I walk some way down the Mussoorie–Tehri road, a fine road to walk on, in spite of the dust from an occasional bus or jeep. From Mussoorie to Chamba, a distance of some thirty-five miles, the road seldom descends below 7,000 feet, and there is a continual vista of the snow ranges to the north and valleys and rivers to the south. Dhanaulti is one of the lovelier spots, and the Garhwal Mandal Vikas Nigam has a rest house here, where one can spend an idyllic weekend. Some years ago I walked all the way to Chamba, spending the night at Kaddukhal, from where a short climb takes one to the Surkhanda Devi temple.

Leaving the Tehri road, one can also trek down to the little Aglar river and then up to Nag Tibba, 9,000 feet, which has good oak forests and animals ranging from barking deer to Himalayan bear; but this is an arduous trek and you must be prepared to spend the night in the open or seek the hospitality of a village.

On this particular day I reach Suakholi and rest at a tea shop, a loose stone structure with a tin roof held down by stones. It serves the bus passengers, mule drivers, milkmen and others who use this road.

I find a couple of mules tethered to a pine tree. The mule drivers, handsome men in tattered clothes, sit on a bench in the shade of the tree, drinking tea from brass tumblers. The shopkeeper, a man of indeterminate age—the cold dry winds from the mountain passes having crinkled his face like a walnut—greets me enthusiastically, as he always does. He even produces a chair, which looks a survivor from one of Wilson's rest houses, and may even be a Sheraton. Fortunately, the Mussoorie kabaris do not know about it or they'd have snapped it up long ago. In any case, the stuffing has come out of the seat. The shopkeeper apologizes for its condition: 'The rats were nesting in it.' And then, to reassure me: 'But they have gone now.'

I would just as soon be on the bench with the Jaunpuri mule drivers, but I do not wish to offend Mela Ram, the tea shop owner; so I take his chair into the shade and lower myself into it.

'How long have you kept this shop?'

'Oh, ten...fifteen years, I do not remember.' He hasn't bothered to count the years. Why should he? Outside the towns in the isolation of the hills, life is simply a matter of yesterday, today and tomorrow. And not always tomorrow.

Unlike Mela Ram, the mule drivers have somewhere to go and something to deliver—sacks of potatoes! From Jaunpur to Jaunsar, the potato is probably the crop best suited to these stony, terraced fields. They have to deliver their potatoes in the Landour bazaar and return to their villages before nightfall; and soon they lead their pack animals away, along the dusty road to Mussoorie.

'Tea or lassi?' Mela Ram offers me a choice, and I choose the curd preparation, which is sharp, sour and very refreshing. The wind soughs gently in the upper branches of the pine trees, and I relax in my Sheraton chair like some eighteenth-century nawab who has brought his own furniture into the wilderness. I can see why Wilson did not want to return to the plains when he came this way in the 1850s. Instead, he went further and higher into the mountains and made his home among the people of the Bhagirathi Valley.

Having wandered some way down the Tehri road, it is quite late by the time I return to the Landour bazaar. Lights still twinkle on the hills, but shop fronts are shuttered and the little bazaar is silent. The people living on either side of the narrow street can hear my footsteps, and I hear their casual remarks, music, a burst of laughter.

Through a gap in the rows of buildings I can see Pari Tibba outlined in the moonlight. A greenish phosphorescent glow appears to move here and there about the hillside. This is the 'fairy light' that gives the hill its name Pari Tibba, Fairy Hill. I have no explanation for it, and I don't know anyone else who has been able to explain it satisfactorily; but often from my window I see this greenish light zigzagging about the hill.

A three-quarter moon is up, and the tin roofs of the bazaar, drenched with dew, glisten in the moonlight. Although the street is unlit, I need no torch. I can see every step of the way. I can even read the headlines on the discarded newspaper lying in the gutter.

Although I am alone on the road, I am aware of the life, pulsating around me. It is a cold night, doors and windows are shut; but through the many clinks, narrow fingers of light reach out into the night. Who could still be up? A shopkeeper going through his accounts, a college student preparing for his exams, someone coughing and groaning in the dark.

Three stray dogs are romping in the middle of the road. It is their road now, and they abandon themselves to a wild chase, almost knocking me down.

A jackal slinks across the road, looking to the right and left—he knows his road-drill—to make sure the dogs have gone. A field rat wriggles through a hole in a rotting plank on its nightly foray among sacks of grain and pulses.

Yes, this is an old bazaar. The bakers, tailors, silversmiths and wholesale merchants are the grandsons of those who followed the mad sahibs to this hilltop in the 1930s and 1940s of the last century. Most of them are plainsmen, quite prosperous, even though many of their houses are crooked and shaky.

Although the shopkeepers and tradesmen are fairly prosperous, the hill people—those who come from the surrounding Tehri and Jaunpur villages—are usually poor. Their small holdings and rocky fields do not provide them with much of a living, and men and boys have to often come into the hill station or go down to the cities in search of a livelihood. They pull rickshaws, or work in hotels and restaurants. Most of them have somewhere to stay.

But as I pass along the deserted street under the shadow of the clock tower, I find a boy huddled in a recess, a thin shawl wrapped around his shoulders. He is wide awake and shivering.

I pass by, my head down, my thoughts already on the warmth of my small cottage only a mile away. And then I stop. It is almost as though the bright moonlight has stopped me, holding my shadow in thrall.

If I am not for myself,
Who will be for me?

And if I am not for others,
What am I?
And if not now, when?

The words of an ancient sage beat upon my mind. I walk back to the shadows where the boy crouches. He does not say anything, but he looks up at me, puzzled and apprehensive. All the warnings of well-wishers crowd in upon me—stories of crime by night, of assault and robbery, 'ill met by moonlight'.

But this is not northern Ireland or Lebanon or the streets of New York. This is Landour in the Garhwal Himalayas. And the boy is no criminal. I can tell from his features that he comes from the hills beyond Tehri. He has come here looking for work and has yet to find any.

'Have you somewhere to stay?' I ask.

He shakes his head; but something about my tone of voice has given him confidence, because now there is a glimmer of hope, a friendly appeal in his eyes.

I have committed myself. I cannot pass on. A shelter for the night—that's the very least one human should be able to expect from another.

'If you can walk some way,' I offer, 'I can give you a bed and blanket.'

He gets up immediately, a thin boy, wearing only a shirt and part of an old tracksuit. He follows me without any hesitation. I cannot now betray his trust. Nor can I fail to trust him.

# Voting at Fosterganj

I am standing under the deodars, waiting for a taxi. Devilal, one of the candidates in the civic election, is offering free rides to all his supporters, to ensure that they get to the polls in time. I have assured him that I prefer walking but he does not believe me; he fears that I will settle down with a bottle of beer rather than walk the two miles to the Fosterganj polling station to cast my vote. He has gone to the expense of engaging a taxi for the day just to make certain of lingerers like me. He assures me that he is not using unfair means—most of the other candidates are doing the same thing.

It is a cloudy day, promising rain, so I decide I will wait for the taxi. It has been plying since 6 a.m., and now it is ten o'clock. It will continue plying up and down the hill till 4 p.m. and by that time it will have cost Devilal over a hundred rupees.

Here it comes. The driver—like most of our taxi drivers, a Sikh—sees me standing at the gate, screeches to a sudden stop, and opens the door. I am about to get in when I notice that the windscreen carries a sticker displaying the Congress symbol of the cow and calf. Devilal is an Independent, and has adopted a cock bird as his symbol.

'Is this Devilal's taxi?' I ask.

'No, it's the Congress taxi,' says the driver.

'I'm sorry,' I say. 'I don't know the Congress candidate.'

'That's all right,' he says agreeably; he isn't a local man and has no interest in the outcome of the election. 'Devilal's taxi will be along any minute now.'

He moves off, looking for the Congress voters on whose behalf he has been engaged. I am glad that the candidates have had to adopt different symbols; it has saved me the embarrassment of turning up in a Congress taxi, only to vote for an Independent. But the real reason for using symbols is to help illiterate voters know whom they are voting for when it comes to putting their papers in the ballot box. All through the hill station's mini-election campaign, posters have been displaying candidates' symbols—a car, a radio, a cock bird, a tiger, a lamp—and the narrow, winding roads resound to the cries of children who are paid to shout, 'Vote for the Radio!' or 'Vote for the Cock!'

Presently my taxi arrives. It is already full, having picked up others on the way, and I have to squeeze in at the back with a stout lalain and her bony husband, the local ration-shop owner. Sitting up front, near the driver, is Vinod, a poor, ragged, quite happy-go-lucky youth, who contrives to turn up wherever I happen to be, and frequently involves himself in my activities. He gives me a namaste and a wide grin.

'What are you doing here?' I ask him.

'Same as you, Bond Sahib. Voting. Maybe Devilal will give me a job if he wins.'

'But you already have a job. I thought you were the games-boy at the school.'

'That was last month, Bond Sahib.'

'They kicked you out?'

'They asked me to leave.'

The taxi gathers speed as it moves smoothly down the

winding hill road. The driver is in a hurry; the more trips he makes, the more money he collects. We swerve round sharp corners, and every time the lalain's chubby hands, covered with heavy bangles and rings, clutch at me for support. She and her husband are voting for Devilal because they belong to the same caste; Vinod is voting for him in the hope of getting a job; I am voting for him because I like the man. I find him simple, courteous and ready to listen to complaints about drains, street lighting and wrongly assessed taxes. He even tries to do something about these things. He is a tall, cadaverous man, with paan-stained teeth; no Nixon, Heath or Indira Gandhi; but he knows that Fosterganj folk care little for appearances.

Fosterganj is a small ward (one of four in the hill station of Mussoorie); it has about 1,000 voters. An election campaign has, therefore, to be conducted on a person-to-person basis. There is no point in haranguing a crowd at a street corner; it would be a very small crowd. The only way to canvass support is to visit each voter's house and plead one's cause personally. This means making a lot of promises with a perfectly straight face.

The bazaar and village of Fosterganj crouch in a vale on the way down the mountain to Dehra. The houses on either side of the road are nearly all English-looking, most of them built before the turn of the century. The bazaar is Indian, charming and quite prosperous: tailors sit cross-legged before their sewing machines, turning out blazers and tight trousers for the well-to-do students who attend the many public schools that still thrive here; halwais—pot-bellied sweet vendors—spend all day sitting on their haunches in front of giant frying pans; and coolies carry huge loads of timber or cement or grain up the steep hill paths.

The police station, the little Church of the Resurrection,

and the ruined brewery were among the earliest buildings in Fosterganj. The brewery is a mound of rubble, but the road that came into existence to serve the needs of the old Crown Brewery is the one that now serves our taxi. Buckle and Co.'s 'Bullock Train' was the chief means of transport in the old days. Mr Bohle, one of the pioneers of brewing in India, started the 'Old Brewery' at Mussoorie in 1830. Two years later he got into trouble with the authorities for supplying beer to soldiers without permission; he had to move elsewhere.

But the great days of the brewery business really began in 1876, when everyone suddenly acclaimed a much-improved brew. The source was traced to Vat 42 in Whymper's Crown Brewery (the one whose ruins we are now passing), and the beer was retasted and retested until the diminishing level of the barrel revealed the perfectly brewed remains of a soldier who had been reported missing some months previously. He had evidently fallen into the vat and been drowned and, unknown to himself, had given the Fosterganj beer trade a real fillip. Apocryphal though this story may sound, I have it on the authority of the owner of the now defunct *Mafasalite Press* who, in a short account of Mussoorie, wrote that 'meat was thereafter recognized as the missing component and was scrupulously added till more modern, and less cannibalistic, means were discovered to satiate the froth-blower.'

Recently, confirmation came from an old Indian hand now living in London. He wrote to me reminiscing of early days in the hill station and had this to say:

> Uncle Georgie Forster was working for the Crown Brewery when a coolie fell in. Coolies were employed to remove scum etc. from the vats. They walked along planks

suspended over the vats. Poor devil must have slipped and fallen in. Uncle often told us about the incident and there was no doubt that the beer tasted very good.

What with soldiers and coolies falling into the vats with seeming regularity, one wonders whether there may have been more to these accidents than met the eye. I have a nagging suspicion that Whymper and Buckle may have been the Burke and Hare of Mussoorie's beer industry.

But no beer is made in Mussoorie today, and Devilal probably regrets the passing of the breweries as much as I do. Only the walls of the breweries remain, and these are several feet thick. The roofs and girders must have been removed for use in other buildings. Moss and sorrel grow in the old walls, and wildcats live in dark corners protected from rain and wind.

We have taken the sharpest curves and steepest gradients, and now our taxi moves smoothly along a fairly level road which might pass for a country lane in England were it not for the clumps of bamboo on either side.

A mist has come up the valley to settle over Fosterganj, and out of the mist looms an imposing mansion, Sikander Hall, which is still owned and occupied by the Skinners, descendants of Colonel James Skinner who raised a body of Irregular Horse for the Marathas. This was absorbed by the East India Company's forces in 1803. The cavalry regiment is still known as Skinner's Horse, but of course it is a tank regiment now. Skinner's troops called him 'Sikander' (a corruption of both Skinner and Alexander), and that is the name his property bears. The Skinners who live here now have, quite sensibly, gone in for keeping pigs and poultry.

The next house belongs to the Raja of K but he is unable

to maintain it on his diminishing privy purse, and it has been rented out as an ashram for members of a saffron-robed sect who would rather meditate in the hills than in the plains. There was a time when it was only the Sahibs and rajas who could afford to spend the entire 'season' in Mussoorie. The new rich are the industrialists and maharishis. The coolies and rickshaw pullers are no better off than when I was a boy in Mussoorie. They still carry or pull the same heavy loads, for the same pittance, and seldom attain the age of forty. Only their clientele has changed.

One more gate, and here is Colonel Powell in his khaki bush shirt and trousers, a uniform that never varies with the seasons. He is an old shikari; once wrote a book called *The Call of the Tiger*. He is too old for hunting now, but likes to yarn with me when we meet on the road. His wife has gone home to England, but he does not want to leave India.

'It's the mountains,' he was telling me the other day. 'Once the mountains are in your blood, there is no escape. You have to come back again and again. I don't think I'd like to die anywhere else.'

Today there is no time to stop and chat. The taxi driver, with a vigorous blowing of his horn, takes the car round the last bend, and then through the village and narrow bazaar of Fosterganj, stopping about a hundred yards from the polling stations.

There is a festive air about Fosterganj today, I have never seen so many people in the bazaar. Bunting, in the form of rival posters and leaflets, is strung across the street. The tea shops are doing a roaring trade. There is much last-minute canvassing, and I have to run the gamut of various candidates and their agents. For the first time, I learn the names of some of the candidates. In all, seven men are competing for this seat.

A schoolboy, smartly dressed and speaking English, is the first to accost me. He says: 'Don't vote for Devilal, sir. He's a big crook. Vote for Jatinder! See, sir, that's his symbol—the bow and arrow.'

'I shall certainly think about the bow and arrow,' I tell him politely.

Another agent, a man, approaches, and says, 'I hope you are going to vote for the Congress candidate.'

'I don't know anything about him,' I say.

'That doesn't matter. It's the party you are voting for. Don't forget it's Mrs Gandhi's party.'

Meanwhile, one of Devilal's lieutenants has been keeping a close watch on both Vinod and me, to make sure that we are not seduced by rival propaganda. I give the man a reassuring smile and stride purposefully towards the polling station, which has been set up in the municipal schoolhouse. Policemen stand at the entrance to make sure that no one approaches the voters once they have entered the precincts.

I join the patient queue of voters. Everyone is in good humour, and there is no breaking of the line; these are not film stars we have come to see. Vinod is in another line, and grins proudly at me across the passageway. This is the one day in his life on which he has been made to feel really important. And he *is*. In a small constituency like Fosterganj, every vote counts.

Most of my fellow voters are poor people. Local issues mean something to them, affect their daily living. The more affluent can buy their way out of trouble, can pay for small conveniences; few of them bother to come to the polls. But for the 'common man'—the shopkeeper, clerk, teacher, domestic servant, milkman, mule driver—this is a big day. The man he is voting for has promised him something, and the voter means to take the successful candidate up on his promise. Not for another five years will the same fuss be made over the local cobblers, tailors and laundrymen. Their votes are indeed precious.

And now it is my turn to vote. I confirm my name, address and roll number. I am down on the list as 'Rusking Bound', but I let it pass: I might forfeit my right to vote if I raise any objection at this stage! A dab of marking-ink is placed on my forefinger—this is so that I do not come around a second time—and I am given a paper displaying the names and symbols of all the candidates. I am then directed to the privacy of a small booth, where I place the official rubber stamp against Devilal's name. This done, I fold the paper in four and slip it into the ballot box.

All has gone smoothly. Vinod is waiting for me outside. So is Devilal.

'Did you vote for me?' asks Devilal.

It is my eyes that he is looking at, not my lips, when I reply in the affirmative. He is a shrewd man, with many years' experience in seeing through bluff. He is pleased with my reply, beams at me, and directs me to the waiting taxi.

Vinod and I get in together, and soon we are on the road again, being driven swiftly homewards up the winding hill road.

Vinod is looking pleased with himself; rather smug, in fact. 'You did vote for Devilal?' I ask him. 'The symbol of the cock bird?'

He shakes his head, keeping his eyes on the road. 'No, the cow,' he says.

'You ass!' I exclaim. 'Devilal's symbol was the cock, not the cow!'

'I know,' he says, 'but I like the cow better.'*

I subside into silence. It is a good thing no one else in the taxi has been paying any attention to our conversation. It would be a pity to see Vinod turned out of Devilal's taxi and made to walk the remaining mile to the top of the hill. After all, it will be another five years before he gets another free taxi ride.

---

*In spite of Vinod's defection, Devilal won in 1974.

# Shahjahanpur

It is forty-five years since I last saw Shahjahanpur, a sleepy little town halfway between Delhi and Lucknow. I doubt if it has changed much. It wasn't the sort of place…that changes. Even in 1960, when I stopped there for a few hours, it looked as though time had been standing still since the dramatic events of the 1857 uprising, which I described in my novella *A Flight of Pigeons*.

Forty years after those events, in 1896 to be exact, my father had been born in Shahjahanpur's 'military camp', according to Grandfather's army service records. Grandfather's regiment, the Scottish Rifles, must have been quartered there for a few months before moving on to Bareilly, Aligarh, Gorakhpur, Lucknow and other cantonment towns across the hot and dusty Gangetic plains.

This was one reason for me to stop there, but I was also keen to visit the cantonment church, where he had probably been baptized, and where, during the outbreak of 1857, the European residents had been slaughtered. Among the few survivors were Ruth Labadoor and her mother. Their story came down to me from my father and other sources, and I was keen to follow it up.

The church was still there, of course, but locked up; a memorial to those who had been killed on that fatal day at the end of May stood in the parade ground (I believe it has since been removed); the mango groves and some old bungalows going back to Mutiny days were still evident; and crossing the little Khannant river was the bridge of boats which had played so important a part for those who were escaping from the town—first, the fleeing Europeans; later, the mutineers or their families when the British had retaken the district.

Founded in the seventeenth century, the town had a large Pathan population, and still does. The crowded city area and mohallas are still home to the descendants of Javed Khan, his friends and relatives, and those who had set fire to the cantonment bungalows. In his film of the story, *Junoon,* Shyam Benegal provided a rather opulent-looking Nawabi setting, but in reality Shahjahanpur's streets were occupied by working or lower-middle-class families, and only the Nawab (who lived elsewhere) would have enjoyed much affluence.

The dramatic events of 1857 led to the loss of many innocent lives on both sides of the conflict, Indian and British. In retelling Ruth's story I tried to show how the common humanity of ordinary folk—Hindu, Muslim, or Christian—could sometimes overcome the forces of hate, revenge and retribution.

On a lighter note: The Rose Rum factory stands a little way outside Shahjahanpur. It dates back to pre-Mutiny times. During the uprising it was sacked by rioters. Some quenched their thirst, while others poured barrels of good rum into the Khannant. Grandfather would have been appalled. I don't know if he was much of a drinker, but we did find these verses among his papers. He was, of course, referring to the Solan Brewery near Shimla. Like the Rosa distilleries, it is over 150 years old.

'Where's Solan?' the private was asking;
'Somewhere near Tibet, I should think.'
'There's a brewery there,

And it's brimming with beer,
But we can't get a mouthful to drink!'
So we route-march from Delhi to Solan
In the dust and the maddening sun,
And we're cursing away like Hades
Well knowing there ain't any ladies
To hear every son-of-a-gun!
And when we have climbed up to Solan
Our language continues profane,
For right well we know
We shall soon have to go
Down from Solan to Delhi again!

I'm not sure if Grandfather wrote the poem, but we'll credit it to him anyway—Henry William Bond, with a few profanities edited out by his grandson.

I should add that young Mr Carew, the proprietor of the Rosa distillery, went into hiding and survived the mutiny. If he had not done so, I would not be enjoying Carew's Gin today.

# The Dehra I Know

Formally, it's known as Dehradun, but in the 1940s and 1950s, when we were young, everyone called it Dehra.

That's where I spent much of my childhood, boyhood, and early manhood, and it was the Dehra I wrote about in many of my books and stories.

It was very different from the Dehradun of today—much smaller, much greener, considerably less crowded; sleepier too, and somewhat laid-back, easy-going; fond of gossip, but tolerant of human foibles. A place of bicycles and pony-drawn tongas. Only a few cars; no three-wheelers. And you could walk almost anywhere, at any time of the year, night or day.

The Dehra I knew really fell into three periods. The Dehra of my childhood, staying in my grandmother's house on the Old Survey Road (not much left of that bungalow now). The Dehra of my schooldays, when I would come home for the holidays to stay with my mother and stepfather—a different house on almost every visit, right up until the time I left for England. And then the Dehra of my return to India, when I lived on my own in a small flat above Astley Hall and wrote many of my best stories.

While I was in England, I wrote my first novel *The Room on the Roof*, which was all about the Dehra I had left and the people and young friends I had known and loved. It was a little immature, but it came straight from the heart—the heart and mind of a seventeen-year-old—and if it's still fresh today, fifty years after its first publication, it's probably because it was so spontaneous and unsophisticated.

Back in Dehra, I wrote a sequel of sorts, *Vagrants in the Valley*. It wasn't as good, probably because I had exhausted my adolescence as a subject for fiction; but it did capture aspects of life in Dehra and the Doon valley in the early fifties.

I had returned to India and Dehra when I was twenty-one, and set up my writing shop, so to speak, in that flat above Bibiji's provision store.

Bibiji was my stepfather's first wife. He and my mother had moved to Delhi, leaving Bibiji with the provision store. I got on very well with her and helped her with her accounts, and she gave me the use of her rooms above the shop. I think it's only in India that you could find such a situation—a young offspring of the Raj, somewhat at odds with his mother and Indian stepfather, choosing to live with the latter's abandoned first wife!

Bibiji made excellent parathas, shalgam (turnip) pickle, and kanji, a spicy carrot juice. And so, romantic though I may have been, I was far from being the young poet starving in a garret, nor was Bibiji to be pitied. She was Dehra's first woman shopkeeper, and she managed very well.

Bibiji was of course much older than me; heavily built, strong. She could toss sacks of flour about the shop. Her son, rather mischievous, kept out of her reach; a cuff about the ears would send him sprawling. She suffered from a hernia, and was immensely grateful to me for bringing her a hernia-belt from England; it provided her with considerable relief.

Early morning she would march off to the mandi to get her

provisions (rice, atta, pulses, etc.) wholesale, and occasionally I would accompany her. In this way I learnt the names of different pulses and lentils—moong, urad, malka, arhar, masoor, channa, lobia, rajma, etc. But I've never been tempted to write a cook book or run a ration shop of my own.

I was quite happy cooking up stories, most of them written after dark by the light of a kerosene lantern. Bibiji hadn't been able to pay the flat's accumulated electricity bills, and as a result the connection had been cut. But this did not bother me. I was quite content to live by candlelight or lamplight. It lent a romantic glow to my writing life.

And a lot of romance went into those early stories. There was the girl on the train in 'The Eyes Are Not Here', and the girl selling baskets on the platform at Deoli, and Aunt Maram's amours behind the Dilaram Bazaar, and romantic episodes in places as unlikely as Shamli and Bijnor (Pipalnagar). I was writing for anyone who would read me. It was only much later that I began writing for children.

Some favourite places for my fictional milieu were the parade-ground or maidaan, the Paltan Bazaar and its offshoots, the lichee gardens of Dalanwala, the tea-gardens, the quiet upper reaches of the Rajpur Road (non-transformed into shopping malls), the sal forests near Rajpur, the approach to Dehra by road or rail, and of course the railway station which is much the same as it used to be.

When I was a boy, many of the bungalows (such as the one built by my grandfather) had fairly large grounds or compounds—flower gardens in front, orchards at the back. Apart from lichees, the common fruit trees were papaya, guava, mango, lemon, and the pomalo, a sort of grapefruit. Most of those large compounds have now been converted into housing-estates.

Dehra's population has gone from fifty thousand in 1950 to over seven lakh at present. Not much room left for fruit trees!

Some of the stories, such as 'A Handful of Nuts' and 'Living Without Money', were written long after I'd left Dehra, but I think the atmosphere of the place comes through quite strongly in them. When a writer looks back at a particular place or period in his life, he tries to capture the essence of the place and the experience.

During the two years I freelanced from Bibiji's flat (1956–1958), I produced over thirty short stories, a couple of novellas, and numerous articles of an ephemeral nature. I managed to sell some of the stories to the BBC's Home service programme—*The Thief, The Night Train to Devli, The Woman on Platform No. 8, The Kitimaber*—others to the *Elizabethan, Illustrated Weekly of India, Sunday Statesman* (over the years, a few have been lost.) In India, ₹50 was the most you got for a short story or article, but you could live quite comfortably on three or four hundred rupees a month—provided your mode of transport was limited to the bicycle. Only successful businessmen and doctors owned cars.

My stepfather was an exception. He was an unsuccessful businessman who used a different car every month. That was because, before leaving Dehra, he ran a motor workshop, and if a car was left with him for repairs or overhauling ('oiling and greasing' he called it) he would use it for a month or two on the pretext of trying it out, before returning it to its owner. This he would do only when the owner's patience had reached its limit; sometimes the car had to be taken away by force. Occasionally my stepfather would relent and return the car of his own accord—along with a bill for having looked after it for so long!

His talents went unappreciated in Dehra. When he moved to Delhi he became a successful salesperson.

Some of the characters in my Dehra stories were fictional, some were based on real people; Granny was real, of course. And so were the boys in *The Room* and *Vagrants*. But did Rusty really make love to Meena Kapoor? It's a question I have often been asked and must leave unanswered. It might have happened. And then again, it might not. I prefer to leave it as a sweet mystery that will never be solved.

One thing is certain. Dehra played an integral part in my development as a writer. More than Shimla, where I did my schooling. More than London, where I lived for nearly four years. More than Delhi, where I spent a number of years. As much as Mussoorie, where I have passed half my life. It must have been the ambience of the place, something about it, that suited my temperament.

But it's a different place now, and no longer do I feel like 'singin' in the rain' as I walk down the Rajpur Road. I am in danger of being knocked down by a speeding vehicle if I try out my old song-and-dance routine. So I keep well to the side of the pavement and look out for known landmarks—an old peepal tree, a familiar corner, a surviving bungalow, a bookshop, the sabzi-mandi, a bit of wasteland where once we played cricket.

There was a wild flower, a weed, that grew all over Dehra and still does. We called it Blue Mint. It grows in ditches, in neglected gardens, anywhere there's a bit of open land. It's there nearly all the year round. I've always associated it with Dehra. The burgeoning human population has been unable to suppress it. This is one plant that will never go extinct. It refuses to go away. I have known it since I was a boy, and as long as it's there I shall know that a part of me still lives in Dehra.

# Desert Rhapsody

A fierce sun beat down on the desert sand. Heat waves shimmered across the barren landscape. *Did anything live out there?* I wondered, as I sat in a cane chair on the veranda of the rest house on the outskirts of the city of Jodhpur.

It was September, and there was no likelihood of rain. I had spent a night in this remote rest house, and now there was nothing for me to do until late evening when I would catch a train to Delhi. The previous day had been spent in Ajmer, where the grounds of the old Mayo School had provided ample shade. But there was no shade outside Jodhpur.

The only relief from the glare was provided by a small pond that existed in a declivity to one side of the rest house. And this too had shrivelled in recent weeks, leaving large cracks in the dry mud where the water had receded.

I had taken my breakfast in the veranda, served by a room-boy who had also done the cooking and was now about to tidy up the rooms. Apparently, the rest house had a staff of one.

'Do you do everything by yourself?' I asked.

He assured me that it was no trouble, as hardly anyone came to stay in the rest house. He gave me a good breakfast—parathas and an omelette—and set about making up the bed.

As he lifted up a pillow, a large black scorpion ran out and scurried across the bed sheets, its tail raised as if to strike.

I was horrified. I had spent the night with my head on that pillow, unaware that it had also sheltered a scorpion.

The room-boy was unperturbed. 'Must be more here,' he said, and lifted the mattress. Several fierce-looking scorpions emerged, running for shelter. I had spent the entire night on a bed of scorpions.

I decided to spend the rest of the day on the veranda. No afternoon siesta for me, no matter how drowsy I felt.

The room-boy assured me that the room was now free of scorpions, and asked me if I would be staying another night. I told him that it was vital that I catch the train to Delhi that evening.

'There is another room,' he told me.

'I don't think I'll need it,' I said.

But the pond looked inviting.

Not that I was about to plunge into it. A green scum covered most of the surface. But at least it looked cool.

And presently, its cool waters attracted a group of youths who drove their buffaloes into the shallows, and then followed them, shouting and splashing around. Had I been a boy, I might well have joined them. But at seventy-five, you don't go leaping into strange ponds, mixing with a herd of buffaloes and their high-spirited keepers. No, I just didn't have the figure for it any more.

So I sat and watched.

After half-an-hour the youths and their buffaloes left the pond and meandered away. Buffaloes have to be fed if you want them to provide for you. Nobody keeps buffaloes because they make nice pets.

The pond was still again. A cormorant arrived, wading into the shallows on its long legs, looking for a small fish or two for breakfast. A kingfisher flew across the pond, a sparkle of colour, but it did not dive or descend; the water was still too muddy.

A small islet, consisting of sand and a fringe of rushes, stood out in the middle of the pond. What I took to be a small boulder turned out to be a tortoise. It hadn't moved since I'd first seen it, and it remained motionless for the rest of the morning.

Three mynas were squabbling on the patch of grass in front of the bungalow. One of them was bald, having lost its feathers in some previous gladiatorial contest. Its companions did not care for its unconventional appearance, and like humans who resent the presence of a nonconforming outsider, they went at it with their beaks and talons until it fled from the field.

The room-boy gave me lunch in the little sitting room, beneath an overhead fan. This young all-rounder, whose name was Bhim, had made the lunch himself. His dal, roti, and aloomattar, was better than any hotel meal; but I couldn't do justice to the very sticky dessert (a sort of pastry stuffed with coconut and various nuts) that he served up afterwards, and he was a little put out that I pushed my plate away after a couple of mouthfuls.

'Mawa-ki-kachori,' he informed me. 'Special to Jodhpur.'

'Too sweet for me,' I said. 'But the dal–roti was perfect.'

He was mollified, and went off on his bicycle to carry out a few errands.

I was left with the sun and the sand and the pond below. The tortoise was still meditating on its islet.

I slept. I overslept. And young Bhim was late in returning from the city. As a result, no taxi turned up to take me to the station.

'Never mind,' he said philosophically. 'You can leave tomorrow. Tonight, I make mutton kebabs and hot bean curry. You will like!'

I did not feel so philosophical, and wondered if Bhim had conspired to keep me in the rest house for another night. He couldn't be having many guests in that remote place.

At sunset, he turned up with a glass, a bottle of soda, and a half-bottle of rum.

'Good Army rum,' he said. 'No headache.'

I gave in. Drank the rum, consumed the kebabs and bean curry, and slept peacefully in the second bedroom. Bhim had made the bed in my presence, convincing me that there were no scorpions or centipedes among the bed sheets. We turned the mattress over. All clear.

I woke at seven, to be greeted by Bhim with a cup of tea.

Then, I went to the bathroom and settled down on the toilet seat; at peace with the world—as I usually am when the bowels are moving freely.

And then I looked down and froze.

A large, glistening snake had wound itself around the base of the toilet-seat. It had a frog in its jaws, and only the back legs of the frog were visible. I have no idea what kind of snake it was—I did not stop to study it, but leapt from the seat and dashed into the bedroom, shouting for the room-boy.

Bhim appeared almost instantly.

'What is wrong, Sir? Breakfast almost ready.'

'A snake!' I shouted. 'There's a huge snake in the bathroom!'

'Not to worry, Sir. Only a *dhaman*, not poisonous. He comes through the drainpipe. Kills the rats. Very helpful.'

'Well, he has a frog this time,' I said. 'And I'm leaving right away. Just as soon as I can find my trousers.'

He went into the bathroom and returned with my trousers.

'Snake gone,' he said. 'Nothing to fear.'

I felt better after putting on my trousers. It's amazing what a pair of trousers can do for one's confidence.

'Thanks,' I said. 'And now you can get me a taxi.'

'But the train doesn't leave till evening.'

'I'm taking a bus,' I said. 'A bus leaves for Jaipur every hour.'

Disappointed, Bhim cycled off to arrange for some transport. I waited on the veranda, taking a last look at the pond. It was certainly safer outside than in the house.

The buffaloes were back. So were there young minders. So was the cormorant. And the tortoise was there too. It was all very peaceful—just another tranquil day in the desert.

# Belting around Mumbai

I have lived to see Bombay become Mumbai, Calcutta become Kolkata, and Madras become Chennai. Times change, names change, and if Bond becomes Bonda I won't object. Place-names may alter but people don't, and in Mumbai I found that people were as friendly and good-natured as ever; perhaps even more than when I was last there twenty-five years ago.

On that occasion, I had travelled on the Doon Express, a slow passenger train that stopped at every small station in at least five states, taking two days and two nights from Dehradun to Bombay. It had been a fairly uneventful journey, except for an incident in the small hours when we stopped at Baroda and a hand slipped through my open window, crept under my pillow, found nothing of value except my spectacles, and decided to take them anyway, leaving me to grope half-blind around Bombay until another pair could be made.

Now I carry three pairs of spectacles: one for reading, one for looking at people, and one for looking far out to sea.

On the Kingfisher flight to Mumbai, I used the second pair, as I like looking at people, especially attractive air hostesses. I found they were looking at me too, but that was because I'd caught my belt (my trouser belt, not my seat-belt) in a fellow-passenger's luggage strap and was proceeding to drag both him and his travel-bag down the aisle. We were diplomatically separated by the aforesaid air hostesses who then guided me to my seat without further mishap.

This reminded me of the occasion many years ago when I auditioned for a role in a Tarzan film.

'Who do you wish to play?' asked the casting director. 'Tarzan, of course,' I said

He gave me a long hard look. Can you swing from one tree to another?' he asked.

'Easily,' I said. 'I can even swing from a chandelier.' And I proceeded to do so, wrecking the hall they sat in, in the process. They begged me to stop.

'Thank you, Mr Bond, you have made your point. But we don't think you have the figure for the part of Tarzan. Would you like to take the part of the missionary who is being cooked to a crisp by a bunch of cannibals? Tarzan will come to your rescue.'

I declined the role with dignity.

And now I was in Mumbai, not to audition for a film, but to inaugurate the Rupa Book Festival. For old time's sake, I arrived at the venue in a horse-drawn carriage. Alighting, my recalcitrant belt-buckle got entangled with the horse's harness and I almost dragged the entire contraption into the Bajaj Exhibition Hall.

However, the evening's entertainment went off without a hitch. Gulzar read from Ghalib, Tom Alter read from Gulzar, Mandira Bedi read from Nandita Puri, and everyone read madly from each other, and I sat quietly in a corner to keep my belt out of further entanglements.

The next day I was taken on a tour of the city by a *Hindustan Times* journalist and a photographer. They asked me to pose on the steps of the Asiatic Society's Library, an imposing colonial edifice. While I stood there being photographed, a group of teenagers walked past and I overheard one of them remark: 'Yeh naya model hain.'

I took it as a compliment. At least they didn't call me a purana model. Perhaps there's still a chance to get that Tarzan role. If not Tarzan, then his grandfather.

The same journalist and photographer took me to a market where you could buy anything from books to bras. They thrust a thousand-rupee note into my willing hands and told me I could buy anything I liked, while they took pictures.

'Can I keep the money?' I asked. 'No, you have to spend it.'

So I bought two ladies handbags and two pairs of ladies slippers.

'For your girlfriends?' asked the journalist.

'No,' I said, 'for their mothers.'

Back at the festival hall, I was presented with a beautiful sky-blue T-shirt by a charming lady who wishes to remain anonymous. I wore it the next morning when I was leaving Mumbai.

At the airport, one of the Kingfisher staff complimented my dress sense; the first time anyone has alone so.

'Your blue shirt matches your eyes,' she said.

After that, I shall definitely fly Kingfisher again.

# Pistols at Twenty Paces: A Duel at Poona

Duels among British officers serving in India were fairly common in the early part of the nineteenth century, but we do not come across many accounts of them, as the penalties for duelling were severe. Such incidents were usually hushed up. And many of the 'resignations' and sudden deaths from 'cholera' were, in fact, the result of duels.

Perhaps the most tragic of these was the duel that was fought at Poona in June 1842. In that year the 27th Foot (Inniskillings), a North of Ireland regiment, whose officers were all Irish Protestants, was quartered at Poona. It had been some three months since an Irishman named Sarsfield, a mere boy of nineteen, belonging to an old and distinguished Catholic family, had been posted to the regiment. One of his ancestors had been James II's general at the Siege of Londonderry and such ancestry and religion told against him in a Protestant regiment. His advent was looked upon as an insult to the regiment and it was decided to make his life so intolerable that he would either resign or ask for a transfer to another regiment.

One night at the mess, Sarsfield, who had been drinking with the others, questioned a statement made by another officer and, on being asked by the latter if he thought it was a lie, replied that he did. Immediately the other officer rose, bowed ceremoniously to Sarsfield, and left the mess room in company with the paymaster. The others followed, leaving Sarsfield, who had a few more drinks before leaving and going home to bed.

At about four in the morning he was aroused by the paymaster, who brought him a challenge or a demand for an apology. Not realizing what he was doing, the young man dazedly signed the document the paymaster gave him, which was an abject apology. The next morning at six he appeared on parade, and, having but the faintest recollection of what had happened, walked up to the group of officers waiting for the parade to be formed. To his cheery good morning they returned a blank and contemptuous stare, and then, each turning on his heel, walked away. To give an apology was considered a most cowardly action.

For the next three months Sarsfield's life was miserable, for he was cut dead by everyone in the garrison. None spoke to him except on a matter of duty, and when he entered the mess, a dead silence fell over the company. The end came after three months, and there can be no doubt that the unfortunate young man was by now half demented.

One night he entered the mess room, and, as usual, conversation ceased abruptly. There was a vacant seat immediately opposite the paymaster and this Sarsfield took. By this time the conversation had been resumed, not the slightest notice being taken of him either by word or glance. He was waited upon by the servants just as the others were and it was only as the table was being cleared for the second course that Sarsfield spoke.

'Will you take wine with me?' he said to the paymaster.

'I do not take wine with a coward,' was the blunt reply.

'But will you take this?' was Sarsfield's rejoinder, as he dashed his wine glass and its contents into the paymaster's face.

In a moment all were on their feet, and amidst a roar of voices Sarsfield was pulled out of the mess room by the doctor.

'You will have to fight now, my boy,' said the doctor, more sorrowfully than might have been expected.

'I know,' said Sarsfield. 'I came for that purpose.'

The whole party now proceeded to a garden on the outskirts of the cantonment where such affairs were usually settled. All the preliminaries were quickly arranged, the captain acting as Sarsfield's second. It was a bright moonlit night, and the result was never for a moment in doubt for the paymaster, at the first exchange of shots, put a bullet through Sarsfield's heart. Sarsfield did not fire. He had made no attempt to discharge his pistol.

The next issue of the *Poona Gazette* contained the following announcement:

'Suddenly, of cholera, in the officers' line of Her Majesty's 27th Foot, Ensign J. S. Sarsfield.'

When an account of the circumstances reached Sarsfield's friends and relatives, a brother arrived at Poona and tried to ascertain the truth. But he could gain nothing more than what the doctor's certificate stated—'death by cholera'—for there was a mutual conspiracy of silence.

# The Last Time I Saw Delhi

I'd had this old and faded negative with me for a number of years and had never bothered to make a print from it. It was a picture of my maternal grandparents. I remembered my grandmother quite well, because a large part of my childhood had been spent in her house in Dehra after she had been widowed; although everyone said she was fond of me, I remembered her as a stern, somewhat aloof person, of whom I was a little afraid.

I hadn't kept many family pictures and this negative was yellow and spotted with damp.

Then last week, when I was visiting my mother in hospital in Delhi, while she awaited her operation, we got talking about my grandparents, and I remembered the negative and decided I'd make a print for my mother.

When I got the photograph and saw my grandmother's face for the first time in twenty-five years, I was immediately struck by my resemblance to her. I have, like her, lived a rather spartan life, happy with my one room, just as she was content to live in a room of her own while the rest of the family took over the house! And like her, I have lived tidily. But I did not know the physical resemblance was so close—the fair hair, the heavy build, the wide forehead. She looks more like me than my mother!

In the photograph she is seated on her favourite chair, at the top of the veranda steps, and Grandfather stands behind her in the shadows thrown by a large mango tree which is not in the picture. I can tell it was a mango tree because of the pattern the leaves make on the wall. Grandfather was a slim, trim man, with a drooping moustache that was fashionable in the 1920s. By all accounts he had a mischievous sense of humour, although he looks unwell in the picture. He appears to have been quite swarthy. No wonder he was so successful in dressing up 'native' style and passing himself off as a street vendor. My mother tells me he even took my grandmother in on one occasion, and sold her a basketful of bad oranges. His character was in strong contrast to my grandmother's rather forbidding personality and Victorian sense of propriety; but they made a good match.

So here's the picture, and I am taking it to show my mother who lies in the Lady Hardinge Hospital, awaiting the removal of her left breast.

It is early August and the day is hot and sultry. It rained during the night, but now the sun is out and the sweat oozes through my shirt as I sit in the back of a stuffy little taxi taking me through the suburbs of Greater New Delhi.

On either side of the road are the houses of well-to-do Punjabis who came to Delhi as refugees in 1947 and now make up more than half the capital's population. Industrious, flashy, go-ahead people. Thirty years ago, fields extended on either side of this road as far as the eye could see. The Ridge, an outcrop of the Aravallis, was scrub jungle, in which the blackbuck roamed. Feroz Shah's fourteenth-century hunting lodge stood here in splendid isolation. It is still here, hidden by petrol pumps and lost in the sounds of buses, cars, trucks and scooter rickshaws. The peacock has fled the forest, the blackbuck is extinct. Only the jackal remains. When, a thousand years from now, the last human has left this contaminated planet for some other star, the jackal and the crow will remain, to survive for years on all the refuse we leave behind.

It is difficult to find the right entrance to the hospital, because for about a mile along the Panchkuian Road the pavement has been obliterated by tea shops, furniture shops, and piles of accumulated junk. A public hydrant stands near the gate, and dirty water runs across the road.

I find my mother in a small ward. It is a cool, dark room, and a ceiling fan whirrs pleasantly overhead. A nurse, a dark, pretty girl from the South, is attending to my mother. She says, 'In a minute,' and proceeds to make an entry on a chart.

My mother gives me a wan smile and beckons me to come nearer. Her cheeks are slightly flushed, due possibly to fever, otherwise she looks her normal self. I find it hard to believe that the operation she will have tomorrow will only give her, at the most, another year's lease on life.

I sit at the foot of her bed. This is my third visit since I flew back from Jersey, using up all my savings in the process; and I will leave after the operation, not to fly away again, but to return to the hills which have always called me back.

'How do you feel?' I ask.

'All right. They say they will operate in the morning. They've stopped my smoking.'

'Can you drink? Your rum, I mean?'

'No. Not until a few days after the operation.'

She has a fair amount of grey in her hair, natural enough at fifty-four. Otherwise she hasn't changed much; the same small chin and mouth, lively brown eyes. Her father's face, not her mother's.

The nurse has left us. I produce the photograph and hand it to my mother.

'The negative was lying with me all these years. I had it printed yesterday.'

'I can't see without my glasses.'

The glasses are lying on the locker near her bed. I hand them to her. She puts them on and studies the photograph.

'Your grandmother was always very fond of you.'

'It was hard to tell. She wasn't a soft woman.'

'It was her money that got you to Jersey, when you finished school. It wasn't much, just enough for the ticket.'

'I didn't know that.'

'The only person who ever left you anything. I'm afraid I've nothing to leave you either.'

'You know very well that I've never cared a damn about money. My father taught me to write. That was inheritance enough.'

'And what did I teach you?'

'I'm not sure… Perhaps you taught me how to enjoy myself now and then.'

She looked pleased at this. 'Yes, I've enjoyed myself between troubles. But your father didn't know how to enjoy himself. That's why we quarrelled so much. And finally separated.'

'He was much older than you.'

'You've always blamed me for leaving him, haven't you?'

'I was very small at the time. You left us suddenly. My father had to look after me, and it wasn't easy for him. He was very sick. Naturally I blamed you.'

'He wouldn't let me take you away.'

'Because you were going to marry someone else.'

I break off; we have been over this before. I am not here as my father's advocate, and the time for recrimination has passed.

And now it is raining outside, and the scent of wet earth comes through the open doors, overpowering the odour of medicines and disinfectants. The dark-eyed nurse comes in again and informs me that the doctor will soon be on his rounds. I can come again in the evening, or early morning before the operation.

'Come in the evening,' says my mother. 'The others will be here then.'

'I haven't come to see the others.'

'They are looking forward to seeing you.' 'They' being my stepfather and half-brothers.

'I'll be seeing them in the morning.'

'As you like…'

And then I am on the road again, standing on the pavement, on the fringe of a chaotic rush of traffic, in which it appears that every vehicle is doing its best to overtake its neighbour. The blare of horns can be heard in the corridors of the hospital, but everyone is conditioned to the noise and pays no attention to it. Rather, the sick and the dying are heartened by the thought that people are still well enough to feel reckless, indifferent to each other's safety! In Delhi there is a feverish desire to be first in line, the first to get anything… This is probably because no one ever gets round to dealing with second-comers.

When I hail a scooter rickshaw and it stops a short distance away, someone elbows his way past me and gets in first. This epitomizes the philosophy and outlook of the Delhiwallah.

So I stand on the pavement waiting for another scooter, which doesn't come. In Delhi, to be second in the race is to be last.

I walk all the way back to my small hotel, with a foreboding of having seen my mother for the last time.

# Street of the Red Well

The sun beats down on the sweltering city of Old Delhi. Not a breath of air stirs in the narrow, winding streets. This old Walled City, now over 300 years old, has no open spaces, no sidewalks, no shady avenues. During the reign of Emperor Shah Jahan, a canal ran down the centre of the main throughfare, Chandni Chowk (street of the silversmiths), but the canal has long since been covered over, and the Yamuna river, from which water has been channelled, lies beyond the emperor's fort, the Red Fort of Delhi, where the prime minister speaks to the multitude every year on Independence Day.

It is not water that I seek most, but shelter from the heat and glare of the overhead sun. I have chosen what is quite possibly the hottest day in May, the temperature over 105 degrees Fahrenheit, to go walking in search of—what? A story, perhaps, and adventure. Or that is what I set out to do. The heat of the day has willed otherwise. I may be ready for an adventure, but no one else is interested. I am the only one walking the streets from choice.

Shopkeepers nod drowsily beneath whirring ceiling-fans. The pavement barber has taken his customer into the shelter of an awning. A fortune-teller has decided that there is nothing to predict and has fallen asleep under the same awning. A vegetable seller sprinkles water on his vegetables in a dispirited fashion.

Those cauliflowers were fresh an hour ago: they look old already. Even the flies are drowsy. Instead of buzzing feverishly from place to place, they stagger about on tired legs.

It is the pigeons who have found all the coolest places. These birds have made the old city their own. New Delhi is for the crows who like to have a tree to sleep in, even if they take their meals from out of kitchens and verandas. But the pigeons prefer buildings and the older the buildings the better. They are familiar with every cool alcove or shady recess in the crumbling walls of neglected mosques and mansions.

A fat, supercilious pigeon watches me from the window ledge above a jeweller's shop. The pigeon's forebears settled here long before the British thought of taking Delhi. Conquerors have come and gone, Nadir Shah the Persian, Madhav Rao the Maratha, Gulam Kadir the Rohilla, and generations of goldsmiths and silversmiths. Hindus and Muslims have made the lost fortunes in the city, but nothing has disturbed the tranquil life of these pigeons. Their gentle cooing can always be heard when there is a lull in the jagged symphony of traffic noise. How do they manage to sound so cool?

But here's welcome relief for humans; a shady corner in Lal Kuan Bazaar (street of the Red Well) where an old man provides drinking water to thirsty wayfarers such as myself. His water is stored in a surahi, an earthenware jug which keeps the water sweet and cool. I bend down, cup my hands, and receive the sparkling liquid as my benefactor tilts the surahi towards me.

Lal Kuan. The Red Well. Of course it is no longer here, but the street still bears its name. And I like to think that here, in the middle of the street, where a bullock has gone to sleep forcing the cyclists to make a detour, there was once a well made of dark red brick, where the water bubbled forth all day. Imprisoned beneath the soil, held down by the crowded commercial houses of this old quarter, the water must still be there; it gives nourishment to an old peepul tree that grows beside a temple. It is the only tree in the street. It juts out from the temple wall growing straight and tall, dwarfing the two-storeyed houses. One of its roots, breaking throughout the ground, has curled up to provide a smooth, well-worn seat. And it is cool here, beneath the peepul. Even when there is no breeze, the slender, heart-shaped leaves revolve prettily, creating their own currents of air. No wonder the sages of old found it a good tree to sit beneath, and no wonder they called it sacred.

On the other side of the road, a tall iron doorway is set in a high wall. Doors like this were only built in the previous century, when a wealthy merchant's house had to be a miniature fortress as well as a residence. I cannot see over the wall and I would like to know what lies behind the door. Perhaps a side street, perhaps a market, perhaps a garden, perhaps...

The door opens, not easily, because it has been left closed for a long time, but slowly and with much complaint. And beyond the door there is only an empty courtyard, cohered with rubble, the ruins of the old house. I am about to turn away when I hear a deep tremendous murmur.

It is the cooing of many pigeons. But where are they?

I advance further into the ruin, and there, opening out in front of me, ready to receive me as the rabbit-hole was ready to receive Alice, is an old, disused well. I peer down into its murky depths. It is dark, very dark down there; but that is where the pigeons live, in the walls of this lost, long-forgotten well shut away from the rest of the city. I cannot see any water. So I drop a pebble over the side. It strikes the wall, and then, with a soft plop, touches water. At that instant there is a rush of air and a tremendous beating of wings, and a flock of pigeons—thirty or forty of them—flies out of the well, streaks upwards, circles the building, and then falling into formation, wheels overhead, the sun gleaming white on the underwings.

I have discovered their secret. Now I know why they look so cool, so refreshed, while we who walk the streets of Old Delhi do so with parched mouths and drooping limbs. The pigeons are the only ones who still know about the Red Well.

# Mathura's Hallowed Haunts

Mathura, most sacred of cities, stands on the right bank of the Yamuna northwest of Agra. All men speak of Mathura with reverence, and it has been said, 'if a man spend in Banaras all his lifetime, he has earned less merit than if he passes but a single day in the sacred city of Mathura.'

It is difficult to pierce the fog which hides the date of the city's birth; but sacred it has always been as the capital of the kingdom of Braj and the birthplace of Lord Krishna: 'Teacher and Soul of the Universe. Destroyer of the earth's tyrant kings, and the First of the Spirits...'

I went to Mathura at the end of the rains. The fields and the trees were alive with strange, beautiful birds: the long-tailed king crow; innumerable doves in shades of blue and green; kingfishers and bluejays and weaver-birds; and, resting on a telegraph pole, the great white-headed kite, which, some say, was Garuda, Vishnu's famous steed. Resplendent, too, were the green and gold parrots, from among whom Kamadeva, the god of love, chose his steed. Armed with his sugarcane bow with its string made of bees, Kamadeva still rides at night over the plains of Mathura. Many are the journeys he makes on nights approaching the full moon. He knows the ways of men and women, and his bow, like Cupid's, is always ready to assist the ardent lover.

In the tanks and 'jheels' around Mathura I saw a variety

of game birds—wild duck, hermits, cranes and snipe—but all life is sacred for many miles around Mathura, and not even the bird trapper is permitted to lay his snares.

Strutting under an old tamarind tree are Krishna's birds, the brilliant peacocks. Centuries ago, they gave the city their name, and today Mathura is still known as the Peacock City. The peacocks seem to know that they are the chosen of Krishna. Spreading out their many-hued fantails, they glance at us drab mortals with an air of disdain.

Near Mathura is Brindavan in whose forests—they have gone now—the boy Krishna and his brother Balram ran wild, playing on their shepherds' pipes. The neighbours found Krishna very mischievous. He was extremely fond of butter and, going by stealth one day to the house of a neighbour, climbed onto a shelf to get at a large jar of butter. He ate the butter as far as he could reach, and then got into the jar. The owner, on returning, found him there and putting a cover on the jar to prevent the boy from escaping went to Krishna's father to make a complaint. But when he arrived at the house it was not the father who met him but the little butter-thief.

There is another story which tells us of the day Krishna stole his mother's curds, and finished them while no one was looking. 'O, you wicked one!' exclaimed his mother when she discovered what had happened. 'Come, let me see your mouth.' And when she looked into his mouth, she saw the Universe—the earth, sea and heavens; the sun and the moon, the planets and all the stars…

Brindavan stands on a tongue of land surrounded by the river, which has curved here in a strange fashion. Legend tells us that Balram, who was very strong, once led a dance on the Yamuna's bank, but moved his giant limbs so clumsily that the river laughed aloud and taunted him, saying: 'Enough, my clumsy child! How can you hope to dance as Krishna, who is divine?' Balram was very angry with the river, and taking his great plough he traced a furrow from the brink of the river; but so deep was the furrow that the river fell into it and was led far astray.

When the tyrant king Kamsa heard of the unusual exploits of Krishna and Balram, he planned to have them killed in case they became a danger to his power. He sent a message to the brothers, inviting them to a contest of arms in the royal city of Mathura. Krishna and Balram accepted the challenge.

On the day of the contest, King Kamsa sat on a lofty throne near the arena. As Krishna and Balram entered, a mighty elephant was sent against them. But Krishna, seizing the animal by the tail, swung it around his head and threw it to the ground. Then each of the brothers taking a tusk, they slew Kamsa's mightiest champions. Kamsa ordered his army to kill the boys, but Krishna sprang up the steps of the throne, seized the king by his hair and hurled him into a deep ravine.

Visitors to Mathura are still shown the mound where Kamsa's throne once stood. And still venerated is that part of the riverfront where the two boys rested after dragging the body of Kamsa down to the funeral pyre.

I wandered in the streets of the city past shops gleaming with brasswork or piled high with pedas, Mathura's famous sweets. From the bridge, I could see the riverfront with its innumerable temples. And below, hundreds of majestic tortoises watched the bathers and the boatmen with speculative eyes. Sometimes a boatman seized one of these long-necked creatures and held it up to view. The tortoise would immediately draw its legs into its shell—a vivid illustration of the theory that nothing is annihilated but only disappears, the effect being absorbed in the cause!

# Jaipur

As we still had a few days left of our holiday, and a little money, and as neither Kamal nor I was anxious to return to Delhi earlier than was necessary, we decided to sneak off to Jaipur for a day or two. We had both been to Jaipur before, but it is a city that one can visit again and again without ever tiring of its charm.

There is an atmosphere about Jaipur—once the most beautiful city in India, and one of the earliest planned cities in the world which even to the casual visitor distinguishes it from other towns. This is probably due to the almost entire absence of any European or Western influence on the architecture and planning of the town.

Founded in 1728 by the brilliant astronomer-king Maharaja Jai Singh II, it is quite unlike any other town in India or Asia: no tortuous gloomy streets or squalid overcrowded bazaars. Its six main streets are very wide and straight, one running the whole length of the town, the others crossing it at right angles, dividing the city into rectangular blocks. These are enclosed by a high wall, its parapets loopholed for musketry, into which are set seven entrance gates.

On the northwest side the hills rise sheer beyond the city, bearing on their summit the Nahargarh or Tiger Fort. Not needed now for purposes of war, it houses much of the wealth of this former states ruler. Guarded not by troops but by men of the robber caste, this wealth lay hoarded for centuries, potential but never used capital, typical of the ways of the East.

In the city itself, narrow streets are found in plenty, for a network of them connects the wide main roads. So narrow are some, that the bougainvillea sprawls from the upper storey of one building to its opposite across the way. But, curiously enough, they are nearly all straight, and a passing glimpse from the main street reveals their whole length. Sometimes these lanes are full of little shops, but many of them contain only private houses, where occasionally a half-open door reveals a glimpse of the grass and fountain of a garden or courtyard beyond.

The great attraction of the main streets is their spaciousness and the beautiful facade of the tall buildings which line them, most colour-washed in a dull, pale old-rose tone, some showing the soft amber or grey of the original limestone. In some of them the plain walls are varied with beautiful little chhattris, while here and there the old carved domes of some Jain temple break the flat line of roofs.

The street walls of these houses—which are really only the walls of the outer courtyard, the main building being behind and cut off from the street altogether—can boast of only the smallest windows, for these were meant to conceal, and not reveal, the zenana quarters behind. The quaint figures of elephants and other animals painted on the walls give them the appearance of dolls' houses when seen from the road below, though many of them are three or four storeys in height and from a distance look very imposing.

The streets themselves are a feast of colour and interest. Every mode of progression can be seen here, from ambling bullock carts and ekkas, with their quaintly shaped and brightly coloured hoods, to buses and streamlined motor cars. There are strings of camels bearing fodder, and elephants that amble up the road to the Amber Palace, and here and there wanders the ubiquitous Brahmani bull. All along the streets and around the squares throng hundreds of pigeons—sacred birds throughout Rajasthan—being fed by the passers-by or helping themselves to food on the stalls.

All along the ground floor of the buildings, and cut off from them by a small projecting tin roof along which the langurs run up and down in play, are the bazaar shops, little hives of industry doing a brisk trade. Busier still are the wide pavements in front; they are chock-a-block with stalls and with groups of artisans plying their trade in the midst of the passers-by.

We saw great piles of yellow maize and corn, of jowar and bajra, heaped upon the pavement, while to one side people were busy grinding the grain on primitive grindstones, laughing and singing as they ceaselessly wound the handle, three of them often working at one grinder. A little further on, what seemed at a distance to be a rich Herati rug flung down resolved itself into masses of chillies spread for yards along the pavement to dry in the sun. Then came the vegetables and fruit piled high in baskets, the countrywomen who had brought them squatting in the midst, sorting and selling and often nursing their babies at the same time.

Next came a little colony of brass workers sitting at the pavement's edge, engraving patterns on brass trays, plates and vessels, and then inlaying them with sticks of coloured enamel. Unlike them, the dyers generally work within their shops. In one of these we saw a whole family variously employed, from the old grandfather, who was mixing brilliant dyes in great brass cauldrons, to the latest infant, sitting in the middle and watching the others with an open mouth, while the family goat and attendant kid ambled in and out at will. Two of the family, a pugree-length of gaudy cloth just freshly dyed between them, walked up and down the pavement, waving it in the air to dry. The street had the appearance of being hung with bunting.

Most amusing of all, we came suddenly on three rows of little boys standing on the pavement with their slates at their feet. To one side stood the enterprising schoolmaster, while in front a small urchin with head craned forward loudly chanted the words of some lesson, which the class, in a medley of hoarse and squeaky voices, repeated after him. The intense concentration of this determined little group seemed in no way upset by the surrounding bustle and confusion.

There are few palaces in India to surpass the grandeur of the famous old palace of Amber. It lies northwest of the city, approached by a narrow pass in the hills which shuts off all view of Jaipur and opens on a little valley almost entirely closed by hills. Above a small lake, built on the barren hillside, stand the still perfect walls of this majestic fortress-palace. Their limestone blocks are mellowed to a soft amber colour, and the marble is now a rich cream.

The palace, now deserted except for its temple to the goddess Kali, is still in perfect condition. Its sun-soaked courtyards are open to the sky, and its empty pillared halls are full of echoes.

# Footloose in Agra

*I went to Agra in 1965, to see the Taj. But what interested me about the city had little to do with Emperor Shah Jahan's grand monument to his love.*

The cycle rickshaw is the best way of getting about Agra. Its smooth gliding motion and leisurely rate of progress are in keeping with the pace of life in this old-world city. The rickshaw boy makes his way through the crowded bazaars, exchanging insults with tonga drivers, pedestrians and other cyclists; but once on the broad Mall or Taj Road, his curses change to carefree song and he freewheels along the tree-lined avenues. Old colonial-style bungalows still stand in large compounds shaded by peepul, banyan, neem and jamun trees.

Looking up, I notice a number of bright paper kites that flutter, dip and swerve in the cloudless sky. I cannot recall seeing so many kites before.

'Is it a festival today?' I ask,

'No, Sahib,' says the rickshaw boy. 'Not even a holiday.'

'Then why so many kites?'

He does not even bother to look up. 'You can see kites every day, Sahib.'

'I don't see them in Delhi.'

'Ah, but Delhi is a busy place. In Agra, people still fly kites. There are kite-flying competitions every Sunday, and heavy bets are sometimes placed on the outcome.'

As we near the city, I notice kites stuck in trees or dangling from electric wires; but there are always others soaring up to take their place. I ask the rickshaw boy to tell me something about the kite-fliers and the kitemakers, but the subject bores him.

'You had better see the Taj today, Sahib.'

'All right take me to it. I can lunch afterwards.'

It is difficult to view the Taj at noon. The sun strikes the white marble, and there is a great dazzle of reflected light. I stand there with averted eyes, looking at everything—the formal gardens, the surrounding walls of red sandstone, the winding river—everything except the monument I have come to see.

It is there, of course, very solid and real, perfectly preserved, with every jade, jasper or lapis lazuli playing its part in the overall design; and after a while, I can shade my eyes and take in a vision of shimmering white marble. The light rises in waves from the paving-stones, and the squares of black and white marble create an effect of running water. Inside the chamber it is cool and dark but rather musty, and I waste no time in hurrying out again into the sunlight.

I walk the length of a gallery and turn with some relief to the river scene. The sluggish Yamuna winds past Agra on its way to its union with the Ganga. I know the Yamuna well. I know where it emerges from the foothills near Kalsi, cold and blue from the melting snows; I know it as it winds through fields of wheat, sugarcane and mustard, across the flat plains of Uttar Pradesh, sometimes placid, sometimes in flood. I know the river at Delhi, where its muddy banks are a patchwork of clothes spread out by the hundreds of washermen who serve the city and I know it at Mathura, where it is alive with huge turtles; Mathura, sacred city, whose beginnings are lost in antiquity.

And then the river winds its way to Agra, to this spot by the Taj, where parrots flash in the sunshine, kingfishers swoop low over the water and a proud peacock struts across the lawns surrounding the monument.

I follow the peacock into a shady grove. It is quite tame and does not fly away. It leads me to a small boy who is sitting in the shade of a tree, feasting on a handful of small green fruit.

I have not seen the fruit before, and I ask the boy to tell me what it is. He offers me what looks like a hard green plum.

'It is the fruit from the Ashok tree,' says the boy. 'There are many such trees in the garden.'

'Are you allowed to take the fruit?'

'I am allowed,' he says, grinning. 'My father is the head gardener.' I bite into the fruit. It is hard and sour but not unpleasant.

'Do you live here?' I ask.

'Over the wall,' he says. 'But I come here everyday, to help my father and to eat the fruit.'

'So you see the Taj Mahal every day?'

'I have seen it every day for as long as I can remember.'

'And I am seeing it for the first time…you're very lucky.'

He shrugs. 'If you see it once, or a hundred times, it is the same. It doesn't change.'

'Don't you like looking at it, then?'

'I like looking at the people who come here. They are always different. In the evening there will be many people.'

'You must have seen people from almost every country in the world.'

'That is so. They all come here to look at the Taj. Kings

and queens and presidents and prime ministers and film stars and poor people too. And I look at them. In that way it isn't boring.'

'Well, you have the Taj to thank for that.'

He gazes thoughtfully at the shimmering monument.

His eyes are accustomed to the sharp sunlight. He sees the Taj every day, but at this moment, he is really looking at it, thinking about it, wondering what magic it must possess to attract people from all corners of the earth, to bring them here, walking through his father's well-kept garden, so that he can have something new and fresh to look at each day.

A cloud—a very small cloud—passes across the face of the sun; and in the softened light I too am able to look at the Taj without screwing up my eyes.

As the boy said, it does not change. Therein lies beauty. For the effect on the traveller is the same today as it was three hundred years ago when Bernier wrote: 'Nothing offends the eye... No part can be found that is not skilfully wrought, or that has not its peculiar beauty.'

And so, for a few moments, this poem in marble is on view to two unimportant people—the itinerant writer and the gardener's boy.

We say nothing; there is really nothing to be said. (But now, a few months later, when I try to recapture the essence of that day, it is not the monument that I remember most vividly. The Taj is there, of course; I still see it as a mirror for the sun. But what remain with me, more than anything else, are the passage of the river and the sharp flavour of the Ashok fruit).

In the afternoon, I walk through the old bazaars which lie to the west of Akbar's great red sandstone fort, and I am not surprised to find a small street which is almost entirely taken up by kite shops. Most of them sell the smaller, cheaper kites, but one small dark shop has in it a variety of odd and fantastic creations. Stepping inside, I find myself face-to-face with the doyen of Agra's kitemakers, Hosain Ali, a feeble old man whose long beard is dyed red with the juice of mehendi leaves. He has just finished making a new kite from bamboo, paper and thin silk, and it lies outside in the sun, firming up. It is a pale pink kite, with a small green tail.

The old man is soon talking to me, for he likes to talk and is not very busy. He complains that few people buy kites these days (I find this hard to believe), and tells me that I should have visited Agra twenty-five years ago, when kite-flying was the sport of kings and even grown men found time to spend an hour or two every day with these dancing strips of paper. Now, he says, everyone hurries, hurries in a heat of hope, and delicate things like kites and daydreams are trampled underfoot.

'Once I made a wonderful kite,' says Hosain Ali nostalgically. 'It was unlike any kite seen in Agra. It had a number of small, very light paper discs trailing on a thin bamboo frame. At the end of each disc I fixed a sprig of grass, forming a balance on both sides. On the first and largest disc I painted a face and gave it eyes made of two small mirrors. The discs, which grew smaller from head to tail, gave the kite the appearance of a crawling serpent. It was very difficult to get this great kite off the ground. Only I could manage it.

'Of course, everyone heard of the Dragon Kite I had made, and word went about that there was some magic in its making. A large crowd arrived on the maidan to watch me fly the kite.

'At first the kite would not leave the ground. The discs made a sharp wailing sound, the sun was trapped in the little mirrors. My kite had eyes and a tongue and a trailing silver tail. I felt it come alive in my hands. It rose from the ground, rose steeply into the sky, moving farther and farther away, with the sun still glinting in its dragon eyes. And when it went very high, it pulled fiercely on the twine, and my son had to help me with the reel.

'But still the kite pulled, determined to be free—yes, it had become a living thing—and at last the twine snapped, and the wind took the kite, took it over the rooftops and the waving trees and the river and the far hills forever. No one ever saw where it fell. Sahib, are you listening? The Dragon Kite is lost, but for you I'll make a bright new poem to fly.'

'Make me one,' I say, moved by his tale, or rather by the manner of its telling. 'I will collect it tomorrow, before I leave Agra. Let it be a beautiful kite. I won't fly it. I'll hang it on my wall, and will not give it a chance to get away.'

It is evening, and the winter sun comes slanting through the intricate branches of a banyan tree, as a cycle rickshaw—a different one this time—brings me to a forgotten corner of Agra that I have always wanted to visit. This is the old Roman Catholic cemetery where so many early European travellers and adventurers lie buried.

Although it is quite probably the oldest Christian cemetery in northern India, it has none of that overgrown, crumbling look that is common to old cemeteries in monsoon lands. It is a bright, even cheerful place, and the jingle of tonga bells and other street noises can be heard from any part of the grounds. The grass is cut, the gravestones are kept clean and most of the inscriptions are still readable.

The caretaker takes me straight to the oldest grave—this is the oldest known European grave in northern India—and it happens to be that of an Englishman, John Mildenhall. The lettering stands out clearly:

> Here lies John Mildenhall, Englishman, who left London in 1599 and travelling to India through Persia, reached Agra in 1605 and spoke with the Emperor Akbar. On a second visit in 1614 he fell ill at Lahore, died at Ajmere, and was buried here through the good offices of Thomas Kerridge, Merchant.

During the seventeenth and eighteenth centuries, the Agra cemetery was considered blessed ground by Christians, and the dead were brought here from distant places. Thomas Kerridge must have put himself to considerable expense to bury his friend in Agra. Mildenhall was a romantic, who styled himself an envoy of Queen Elizabeth. Unfortunately, he left no account of his travels, although a couple of his letters are quoted in the writings of Purchas, another English merchant, who lies buried in the Protestant cemetery a couple of furlongs away.

Nearby is the grave of the Venetian, Jerome Veronio, who died at Lahore. According to some old records, he had a hand in designing the Taj, modelling it on Humayun's tomb in Delhi. There had for long been a belief that this 'architect' of the Taj lay buried in the cemetery but no one knew where. Then, in 1945, Father Hyacinth, Superior Regular of Agra, scraped the moss off a tombstone, revealing the simple epitaph: 'Here lies Jerome Veronio, who died at Lahore.'

Actually, there is no evidence that Veronio designed the Taj, and even if he had something to do with it, he was only one of a number of artists and architects who worked on its construction. The chief architect was Muhammed Sharif of Samarkand. Each drew a salary of one thousand rupees per month. Ismail Khan of Turkey was the dome-maker. A number of inlay workers, sculptors and masons were Hindus, including Manohar Singh of

Lahore and Mohan Lal of Kanauj, both famous inlay workers.

A man of more authentic accomplishments was the Italian lapidary, Horten Bronzoni, whose grave lies at a short distance from Veronio's. He died on 11 August 1677. According to Tavernier, it was Bronzoni who cut the Koh-i-noor diamond; and, says Tavernier, he cut the stone very badly.

Bronzoni is again mentioned as having manufactured a model ship of war for Aurangzeb, who had been annoyed by the depredations of Portuguese pirates and was anxious to create a navy. The ship was floated in a huge tank and manoeuvred by a number of European artillerymen. It made a ridiculous sight and convinced the Emperor that a navy was out of the question.

There are over eighty old Armenian graves in the cemetery, but the only one that interests me is the tomb of Shah Azar Khan, an expert in the art of moulding a heavy cannon. One of these, 'Zamzamah', earned a measure of immortality in Kipling's *Kim*—'who holds *Zam-Zammah,* that 'fire-breathing dragon', holds the Punjab, for the great green–bronze piece is always first of the conqueror's loot.' The gun was 14.6 feet long, and is still at Lahore.

Other historic tombs lie scattered about the cemetery, but the most striking and curious of them is the grave of Colonel Jon Hessing, who died in 1803. It is a miniature Taj Mahal, built of red sandstone. Although small compared to a Mughal tomb, it is large for a Christian grave, and could easily accommodate a living family of moderate proportions. Hessing came to India from Holland, and was one of a colourful band of freelance soldiers (most of them deserters) who served in Sindhia's Maratha army. Hessing, we are told, was a good, benevolent man and a great soldier. The tomb was built by his wife Alice, who it must be supposed, felt as tenderly towards the Colonel as

Shah Jahan felt towards his queen. She could not afford marble. Even so, her 'Taj' cost a lakh of rupees.

Outside, in the street, people move about with casual unconcern. Street-vendors occupy the pavement, unwilling that their rivals should take advantage of a brief absence. In the banyan tree, the sparrows and bulbuls are settling down for the night. A kite lies entangled in the upper branches.

# Rishikesh

'*Ganga Mai ki jai!*' Everyone raised the cry as the Haridwar bus moved out of Meerut. Most of the passengers, including Kamal and I, were going to take darshan of Mother Ganga. But while many were bound for Haridwar, we were going to Rishikesh, a more secluded temple town, situated on the banks of the Ganga at the point where the river emerges from the mountains and, hemmed in no longer by rocks and trees, stretches itself across the plains of Uttar Pradesh and Bihar, flowing past great cities like Kanpur, Allahabad, Benares and Patna, and into Bengal.

Just next to us sat a well-built woman with three small children. The eldest, a boy of about six, took a fancy to Kamal, and was soon lolling about on his knees. In front of us, obliterating the view, sat a stout lala and his devoted wife. Lalaji proved to be an impatient and ill-tempered man. He quarrelled with the conductor, the driver and the ticket seller. In order to travel in comfort he had reserved three front seats, but was unwilling to pay toll on the third seat which, he insisted, would only be occupied by his and his wife's feet. They gave in to him eventually. An urchin who inadvertently touched the sleeve of his kurta received a stinging slap. But he became more tolerant as time went on, and once, when engaged in an argument with a passenger at the other end of the bus, favoured me with a smile.

The countryside was monotonous up to Roorkee.

Then the road took us along the Ganga canal, and Kamal sat up and began to look at things. We changed buses at Haridwar, and got into a very old and wheezy contraption which surprised us by going much faster than the government roadways bus. Probably the driver was trying to make up for time lost in stopping every five minutes to pick up some acquaintance on the road. We stopped for ten minutes at the Sat Narain temple, once famous for the tiger that used to visit it every evening. Rattling through the Motichur forest block, we saw two elephants—tame ones, possibly—and a variety of monkeys.

We left the bus at Rishikesh and went in search of my friend Jhardari, with whom we were to stay. He lived at Muni-ki-Reti, two miles upstream, where the wealthier ashrams were situated. His rooms, adjoining Swami Sivanandas Ashram, were on the right-hand bank of the Ganga.

Jhardhari was away, on a routine trip to Devprayag. As secretary of the Tehri-Garhwal Motor Mazdoor Sangh Workers' Union, he has to travel all over the district to keep in touch with the men who drive the trucks and buses on the dangerous hill roads. The buses are privately owned; the government only nationalizes those services that use first-class roads. The state is very cautious about taking over the responsibility of transporting people to remote hill towns like Tehri and Pipalkoti, where pilgrims on the way to Gangotri or Badrinath must start their journey on foot. The motor roads in the interior are narrow, precipitous and unmetalled. To mention this is not to condemn them. Till a few years ago many of these regions had no roads at all. And Garhwalis are excellent drivers—many have experience of Army trucks—and serious accidents are uncommon.

Jhardhari's roommate made us at home, and prepared hot,

strong tea. Garhwalis drink more tea than Englishmen, and seldom take water. We were to become accustomed to drinking tea at almost hourly intervals.

One of the first things we did was to dip ourselves in the river. The water was icy cold, and it was impossible to stay in for more than ten minutes. Shivering, we climbed on to the bathing steps to dry ourselves. Our clothes felt hot against our bodies.

Down at the Rishikesh bathing ghat, hundreds of people would be dipping themselves in the sacred waters; but at Muni-ki-Reti (which is in Tehri-Garhwal district, while the town of Rishikesh is in Dehradun district), there were only a few people by the river—a few pilgrims from Bengal, Andhra and Madras—disciples from Swami Sivananda's Ashram—and a number of boys who work in the area.

Logs were always floating downstream, and boys would get across them, lying flat on their stomachs and paddling the planks through the water. Two of the more daring youths paddled their logs right across the river, to the temples on the opposite bank. They were good swimmers, but had they been parted from their floats, they would have been carried away by the current and quite possibly drowned.

We walked down to Rishikesh in the evening, and saw over a hundred sadhus emerging from an ashram where they were given their evening meal. In their saffron robes, they flooded the dusty road, talking animatedly among themselves. Many of them were young men, probably novices. One was a strapping youth of about twenty, a Hercules gracefully wearing the robe of renunciation.

They looked well fed and contented. Most of them spoke a little English. What had brought them to Rishikesh, I wondered, to live as recluses and ascetics? Personal tragedy, the stress of modern city life or the failure of material pursuits... Or did the career of a religious mendicant hold out profitable prospects? Later on, I was told that some of the novitiates should really have been in prison. But perhaps the rigours of their monastic existence rid them of early criminal tendencies; and if that was so then surely ashrams were better places for them than jails.

Little shacks lined the river banks and though few people bathed late in the evening, hundreds were beside the water. Offerings of flowers in little leaf boats went sailing downstream. They were lighted by wicks dipped in oil and went bobbing up and down on the water, sometimes for a considerable distance. Kamal sent an offering downstream and requested Mother Ganga to grant him success as an artist. His boat, though, did not go very far.

Undeterred, Kamal fed little balls of flour to the fish. They were huge, completely tame and came to the bank in shoals to be fed by the bathers. Sometimes, they fought among themselves, and a few of them were a raw pink where they had been savagely bitten.

That night, we slept in the open, on a wide ledge above the riverbed. The lights from the temples and ashrams on the opposite bank reflected gently on the water. There was a human quietness everywhere. The sounds were of the river—the distant roar of the rapids, the nearby lapping of water on the bathing steps.

We bathed again in the river as the sun came up over the mountain known as Manikoot Parbat. There is an unbroken ridge along the top of this mountain, stretching all the way to the snows of Badrinath, some two hundred miles away. Only a few hermits live on the mountain. It belongs to the elephants who sometimes visit the river in herds to bathe and drink.

Jhardhari had returned, looking quite fresh after a one

hundred and fifty-mile bus journey; and he offered to take us up to Narindernagar, a little town on a hilltop, which, though smaller and less central than Tehri, is the capital of the district. The former Maharaja had preferred it to the less congenial valley town of Tehri on the banks of the Bhagirathi; and Narindernagar became the Maharaja's summer capital.

The buses were all full, and we had to travel up separately, one to each bus—first Kamal, then I and last of all Jhardhari.

⁂

Narindernagar is only ten miles from Rishikesh, but it is also two thousand feet higher, and the bus has to climb a dizzy, winding road on which there can be no two-way traffic. But the buses go faster than their counterparts in the plains. With speedometers conveniently out of order, buses and trucks come downhill at a speed of thirty to thirty-five miles an hour. But, as have said before, Garhwalis are very good drivers. Along the main highways of the Punjab are the wrecks of numerous trucks, some jammed up against trees, others in head-on collisions. But in the hills there is no driving at night, and the drivers prefer smoking bidis to drinking rum or country liquor. Mechanical failure is usually the cause of the few accidents that do occur.

From Narindernagar, we went on for another eight miles, and eventually got down at Agra-khal, a pass in the mountains at a height of about five thousand feet. The motor road, soon becoming kachcha, continues to Tehri and Dharasu, and from the latter, pilgrims must proceed on foot to the shrines and temples of Gangotri.

After eating some hot puris, we walked back to Narindernagar, leaving the main road and hiking through a forest of oak and pine. Kamal, who was seeing real mountains for the first time, was very excited and asked me innumerable questions about plants and streams and trees and rocks. He chattered away until Jhardhari said something flattering about his many and varied interests, and this embarrassed Kamal so much that he stopped talking altogether. I enjoyed the shade of the gnarled, untidy oaks and the soft, slippery carpet of pine needles.

But after the forest, there was bare hillside, the sun was scorching hot, and we had soon emptied the water bottle. So, we rejoined the main road and stopped a truck going down to Rishikesh.

It was the first time Kamal and I sat in the back of a truck travelling at speed down a mountain. It was impossible to anchor oneself on the floor. A kindly sadhu, also at the back, placed his blanket on a tyre and invited us to share it with him; but at every hairpin bend the tyre slid violently about the floor and we were pitched off it. Kamal and I clung to each other to avoid being thrown against the sides of the truck; Jhardhari hung on to an iron bar; we were all feeling quite sick. Only the sadhu appeared unperturbed. He retained his seat on the tyre, even when it went skidding from one end of the truck to the other.

When we reached Rishikesh, we went straight to the river. Never had Mother Ganga's waters been so refreshing. The giddiness disappeared. Then, we lay down on the sand, and Kamal, like the sleepy giant Kumbhakarna in the Ramayana, did not come to life until it was time to eat.

We slept well that night. In the morning, we would go to Lachhman Jhula and, passing the suspension bridge, walk a little way up Manikoot Parbat.

As the sun rose, turning the river to gold, we climbed into the boat that took pilgrims across to the temples on the other bank. The oarsmen sat in the prow, straining against the current, and the people in the boat raised the same ageless cry: 'Ganga Mai ki jai!'

Climbing ashore, we passed through groves of mango trees, planted by rich pilgrims for the benefit of the sadhus. Then, leaving behind Lachhman Jhula, we walked along the pilgrim route to Badrinath until we came to a dharamshala called Garur Chatti. Here, we drank tea, the inevitable but welcome tea, and set off up the hillside in search of a waterfall Jhardhari had told us about

It did not take us long to reach the waterfall. Set amidst rocks and ferns, it fell about thirty feet onto a platform of smooth yellow rocks and pebbles. Here, it formed a small pool, about waist deep, into which we leapt without hesitation. The water wasn't as cold as the Ganga, and we could splash about for as long as we liked while the waterfall sprayed down on our heads. The water was very clear and fresh, though it had a slightly bitter taste, evidence, I suppose, of a strong mineral content.

Further down the stream, we found a lot of old bones, which Kamal insisted were the remains of a tiger's kill as, indeed, they might have been, tigers having been seen on the mountain. But no tiger troubled us; only a band of langurs, swinging from tree to tree, that seemed resentful of our presence and urged us to leave.

This we did at our leisure and, after more tea at Garur Chatti and a visit to a small temple—where the courtyard floor was so hot to our bare feet that we had to skip about in agony—we trudged back to Muni-ki-Reti.

It was our last night sleeping beside the Ganga, and we rested with our chins in our hands, watching the river move silently past us, surging onward, India's lifeblood, inexorable and irresistible.

ON THE ROAD IN INDIA

# The India I Carried with Me

I am now going back in time, to a period when I was caught between East and West, and had to make up my mind just where I belonged. I had been away from India for barely a month before I was longing to return. The insularity of the place where I found myself (Jersey, in the Channel Islands) had something to do with it, I suppose. There was little there to remind me of India or the East, not one brown face to be seen in the streets or on the beaches. I'm sure it's a different sort of place now; but fifty years ago it had nothing to offer by way of companionship or good cheer to a lonely, sensitive boy who had left home and friends in search of a 'better future'.

I had come to England with a dream of sorts, and I was to return to India with another kind of dream; but in between (there were to be four years of dreary office work, lonely bed-sitting rooms, shabby lodging houses, cheap snack bars, hospital wards, and the struggle to write my first book and find a publisher for it.

I started work in a large departmental store called *Le Riche*. At eight in the morning, when I walked to the store, it was dark. At six in the evening, when I walked home, it was dark again. Where were all those sunny beaches Jersey was famous for? I would have to wait for summer to see them, and a Saturday afternoon to take a dip in the sea.

Occasionally, after an early supper, I would walk along the

deserted seafront. If the tide was in and the wind approaching gale-force, the waves would climb the sea wall and drench me with their cold salt spray. My aunt, with whom I was staying, thought I was quite mad to take this solitary walk; but I have always been at one with nature, even in its wilder moments, and the wind and the crashing waves gave me a sense of freedom, strengthened my determination to escape from the island and go my own way.

When I wasn't walking along the seafront, I would sit at the portable typewriter in my small attic room, and hammer out the rough chapters of the book that was to become my first novel. These were characters and incidents based on the journal I had kept during my last year in India. It was 1951, recalled in late 1952. An eighteen-year-old looking back on incidents in the life of a seventeen-year-old! Nostalgia and longing suffused those pages. How I longed to be back with my friends in the small town of Dehradun—a leafy place, sunny, fruit-laden, easy-going, every familiar corner etched clearly in my memory. Somehow, it had been that last year in Dehra that had brought me closer to the India that I had so far only taken for granted. An India of close and sometimes sentimental friendships. Of striking contrasts: a small cinema showing English pictures (a George Formby comedy or an American musical) and only a couple of hours away thousands taking a dip in the sacred water of the Ganga. Or outside the station, hundreds of pony-drawn tongas waiting to pick up passengers, while the more affluent climbed into their Ford Convertibles, Morris Minors, Baby Austins or flashy Packards and Daimlers.

But of course Dehra in the fifties was a town of bicycles. Students, shopkeepers, Army cadets, office workers, all used them. The scooter (or Lanlbretta) had only just been invented, and it would be several years before it took over from the bicycle. It was still unaffordable for the great majority.

I was awkward on a bicycle and frequently fell off, breaking my arm on one occasion. But this did not prevent me from joining my friends on cycle rides to the Sulphur springs, or to Premnagar (where the Military Academy was situated) or along the Haridwar road and down to the riverbed at Lachiwala.

In Jersey, I found an old cycle belonging to my cousin, and I rode from St. Helier, where we lived, to St. Brelade's Bay, at the other end of the island. But returning after dark, I was hauled up for riding without lights. I had no idea that cycles had also to be equipped with lights. Back in Dehra, we never used them!

The attic room had no view, so one of my favourite occupations, gazing out of windows, came to a stop. But perhaps this was helpful in that it made me concentrate on the sheet of paper in my typewriter. After about six months, I had a book of sorts ready for submission to any publisher who was prepared to look at it. Meanwhile, I had been through at least three jobs and had even been offered a post in the Jersey Civil Service, having successfully taken the local civil service exam—something I had done out of sheer boredom, as I had no intention of settling permanently on the island.

I had been keeping a diary of sorts and in some of the entries I had expressed my desire to get back to India, and my discontent at having to stay with relatives who were unsympathetic, not only to my feelings for India but also to my ambitions to become a writer. The diary fell into my uncle's hands. He read it, and was naturally upset. We had a row. I was contrite; but a few days later I packed my suitcases (all two of them) and stepped on to the ferry that was to take me to Southampton and then to London. Lesson one: don't leave your personal diaries lying around!

But perhaps it was all for the best, otherwise I might have hung around in Jersey for another year or two, to the detriment of my personal happiness and my writing ambitions.

I arrived in London in the middle of a thick yellow November fog—those were the days of the killer London fogs— and after a search found the Students' Hostel where I was given a cubicle to myself. But I did not stay there very long; the available food was awful. As soon as I got an office job—not too difficult in the 1950s—I rented an attic room in Belsize Park, the first of many bed-sitters that I was to live in during my three-year sojourn in London.

From Belsize Park I was to move to Haverstock Hill (close to Hampstead Heath), then to South London for a short time, and finally to Swiss Cottage. Most of my landladies were Jewish— refugees from persecution in pre-war Europe—and I too was a refugee of sorts, still very unsure of where I belonged. Was it England, the land of my father, or India, the land of my birth? But my father had also been born in India, had grown up and made a living there, visiting *his* father's land, England, only a couple of times during his life.

The link with Britain was tenuous, based on heredity rather than upbringing. It was more in the mind. It was a literary England I had been drawn to, not a physical England. And in fact, I took several exploratory walks around 'literary' London, visiting houses or streets where famous writers had once lived; in particular the East End and Dockland, for I had grown up on the novels and stories of Dickens, Smollett, Captain Marryat, and W.W. Jacobs. But I did not make many English friends. If they were a reserved race, I was even more reserved. Always shy,

I waited for others to take the initiative. In India, people will take the initiative, they lose no time in getting to know you. Not so in England. They were too polite to look at you. And in that respect, I was more English than the English.

The gentleman who lived on the floor below me occasionally went so far as to greet me with the observation, 'Beastly weather, isn't it?'

And I would respond by saying, 'Oh, perfectly beastly,' and pass on.

How different it was when I bumped into a Gujarati boy, Praveen, who lived on the basement floor. He gave me a winning smile, and I remember saying, 'Oh, to be in Bombay now that winter's here,' and immediately we were friends.

He was only seventeen, a year or two younger than me, and he was studying at one of the polytechnics with a view to getting into the London School of Economics. At that time, most of the Indians in London were students, the great immigration rush was still a long way off, and racial antagonisms were directed more at the recently arrived West Indians than at Asians.

Praveen took me on the rounds of the coffee bars, then proliferating all over London, and introduced me to other students, among them a Vietnamese, called Thanh, who cultivated my friendship because, as he said, 'I want to speak English.' When he discovered that my accent was very un-English (you could have called it Welsh with an Anglo-Indian interaction), he dropped me like a hot brick. He was very frank, he was not interested in friendship, he said, only in improving his accent. I heard later that he'd attached himself to a young journalist from up north, who spoke broad Yorkshire.

Most evenings I remained in my room and worked on my novel. From being a journal it had become a first person narrative, and now I was turning it into fiction in the third person. The title had also undergone a few changes, but finally I settled on *The Room on the Roof*.

Into it, I put all the love and affection I felt for the friends I had left behind in Dehra. It was more than nostalgia, it was a recreation of the people, places and incidents of that last year in India. I did not want it to fade away. The riverbanks at Haridwar, the mango-groves of the Doon, the poinsettias and bougainvillaea, the games on the parade ground, the chaat shops near the Clock Tower, the summer heat, the monsoon downpours, romping naked in the rain, sitting on railway platforms, gnawing at a stick of sugar cane, listening to street cries... All this and more came crowding upon me as I sat writing before the gas fire in my little room.

When it grew very cold, I used an old overcoat given to me by Diana Athill, the junior partner at Andre Deutsch, who had promised to publish *The Room* if I rewrote it as a novel. Another who encouraged me was a BBC producer, Prudence Smith, who got me to give a couple of talks on Radio's Third Programme. I felt I was getting somewhere; and when I found myself confined to the Hampstead General Hospital for almost a month, with a mysterious disease which had affected the vision in my right eye, I used the left to catch up on my reading and to write a couple of short stories.

A nurse brought a tray of books around the ward every afternoon, and thanks to this courtesy, I was able to discover the delightful stories of William Saroyan and Denton Welch's sensitive first novel *Maiden Voyage*. Saroyan, a Pulitzer Prize winner for his play *The Time of Your Life,* was then very successful and popular. Denton's promising career had been cut short by a terrible accident. Out cycling on a country road, he had been knocked down by a speeding motorist. He had lived for several years, struggling against crippling injuries and almost completing his sensitive autobiography A *Voice in the Clouds*. He was thirty-one when he died. Towards the end, he could only work for three or four minutes at a time. Complications set in, and the left side of his heart started failing. Even then he made a terrific effort to finish his book. His friend Eric wrote—'Denton was upheld by the high courage which seemed somehow the fruit of his rare intelligence.'

The work of these writers, together with the bottle of Guinness I was given every day as a tonic (they had found me somewhat undernourished), meant that I walked out of the hospital with a spring in my step and a determination to succeed.

But Andre Deutsch was still dithering over my book. The firm was doing well, but he didn't like taking risks. No publisher likes losing money. And he wasn't going to make much out of my novel, a subjective and unsensational work.

But I resented his indecision. So I returned the small amount he'd paid me by way of an option, and demanded the return of my manuscript. Back came an apologetic letter and an advance (then £50) against publication.

Today, almost fifty years later, the firm of Andre Deutsch has gone, but *The Room on the Roof* is still in print, still making friends. This is not something that I gloat over, it only goes to show that books are unpredictable commodities, and that the most successful authors and publishers often fall by the wayside. Publishers go out of business, writers fade from the public mind. Even Saroyan is forgotten now. I'll be forgotten too, someday.

There were to be further delays before The *Room* was published, and I was back in India when it did come out. By then I'd almost forgotten about the book! But it picked up the John Llewellyn Rhys Prize, an award that also went to V.S. Naipaul a year later, for his first book. It was then worth only £50. There were no big sponsors in those days. It is now sponsored by a British newspaper and is worth £5,000. This was turned down last year by another Indian writer, who disagreed with the paper's policies.

Meanwhile, in London, there were other distractions. I loved stage musicals, and if I had a little money to spare I went to the theatre, taking in such productions as *Porgy and Bess, Paint Your Wagon, Pal Joey, Teahouse of the August Moon,* and the occasional review. And of course the annual presentation of *Peter Pan* at the Scala Theatre, not far from where I worked. I had grown up on Peter Pan, first read to me by my father in distant Jamnagar, and at school I had read Barrie's other plays and been charmed by them; but, like operetta, they had gone out of fashion and only the ageless Peter remained. 'Do you believe in fairies?' he asks in the play. And to save Tinker Bell from extinction, I clapped with the rest of the audience. But did I really believe in fairies? I looked for them in Kensington Gardens, where Peter Pan's statue stood, and found a few mothers pushing their perambulators, but no fairies. And I looked in Hyde Park, but found only courting couples. And I looked all over Leicester Square, but instead of fairies I found prostitutes soliciting business. As I was still looking for romance, I crept back to my room and my portable typewriter—I would have to create my own romance.

The small portable had been in the windows of a Jersey department store, and every time I passed the store I glanced at the window to see if the typewriter was still there. It seemed to be waiting for me to come in and take it away. I longed to buy it, partly because I had to type out the final drafts of my book, and also because it looked very dainty and attractive. It was definitely out to seduce me. Finally, with the help of a loan from Mr Bromley, a kindly senior clerk, I bought the machine. It cost only £12, but that was three month's wages at the time. It accompanied me to London, and then a couple of years later to India, giving me good service in Dehradun, New Delhi, and then Mussoorie where it finally succumbed to the damp monsoon climate.

My worldly possessions had increased, not only by the typewriter, but also by a record player which I had bought second-hand from a Thai student. I had become an ardent fan of the Black singer, Eartha Kitt, and had bought all her records; but they were no good without a player until the Thai boy came to my rescue. Then the sensual, throaty voice of Eartha reverberated through the lodging house, bringing complaints from the landlady and the gentleman downstairs. I had to keep the volume low, which wasn't much fun.

I was also fond of the clarinet (turj) playing of an Indian musician, Master Ibrahim, and I had some of his recordings which transported me back to the streets and bazaars of small-town India. Light, lilting and tuneful, I preferred this sort of flute music to the warblings of the more popular songsters.

Praveen liked gangster films and wanted me to accompany him to anything which featured Humphrey Bogart, James Cagney, George Raft and other tough guys. Praveen wanted to be a tough guy himself and often struck a Bogart-like pose, cigarette dangling from the side of his mouth. There was nothing tough about Praveen, who was really rather delicate, but his affectations were charming and risible.

One day he announced that he was returning to India for a few months, as his ailing mother was anxious to see him. He asked me to come along too, to give him company during the three week voyage. To do so, I would have to throw up my job, but I had already thrown up several jobs. They were simply stop-gaps until I could establish myself as a writer. I hadn't the slightest intention or ambition of being a senior clerk or even an executive for the firm in which I was working. The only problem in leaving England then was that I would have to leave my book in limbo, as there was still no guarantee that Deutsch would publish it. But it was time I went on to write other things; time to strike out on my own, to take a chance with India. The ships were full of British and Anglo-Indian families coming to England, to make a 'better future' for themselves. I would do the opposite, go into reverse, and make my future, for good or ill, in the land of my birth.

My passport was in order, and I had only to give a week's notice to my employers. I had saved up about £200, and of this £50 went on the cost of my passage, London to Bombay. Praveen and I boarded the *S.S. Balory*, a Polish liner with a reputation for running into trouble. We had no difficulty in securing berths in tourist class. Praveen had every intention of returning to England to complete his studies. My own intentions were very vague. I knew there would be no job for me in India, but I was quietly confident that I could make a living from writing, and that too in the English language.

The *Balory* lived up to its reputation. Some of the crew went missing at Gibraltar. A passenger fell overboard in the Red Sea. Lifeboats were lowered, but he could not be found.

Praveen fell in love with an Egyptian girl who disembarked at Aden. He followed her ashore, and I had to run after him and get him back to the ship. As we docked at Ballard Pier, a fire broke out in one of the holds, but by then we were safely ashore. Praveen was swamped by relatives who carried him off to the suburbs of Bombay. I made my way to Victoria Terminus and boarded the Dehradun Express. It was a slow passenger train, which went chugging through several states in the general direction of northern India. Two days and two nights later we crawled through the eastern Doon. It was early March. The mango trees were in blossom, the peacocks were calling, and Belsize Park was far away.

# The Road to Badrinath

If you have travelled up the Mandakini Valley, and then cross over into the valley of the Alaknanda, you are immediately struck by the contrast. The Mandakini is gentler, richer in vegetation, almost pastoral in places; the Alaknanda is awesome, precipitous, threatening—and seemingly inhospitable to those who must live, and earn a livelihood, in its confines.

Even as we left Chamoli and began the steady, winding climb to Badrinath, the nature of the terrain underwent a dramatic change. No longer did green fields slope gently down to the riverbed. Here they clung precariously to rocky slopes and ledges that grew steeper and narrower, while the river below, impatient to reach its confluence with the Bhagirathi at Deoprayag, thundered along the narrow gorge.

Badrinath is one of the four dhams, or four most holy places in India. (The other three are Rameshwaram, Dwarka and Jagannath Puri.) For the pilgrim travelling to this holiest of holies, the journey is exciting, possibly even uplifting; but for those who live permanently on these crags and ridges, life is harsh, a struggle from one day to the next. No wonder so many young men from Garhwal find their way into the army. Little grows on these rocky promontories; and what does, is at the mercy of the weather. For most of the year the fields lie fallow. Rivers, unfortunately, run downhill and not uphill.

The harshness of this life, typical of much of Garhwal, was brought home to me at Pipalkoti, where we stopped for the night. Pilgrims stop here by the coachload, for the Garhwal Mandal Vikas Nigam's rest house is fairly capacious, and small hotels and dharamshalas abound. Just off the busy road is a tiny hospital, and here, late in the evening, we came across a woman keeping vigil over the dead body of her husband. The body had been laid out on a bench in the courtyard. A few feet away the road was crowded with pilgrims in festival mood; no one glanced over the low wall to notice this tragic scene.

The woman came from a village near Helong. Earlier that day, finding her consumptive husband in a critical condition she had decided to bring him to the nearest town for treatment. As he was frail and emaciated, she was able to carry him on her back for several miles, until she reached the motor road. Then, at some expense, she engaged a passing taxi and brought him to Pipalkoti. But he was already dead when she reached the small hospital. There was no morgue; so she sat beside the body in the courtyard, waiting for dawn and the arrival of others from the village. A few men arrived next morning and we saw them wending their way down to the cremation ground. We did not see the woman again. Her children were hungry and she had to hurry home to look after them.

Pipalkoti is hot (and peepul trees are conspicuous by their absence), but Joshimath, the winter resort of the Badrinath temple establishment, is about 6,000 feet above sea level and has an equable climate. It is now a fairly large town, and although the surrounding hills are rather bare, it does have one great tree that has survived the ravages of time. This is an ancient mulberry, known as the Kalpa Vriksha (Immortal Wishing Tree), beneath which the great Sankaracharya meditated, a few centuries ago. It is reputedly over 2,000 years old, and is certainly larger than my modest four-roomed flat in Mussoorie. Sixty pilgrims holding hands might just about encircle its trunk.

I have seen some big trees, but this is certainly the oldest and broadest of them. I am glad Sankaracharya meditated beneath it and thus ensured its preservation. Otherwise it might well have gone the way of other great trees and forests that once flourished in this area.

A small boy reminds me that it is a Wishing Tree, so I make my wish. I wish that other trees might prosper like this one.

'Have you made a wish?' I ask the boy.

'I wish that you will give me one rupee,' he says. His wish comes true with immediate effect. Mine lies in the uncertain future. But he has given me a lesson in wishing.

Joshimath has to be a fairly large place, because most of Badrinath arrives here in November, when the shrine is snowbound for six months. Army and PWD structures also dot the landscape. This is no carefree hill resort, but it has all the amenities for making a short stay quite pleasant and interesting. Perched on the steep mountainside above the junction of the Alaknanda and Dhauli Rivers, it is now vastly different from what it was when Frank Smythe visited it fifty years ago and described it as 'an ugly little place...straggling unbeautifully over the hillside. Primitive little shops line the main street, which is roughly paved in places and in others has been deeply channelled by the monsoon rains. The pilgrims spend the night in single-storeyed rest houses, not unlike the hovels provided for the Kentish hop-pickers of former days, some of which are situated in narrow passages running off the main street and are filthy and evil-smelling.'

Those were Joshimath's former days. It is a different place

today, with small hotels, modern shops, a cinema; and its growth and comparative modernity date from the early sixties, when the old pilgrim footpath gave way to the motor road which takes the traveller all the way to Badrinath. No longer does the weary, footsore pilgrim sink gratefully down in the shade of the Kalpa Vriksha. He alights from his bus or luxury coach and drinks a cola or a Thums-up at one of the many small restaurants on the roadside.

Contrast this comfortable journey with the pilgrimage fifty years ago. Frank Smythe again: 'So they venture on their pilgrimage... Some borne magnificently by coolies, some toiling along in rags, some almost crawling, preyed on by disease and distorted by dreadful deformities... Europeans who have read and travelled cannot conceive what goes on in the minds of these simple folk, many of them from the agricultural parts of India, wonderment and fear must be the prime ingredients. So the pilgrimage becomes an adventure. Unknown dangers threaten the broad, well-made path, at any moment the gods, who hold the rocks in leash, may unloose their wrath upon the hapless passer-by. To the European it is a walk to Badrinath, to the Hindu pilgrim it is far, far more.'

Above Vishnuprayag, Smythe left the Alaknanda and entered the Bhyundar Valley, a botanist's paradise, which he called the Valley of Flowers. He fell in love with the lush meadows of this high valley, and made it known to the world. It continues to attract the botanist and trekker. Primulas of subtle shades, wild geraniums, saxifrages clinging to the rocks, yellow and red potentillas, snow-white anemones, delphiniums, violets, wild roses, all these and many more flourish there, capturing the mind and heart of the flower lover.

'Impossible to take a step without crushing a flower.' This

may not be true any more, for many footsteps have trodden the Bhyundar in recent years. There are other areas in Garhwal where the hills are rich in flora—the Har-ki-doon, Harsil, Tungnath, and the Khiraun valley where the balsam grows to a height of eight feet—but the Bhyundar has both a variety and a concentration of wild flowers, especially towards the end of the monsoon. It would be no exaggeration to call it one of the most beautiful valleys in the world. The Bhyundar is a digression for lovers of mountain scenery; but the pilgrim keeps his eyes fixed on the ultimate goal—Badrinath, where the gods dwelt and where salvation is to be found.

There are still a few who do it the hard way—mostly those who have taken sanyas and renounced the world. Here is one hardy soul doing penance. He stretches himself out on the ground, draws himself up to a standing position, then flattens himself out again. In this manner he will proceed from Badrinath to Rishikesh, oblivious of the sun and rain, the dust from passing buses, the sharp gravel of the footpath.

Others are not so hardy. One saffron-robed scholar, speaking fair English, asks us for a lift to Badrinath, and we find a space for him. He rewards us with a long and involved commentary on the Vedas, which lasts through the remainder of the journey. His special field of study, he informs us, is the part played by aeronautics in Vedic literature.

'And what,' I ask him, 'is the connection between the two?'

He looks at me pityingly.

'It is what I am trying to find out,' he replies.

The road drops to Pandukeshwar and rises again, and all the time I am scanning the horizon for the forests of the Badrinath region I had read about many years ago in James B. Fraser's *The Himalaya Mountains*! Walnuts grow up to 9,000 feet, deodars and 'bilka' up to 9,500 feet, and 'amesh' and 'kiusu' for up to a similar height—but, apart from strands of long-leaved excelsia pine, I do not see much, certainly no deodars. What has happened to them, I wonder. An endless variety of trees delighted us all the way from Dugalbeta to Mandal, a well-protected area, but here on the high ridges above the Alaknanda, little seems to grow; or, if ever they did, have long since been bespoiled or swept away.

Finally we reach the wind-swept, barren valley which harbours Badrinath—a growing township, thriving, lively, but somewhat dwarfed by the snow-capped peaks that tower above it. As at Joshimath, there is no dearth of hostelries and dharamshalas. Even so, every hotel or rest house is filled to overflowing. It is the height of the pilgrim season, and pilgrims, tourists and mendicants of every description throng the riverfront.

Just as Kedar is the most sacred of the Shiva temples in the Himalayas, so Badrinath is the supreme place of worship for the Vaishnav sects.

According to legend, when Sankaracharya in his digvijaya travels visited the Mana Valley he arrived at the Narada–Kund and found fifty different images lying in its waters. These he rescued, and when he had done so, a voice from Heaven said, 'These are the images for the Kaliyug, establish them here.' Sankaracharya accordingly placed them beneath a mighty tree which grew there and whose shade extended from Badrinath to Nandprayag, a distance of over eighty miles. Close to it was the hermitage of Nar-Narayana (or Arjuna and Krishna), and in course of time temples were built in honour of these and other manifestations of Vishnu. It was here that Vishnu appeared to his followers in person, as the four-armed, crested and adorned with pearls and garlands.' The faithful, it is said, can still see him on the peak of Nilkantha, on the great Kumbha day. It is, in fact, the Nilkantha peak that dominates this crater-like valley where a few hardy thistles and nettles manage to survive. Like cacti in the desert, the pricklier forms of life seem best equipped to live in a hostile environment.

Nilkantha means blue-necked, an allusion to the god Shiva's swallowing of a poison meant to destroy the world. The poison remained in his throat, which was rendered blue thereafter. It is a majestic and awe-inspiring peak, soaring to a height of 21,640 feet. As its summit is only five miles from Badrinath, it is justly held in reverence. From its ice-clad pinnacle three great ridges sweep down, of which the southern one terminates in the Alaknanda valley.

On the evening of our arrival we could not see the peak, as it was hidden in clouds. Badrinath itself was shrouded in mist. But we made our way to the temple, a gaily decorated building about fifty feet high, with a gilded roof. The image of Vishnu, carved in black stone, stands in the centre of the sanctum, opposite the door, in a dhyana posture. An endless stream of people passes through the temple to pay homage and emerge the better for their proximity to the divine.

From the temple, flights of steps lead down to the rushing river and to the hot springs which emerge just above it. Another road leads through a long but tidy bazaar where pilgrims may buy mementos of their visit—from sacred amulets to pictures of the gods in vibrant technicolour. Here at last I am free to indulge my passion for cheap rings, with none to laugh at my foible. There are all kinds, from rings designed like a coiled serpent (my favourite) to twisted bands of copper and iron and others containing the pictures of gods, gurus and godmen. They do not cost more that two or three rupees each, and so I am able to fill my pockets. I never wear these rings. I simply hoard them away. My friends are convinced that in a previous existence I was a jackdaw, seizing upon and hiding away any kind of bright and shiny object: so be it...

Even those who have renounced the world appear to be cheerful—like the young woman from Gujarat who had taken sanyas and who met me on the steps below the temple. She gave me a dazzling smile and passed me an exercise book. She had taken a vow of silence; but being, I think, of an extrovert nature, she seemed eager to remain in close communication with the rest of humanity, and did so by means of written questions and answers. Hence the exercise book

Although at Badrinath I missed the sound of birds and the presence of trees, it was good to be part of the happy throng at its colourful little temple, and to see the sacred river close to its source. And early next morning I was rewarded with the liveliest experience of all.

Opening the window of my room, and glancing out, I saw the rising sun touch the snow-clad summit of Nilkantha. At first the snows were pink; then they turned to orange and gold. All sleep vanished as I gazed up in wonder at that magnificent pinnacle in the sky. And had Lord Vishnu appeared just then on the summit I would not have been in the least surprised.

# The Grand Trunk Road

There is a fantasy journey that I have always wanted to make, but one that I know I never will: the long, long journey along the Grand Trunk Road from Calcutta to Peshawar.

For the Grand Trunk Road is a river. It may not be as sacred as the Ganga, which it greets at Kanpur and Varanasi, but it is just as permanent. It's a river of life, an unending stream of humanity intent on reaching their destination and getting there most of the time.

A long day's journey into night, that's how I would describe the saga of the truck driver, that knight errant, or rather errant knight, of India's Via Appia. Undervalued, underpaid and often disparaged, he drives all day and sometimes all night, carrying the country's goods and produce for hundreds of miles on the GT Road, across state borders, through lawless tracts, at all seasons and in all weathers. We blame him for hogging the middle of the road, but he is usually overloaded and if he veers too much to the left or right, he is quite likely to topple over, burying himself and his crew under bricks or gas cylinders, sugarcane or TV sets. More than the railway man, the truck driver is modern India's lifeline, and yet his life is held cheap. He drinks, he swears, occasionally he picks up HIV, and frequently he is killed or badly injured. But we cannot do without him.

# The Grand Trunk Road

In the old, old days, when Muhammad Tughlaq, Sultan of Delhi, streamlined the country's roads, bullock carts and camel caravans were the chief transporters. In 1333, when the Moroccan traveller Ibn Battuta visited India, he was deeply impressed by the Sultan's road network. Sher Shah Suri, who ruled from 1540 till 1545, made further improvements, especially to the GT Road. He built caravanserais and inns for travellers, and planted fine trees along the GT Road and other important highways. Horsemen, carts and palanquin bearers jostled for pride of position, much as our motorists do today. Traffic was slow-moving, and the best way to get ahead was to mount a horse and canter from stage to stage, that is, between twelve and fifteen miles a day.

Invading armies had, of course, made use of the road long before the British gained control of northern India. On this same stretch of the highway, the Persian invader Nadir Shah defeated the Mughal Emperor in 1739. In a battle lasting two hours, over 20,000 of the Emperor's soldiers were killed. The next day, Nadir Shah marched to Delhi, to ransack the city and massacre its inhabitants. The treasure harvest of Delhi was fair game for acquisitive kings and warlords.

When the British consolidated their power in India, they found the Road, stretching as it did from Calcutta to Peshawar, a great line of communication. Kipling's 'regiment a-marchin' down the GT Road' was a common enough sight throughout the nineteenth century. During the 1857 uprising, after the British were ousted from Delhi, their army assembled at Ambala and came marching down the GT Road to lay siege to the city of Delhi. A few years later, a junior officer, recalling the march, wrote:

> The stars were bright in the dark deep sky and the fireflies flashed from bush to bush... Along the road came the heavy roll of the guns, mixed with the jangling of bits and the clanking of the scabbards of the cavalry. The infantry marched behind with a deep, dull tread. Camels and bullock carts, with innumerable camp servants, toiled away for miles in the rear, while gigantic elephants, pulling the heavy guns, came lumbering down the road.

Some thirty years after the 1857 uprising came the Afghan Wars, and the GT Road became an all-important route for the British army proceeding towards Peshawar and the Khyber Pass. Those were the days of military manoeuvres all over North India, and my grandfather, a foot-soldier in the mould of Kipling's 'soldiers three', found himself 'route marching', that is, foot-slogging all over northern and central India. Wives and children followed the regiment wherever it was sent, and military camps and cantonments sprang up everywhere. Children were often born in the course of these marches and troop movements: my father at Shahjahanpur (not far from the road), his brothers and sisters at places as far apart as Barrackpore, Campbellpur and Dera Ismail Khan!

The tedium of the march was broken only by the sight of fields of golden corn stretching towards the horizon, with mango groves rising like islands from the flat plain; but for the most part it was monotonous tramping, exemplified in this marching song of Kipling's:

> Oh, there's them Indian temples to admire when you see,
> There's the peacock round the corner
> An' the monkey up the tree.
> With our best foot first
> And the road a-sliding past,

> An every bloomin' camping-ground
> Exactly like the last.

Kipling immortalized the Road in *Kim* and *Barrack-Room Ballads* (he had a strong empathy with the common soldier); but for him, few outside of India would have heard of the Grand Trunk Road. But Kipling would not recognize the road today. Cars, buses, tractors, trucks, all thunder down the highway, and even the bullock carts are equipped with heavy tyres. It's a very democratic mix. Nowhere else in the world are you likely to find such a variety of traffic, or so many impediments to vehicular progress—cows, cart-horses, buffaloes, cyclists, stray hens, stray villagers, stray policemen.

'Proceed at your own risk.' You could call this the motto of the road, a motto vividly illustrated by overturned lorries lying in ditches, buses upended against trees or dangling over culverts, fancy cars crushed into concertina shapes, squashed cats and dogs, mangled drivers and passengers. These are common sights, along with the endless panorama of field, factory, village or township.

For the towns and cities grow bigger by the day. They spread octopus-like over the rural landscape, and the traffic spills out in an endless, honking procession of humankind on wheels. 'OK Tata', proclaims the truck in front of you, and it would be wise to keep your distance. What's your choice of vehicle for making progress on the road? Motorcycle, taxi, limousine, or buffalo cart? Mine's a steamroller. No one pushes it around.

⁓∞⁓

I have never travelled the entire length of the road, but I have driven along stretches of it. The most memorable one was with Gurbachan Singh.

As his taxi weaved its way in and out of the Amritsar traffic, and headed for Delhi, Gurbachan Singh took his hand off the horn and gave me a brief triumphant look.

'What do you think of my horn?' he asked.

'Oh, it's a fine horn,' I said, wringing out my ears. 'It couldn't be louder.'

'You can hear it half a mile ahead,' said Gurbachan proudly, as he blasted off at two young men who were sharing a bicycle. They moved out of the way with alacrity.

'It makes a lot of noise in the car, too,' I said, and added hastily, 'not that I object, you know…'

'Doesn't your horn have more than one tone of voice?' asked a fellow traveller with a trace of irritation.

'Two!' claimed Gurbachan. 'Male and female. Just see!' And he produced a high note and then a low note on the horn, both equally ear-shattering. Ahead of us, a tonga ran off the road and on to the cart track.

'This is one terrific horn,' said Gurbachan. I have had it made especially for this taxi. No foreign horns for me. They are not loud enough. Indian horns are best.'

'Indian noise is best,' said the fellow traveller.

In an interval of comparative quiet, I found myself reflecting on the nature of sound—the unpleasantness of some sounds, and the sweetness of others, and why certain sounds (like motor horns) can be sweet to some and hideous to others. The sweetest sound of all, I decided, was silence. There are many kinds of silence—the silence of an empty room, the silence of the mountains, the silence of prayer or the enforced silence of loneliness—but the best kind of silence, I concluded, was the silence that comes after the cessation of noise.

'It was made in the Jama Masjid area,' continued Gurbachan,

interrupting my thoughts. 'Seventy-five rupees only. Made by hand, to my own specification. There's only one drawback: it must not get wet!'

As his hand settled down on the horn again, I thought of praying for rain, but the sky being clear and blue, I decided that a prayer would be an unreasonable demand on the Creator.

'Ah, but you don't know what it is to have a horn like this one. Try it, sir. Why don't you try it for yourself?'

'Oh, that's all right,' I assured him. 'You have proved its excellence already.'

'No, you must try it. I insist that you try it!' He was like a big boy, suddenly generous, determined on sharing a new toy with a younger brother.

He grabbed my hand and placed it on the horn, and, as I felt it give a little, a thrill of pleasure rushed up my arm. I pressed hard, and a stream of music flowed in and out of the car. Now I could understand the happiness and the supreme self-confidence of Gurbachan and all drivers like him; for, with a horn like his, one felt the power and glory that belongs to the kings of the road.

For the rest of the journey, Gurbachan drove and I blew the horn.

The fellow passenger, no doubt realizing that he was locked into a taxi with two lunatics, was too terrified to say a word.

# On the Road to Delhi

Road travel can involve delays and mishaps, but it also provides you with the freedom to stop where you like and do as you like. I have never found it boring. The seven-hour drive from Mussoorie to Delhi can become a little tiring towards the end, but as I do not drive myself, I can sit back and enjoy everything that the journey has to offer.

I have been to Delhi five times in the last six months—something of a record for me—and on every occasion I have travelled by road. I like looking at the countryside, the passing scene, the people along the road, and this is something I don't see any more from trains; those thick windows of frosted glass effectively cut me off from the world outside.

On my last trip we had to leave the main highway because of a disturbance near Meerut. Instead we had to drive through about a dozen villages in the prosperous sugarcane belt that dominates this area. It was a wonderful contrast, leaving the main road with its cafés, petrol pumps, factories and management institutes and entering the rural hinterland where very little had changed in a hundred years. Women worked in the fields, old men smoked hookahs in their courtyards, and a few children were playing guli-danda instead of cricket! It brought home to me the reality of India—urban life and rural life are still poles apart.

These journeys are seldom without incident. I was sipping a coffee at a wayside restaurant, when a foreign woman walked in, and asked the waiter if they had '*à la carte*'. Roadside stops seldom provide menus, nor do they go in for French, but our waiter wanted to be helpful, so he led the tourist outside and showed her the way to the public toilet. As she did not return to the restaurant, I have no idea if she eventually found *à la carte*.

My driver on a recent trip assured me that he knew Delhi very well and could get me to any destination. I told him I'd been booked into a big hotel near the airport, and gave him the name. 'Not to worry', he told me, and drove confidently towards Palam. There he got confused, and after taking several unfamiliar turnings, drove straight into a large piggery situated behind the airport. We were surrounded by some fifty or sixty pigs and an equal number of children from the mohalla. One boy even asked me if I wanted to purchase a pig. I do like bit of bacon now and then, but unlike Lord Emsworth I do not have any ambition to breed prize pigs, so I had to decline. After some arguments over right of way, we were allowed to proceed and finally made it to the hotel.

Occasionally I have shared a taxi with another passenger, but after one or two disconcerting experiences I have taken to travelling alone or with a friend.

The last time I shared a taxi with someone, I was pleased to find that my fellow passenger, a large gentleman with a fierce moustache, had bought one of my books, which was lying on the seat between us.

I thought I'd be friendly and so, to break the ice, I remarked 'I see you have one of my books with you,' glancing modestly at the paperback on the seat.

'What do you mean, your book?' he bridled, giving me a

dirty look. 'I just bought this book at the news agency!'

'No, no,' I stammered, 'I don't mean it's mine, I mean it's my book—er, that is, I happened to write it!'

'Oh, so now you're claiming to be the author!' He looked at me as though I was a fraud of the worst kind. 'What is your real profession, may I ask?'

'I'm just a typist,' I said, and made no further attempt to make friends.

Indeed, I am very careful about trumpeting my literary or other achievements, as I am frequently misunderstood.

Recently, at a book reading in New Delhi, a little girl asked me how many books I'd written.

'Oh, about sixty or seventy,' I said quite truthfully.

At which another child piped up: 'Why can't you be a little modest about it?'

Sometimes you just can't win.

My author's ego received a salutary beating when on one of my earlier trips, I stopped at a small book-stall and looked around, hoping (like any other author) to spot one of my books. Finally, I found one, under a pile of books by Deepak Chopra, Khushwant Singh, William Dalrymple and other luminaries. I slipped it out from the bottom of the pile and surreptitiously placed it on top.

Unfortunately the bookseller had seen me do this.

He picked up the offending volume and returned it to the bottom of the pile, saying 'No demand for this book, Sir'.

I wasn't going to tell him I was the author. But just to prove him wrong, I bought the poor neglected thing.

'This is a collector's item,' I told him.

'Ah,' he said, 'At last I meet a collector.'

The number of interesting people I meet on the road is matched only by the number of interesting drivers who have carried me back and forth in their chariots of fire.

The last to do so, the driver of a Qualis, must have had ambitions to be an air pilot. He used the road as a runway and was constantly on the verge of taking off. Pedestrians, cyclists, and drivers of smaller vehicles scattered to left and right, often hurling abuse at my charioteer, who seemed immune to the most colourful invectives. Trucks did not give way but he simply swerved around them, adopting a zigzag approach to the task of getting from Delhi to Dehradun in the shortest possible time.

'There's no hurry,' I told him more than once, but his English was limited and he told me later that he thought I was saying 'Please hurry!'

Well, he hurried and he harried until at a railway-crossing where we were forced to stop, an irate scooterist came abreast and threatened to turn the driver over to the police. A long and heated argument followed, and it appeared that there would soon be a punch-up, when the crossing-gate suddenly opened and the Qualis flew forward, leaving the fuming scooterist far behind.

As I do not drive myself, I am normally the ideal person to have in the front seat; I repose complete confidence in the man behind the wheel. And sitting up front, I see more of the road and the passing scene.

One of Mussoorie's better drivers is Sardar Manmohan Singh who drives his own taxi. He is also a keen wildlife enthusiast. It always amazes me how he is able, to drive through the Siwaliks, on a winding hill road, and still be able to keep his eye open for denizens of the surrounding forest.

'See that cheetal!' he will exclaim, or 'What a fine sambhar!' or 'Just look at that elephant!'

All this at high speed. And before I've had time to get more than a fleeting glimpse of one of these creatures, we are well past them.

Manmohan swears that he has seen a tiger crossing the road near the Mohand Pass, and as he is a person of some integrity, I have to believe him. I think the tiger appears especially for Manmohan.

Another wildlife enthusiast is my old friend Vishal Ohri, of State Bank fame. On one occasion he drove me down a forest road between Haridwar and Mohand, and we did indeed see a number of animals, cheetal and wild boar.

Unlike our car drivers, he was in no hurry to reach our destination and would stop every now and then in order to examine the footprints of elephants. He also pointed out large dollops of fresh elephant dung, proof that wild elephants were in the vicinity. I did not think his old Fiat would outrun an angry elephant and urged him to get a move on before nightfall.

Vishal then held forth on the benefits of elephant dung and how it could be used to reinforce mud walls. I assured him that I would try it out on the walls of my study, which were in danger of falling down.

Vishal was well ahead of his time. Only the other day I read in one of our papers that elephant dung could be converted into good quality paper. Perhaps they'll use it to make bank notes. Reserve Bank, please note.

∞

Other good drivers who have taken me here and there include Ganesh Saili, who is even better after a few drinks; Victor

Banerjee who is better before drinks; and young Harpreet who is a fan of Kenny G's saxophone playing. On the road to Delhi with Harpreet, I had six hours of listening to Kenny G on tape. On my return, two days later, I had another six hours of Kenny G. Now I go into a frenzy whenever I hear a saxophone.

My publisher has an experienced old driver who also happens to be quite deaf. He blares the car horn vigorously and without respite. When I asked him why he used the horn so much, he replied, 'Well, I can't hear their horns, but I'll make sure they hear mine!' As good a reason as any.

It is sometimes said that women don't make good drivers, but I beg to differ. Mrs Biswas was an excellent driver but a dangerous woman to know. Her husband had been a well-known shikari, and he kept a stuffed panther in the drawing room of his Delhi farmhouse. Mrs Biswas spent the occasional weekend at her summer home in Landour. I'd been to one or two of her parties, attended mostly by menfolk.

One day, while I was loitering on the road, she drove up and asked me if I'd like to accompany her down to Dehradun.

'I'll come with you,' I said, 'provided we can have a nice lunch at Kwality.'

So down the hill we glided, and Mrs Biswas did some shopping, and we lunched at Kwality, and got back into her car and set off again—but in a direction opposite to Mussoorie and Landour.

'Where are we going?' I asked.

'To Delhi, of course. Aren't you coming with me?'

'I didn't know we were going to Delhi. I don't even have my pyjamas with me.'

'Don't worry,' said Mrs B. 'My husband's pyjamas will fit you.'

'He may not want me to wear his pyjamas,' I protested.
'Oh, don't worry. He's in London just now.'

I persuaded Mrs Biswas to stop at the nearest bus stop, bid her farewell, and took the bus back to Mussoorie. She may have been a good driver but I had no intention of ending up stuffed alongside the stuffed panther in the drawing room.

# The Great Indian Rope Trick

Everyone has heard of the great Indian rope trick, but I am probably the only person who has actually seen it performed.

It was many years ago, when I was wandering around in the small towns of North India, making a living by writing the occasional story or newspaper article, and staying in cheap hotels or small rented rooms.

I was visiting Kalsi, on the road to Chakrata, with the intention of writing a piece on the rock edicts of the great King Asoka, edicts that had survived in stone for thousands of years.

On a hillock nearby, a small but lively crowd had collected—mostly village folk from the surrounding farmlands—and, like most rustic folk, they were more interested in magic than in history. Come to think of it, so was I!

The object of their interest was a man in a mustard-coloured robe, accompanied by a skinny young boy wearing nothing but a loincloth, or langoti. With the help of his acolyte, the man had been performing various feats of magic, to the amusement of the gathering.

The magician claimed that he could invert the order of nature, and someone in the crowd challenged him to produce out of thin air, a bunch of coconuts, well knowing that coconuts grew by the sea and not in the Himalayan foothills.

'Well, you won't find coconuts growing here,' said the magician, 'but perhaps there are some to be found above the clouds, in the land of the gods.'

'But how are we to fetch them?' asked the boy.

'I have the means,' said the man, and proceeded to take from a large round tin box, a cord some tens of feet in length. After carefully arranging the cord, he threw one end of it high up in the air—and there, to everyone's astonishment, it remained as if caught by something. He now paid out the corded rope, which kept going up higher and higher until it disappeared in the mist, leaving only a short length in his hands. He then told the crowd that as he was too heavy to climb the rope himself, he would ask the boy to do so. And handing the end of the rope to the boy, he told him to go ahead.

At first the boy demurred, saying that if he fell from a great height, he would surely be killed. But on being thumped on the head by his angry mentor, he seized the rope and swarmed up it, looking rather like a small spider running up a hanging thread from a wall.

In a few moments, the boy was out of sight, and the crowd fell silent, wondering what would happen next.

Presently, down fell a large coconut—a real coconut—which the pleased magician presented to someone in the crowd. It was followed by several more coconuts.

Then, suddenly, the rope came down, without the boy, and the magician shrieked, 'Someone has cut the rope! What will my boy do now?'

A minute later, down came the boy's head. It bounced on the ground, like a coconut.

This was followed by the boy's arms, legs and body, all falling to the ground one after another.

The mesmerized crowd had been watching these startling events in horror and amazement when suddenly the lid of the tin box flew open and the boy popped out and bowed to the crowd.

A cheer went up, and coins were thrown to the smiling performers. They thanked the crowd with folded hands.

How had they done this trick—if indeed it was a trick? Mesmerism, hypnotism, the powers of suggestion?

The coil of rope was back in its box; the fallen limbs were nowhere to be seen.

As the magician passed me, he smiled and held out a coconut, which I took in both hands. It seemed to quiver as I held it!

Then, as I looked down at the coconut, I saw it change into a human face. Two eyes looked out at me, and a wide mouth broke into a sly grin. This transformation lasted only for seconds, and then it was a coconut again.

I dropped the coconut. It rolled away, and was seized upon by several street urchins, who made off with it.

I turned to see if the magician was still around, and was just in time to catch a glimpse of the man and the boy and the tin box as they disappeared into the crowd—into the mystery and multitude that was India.

# The Last Days of the Tonga

Tongas, along with tramcars, haircuts and the Indian rhinoceros, will soon be extinct. In many towns where, ten years ago, there were two or three hundred tongas on the roads, there are now some twenty or thirty. Buses, taxis and, above all, the ubiquitous scooter-rickshaws are slowly but surely putting the pony-drawn carriage out of business and existence.

This is nowhere more apparent than in Delhi. During World War II, when I was a young boy, the Delhi tonga was the accepted mode of conveyance for high-ranking officers and officials and for their wives and families. My father and I thought nothing of taking a tonga from Humayun Road to Connaught Place in order to visit a cinema or the famous Davicos restaurant. There was no bus service then, cars were few, the scooter had not been invented and the only public transport, the tramcar (now obsolete) plied exclusively in Chandni Chowk and environs. In today's Delhi, no one of any standing would think of taking a tonga; it would be infra dig. And if a foreign tourist should find a tonga-ride exhilarating, we look on him with the tolerant amusement reserved for eccentrics.

This is all very sad for those who, like this writer, grew up in a tonga-driven world.

When I was very small, I travelled some thirty miles from Dehradun to Haridwar in a tonga. There were a few cars about in those days, but a tonga was considered just as good, almost as fast and certainly more dependable when it came to crossing the Song River—a small tributary of the Ganga.

During the rains, when the river flowed strong and deep, it was impossible to get across except by a hand-operated ropeway (which is still in use in some areas); but during the dry months, when the river was a small stream, the tonga-pony went splashing through, carriage wheels churning through the clear mountain water. If the pony found the going difficult, we removed our shoes, rolled up our trousers and waded across, while the driver led his pony by the muzzle.

Long before my time, in fact before the turn of the century, when the 'Scinde, Punjab and Delhi Railway' went no further than Saharanpur, the only way of getting to Dehra was by the night-mail, better known as the dak-ghari.

Dak-ghari ponies were difficult animals, always attempting to turn around and get into the carriage with the passengers. It was only when the coachman used his whip liberally and reviled the ponies' ancestors as far back as their third and fourth generations that the beasts could be persuaded to move. And once they started, there was no stopping them; it was a gallop all the way to the first stage, where the ponies were changed to the accompaniment of a bugle blown by the coachman in true Dickensian fashion.

The journey through the Siwaliks really began—as it still does today—at the Mohand Pass. The ascent starts with a gradual gradient, which increases as the road becomes more steep and winding. The hills are abrupt and perpendicular on the southern side, but slope gently away to the north.

At this stage of the journey, drums were beaten (if it was day) and torches were lit (if it was night) because sometimes wild elephants resented the approach of the dak-ghari and, trumpeting a challenge, would throw the ponies into confusion and panic and send them racing back to the plains.

There are no wild elephants to be found near Mohand today, and very few other animals. Poachers have seen to that. Tigers, once a fairly common sight, are now almost as rare as dak-gharis.

And now it is the tonga that is nearing extinction. With the emergence of a fairly prosperous middle class in many cities, the machine has taken precedence as a means of conveyance. Trucks, buses, cars, motorcycles and scooters now ply on routes that were once the monopoly of cycles and tongas. If this can be taken as a measure of a country's progress then we have certainly forged ahead; but our roads, never meant for such heavy traffic, are frequently cracking.

Tongas are still to be found, but they are usually confined to roads where buses and taxis do not penetrate. Most tonga-drivers refuse to change with the times, despite a diminishing income. Their ponies seem to have more traffic sense than some of our taxi drivers and are involved in fewer accidents.

But give a tonga a straight clear stretch of road, and it will go into action, racing at breakneck speed while the passengers cling to their seats for their lives and the exhilarated driver, shouting his challenge to the machine-age, cracks his whip, calls an endearment to his pony and bursts into song.

Tonga-drivers vary according to the towns they belong to. In Lucknow, they are courteous, garrulous, self-styled descendants of nawabs. In Delhi, they are aggressive and shrewd, matching the temper of the city. Some of them are selling their ponies and buying scooters. Everywhere, tongas are fading away, becoming part of our nostalgia for the past.

# The Open Road

As the years go by, I do not walk as far or as fast as I used to; but speed and distance were never my forte. Like J. Krishnamurti, I believe that the journey is more important than the destination. But, then, I have never really had a destination. The glory that comes from conquering the Himalayan peaks is not for me. My greatest pleasure lies in taking a path—any old path will do—and following it until it leads me to a forest glade or village or stream or windy hilltop.

This sort of tramping (it does not even qualify as trekking) is a compulsive thing with me. You could call it my vice, since it is stronger than the desire for wine, women or song. To get on to the open road fills me with joie de vivre, gives me an exhilaration not found in other, possibly more worthy pursuits.

Only this afternoon I had one of my more enjoyable tramps. I had been cooped up in my room for several days, while outside it rained and hailed and snowed and the wind blew icily from all directions. It seemed ages since I'd taken a long walk. Fed up with it all, I pulled on my overcoat, banged the door shut and set off up the hillside.

I kept to the main road, but because of the heavy snow there were no vehicles on it. Even as I walked, flurries of snow struck my face, and collected on my coat and head. Up at the top of the hill, the deodars were clothed in a mantle of white.

It was fairyland: everything still and silent. The only movement was the circling off an eagle over the trees. I walked for an hour, and passed only one person, the milkman on his way back to his village. His cans were crowned with snow. He looked a little tipsy. He asked me the time, but before I could tell him he shook me by the hand and said I was a good fellow because I never complained about the water in the milk. I told him that as long as he used clean water, I'd contain my wrath.

On my way back, I passed a small group. It consisted of a person in some sort of uniform (because of the snow I couldn't really make it out), who was hurling epithets at several small children who were busy throwing snowballs at him. He kept shouting: 'Do you know who I am? Do you know who I am?' The children did not want to know. They were only interested in hitting their target, and succeeded once in every five or six attempts.

I came home exhilarated and immediately sat down beside the stove to write this piece. I found some lines of Stevenson's which seemed appropriate:

And this shall be for music when no one else is near,
The fine song for singing, the rare song to hear!
That only I remember, that only you admire,
Of the broad road that stretches, and the roadside fire.

He speaks directly to me, across the mists of time: R.L. Stevenson, prince of essayists. There is none like him today. We hurry, hurry in a heat of hope—and who has time for roadside fires, except, perhaps, those who must work on the roads in all weathers?

Whenever I walk into the hills, I come across gangs of road workers breaking stones, cutting into the rocky hillsides, building retaining walls. I am not against more roads—especially in the hills, where the people have remained impoverished largely because of the inaccessibility of their villages. Besides, a new road is one more road for me to explore, and in the interests of progress I am prepared to put up with the dust raised by the occasional bus. And if it becomes too dusty, one can always leave the main road. There is no dearth of paths leading off into the valleys.

On one such diversionary walk, I reached a village where I was given a drink of curd and a meal of rice and beans. That is another of the attractions of tramping to nowhere in particular—the finding of somewhere in particular; the striking up of friendships; the discovery of new springs and waterfalls, unusual plants, rare flowers, strange birds. In the hills, a new vista opens up at every bend in the road.

That is what makes me a compulsive walker—new vistas, and the charm of the unexpected.

# A Wayside Tea Shop

The Jaunpur range in Garhwal is dry, brown and rocky. Water is hard to find, and green fields are to be seen only far down in the valley, near the Aglar or some smaller stream. Elsewhere only monsoon crops are grown.

I have walked five miles without finding a spring or even a shady spot along the sun-blistered path, and I am beginning to wonder if the only living creatures in the area are the big lizards, who slither about on the hot surface of the rocks and stare at me with unblinking eyes. Just as I am asking myself if it is better to be a lizard than a thirsty trekker, I round a bend and discover a small mountain oasis: a crooked little shack tucked away in a cleft of the hillside. Growing beside the shack is a single pine tree, humming softly in the faint breeze that drifts across the mountains.

When one tree suddenly appears in this way, lonely and dignified in the midst of a vast treeless silence, it can be more beautiful than a forest.

There is no glamour about the shack, a loose stone structure with a tin roof held down by stones. But it is a tea shop, one of those little pockets of pioneering mankind that spring up in the mountain wilderness to serve the weary traveller. Go where you will in Garhwal, you will always find a tea shop to sustain you just when you feel you have reached the end of your tether.

The shopkeeper, Megh Chand, a man of indeterminate age—the cold dry winds from the snows have crinkled his face like a walnut but his teeth are sound and his eyes are clear—greets me as a long-lost friend, although we are meeting for the first time.

'Do you live here alone?' I ask.

'Sometimes I am alone,' he says. 'My family is down in the village, looking after the fields. It is quite far—six miles. So I go home once a week, and then my son comes up to look after the shop.

Megh Chand tells me that he has been starved of good conversation. 'Next year,' he says, sitting down on the steps of his shop, 'the government will be widening the road, and then the buses will be able to stop here. For many years, I have depended on the mule drivers, but they do not have much money to spend. Once the buses come, I will have many customers. Then, perhaps I will be able to afford to go to Delhi for my operation.'

'What operation?'

'Oh, a rasoli—a growth—in my stomach. Sometimes, the pain is very bad. I went to the hospital in Mussoorie, but they told me I would have to go to Delhi for an operation. Whenever someone is seriously ill, they say, "Go to Delhi!" Does the whole world go to Delhi to get treated? My uncle was told to go to Delhi for an operation. He went from one hospital to another until his money was finished, and then he came back to the village and died within a week. So maybe, I won't go for the operation. The money is needed here. Once the buses come, I will have to keep sweets and biscuits and other things, and a boy to help me cook a few meals. All I can offer you today is a bun. It was made in Delhi, I am told.

'I'd rather have your lassi than a Delhi bun,' I protest. 'But where do you get your water?' I ask.

'Come, I will show you,' he says, and takes me round to the back of the shack and through an unexpected gap in the hillside. It gives me a breathtaking glimpse of snow-clad mountains striding into the sky. It is cool and shady on the northern face of the hill, and here, issuing from a rock, is a trickle of water. Yellow primulas grow in clusters along the edges of a damp, dripping rock face. The water collects in a small stone trough.

'There is no other *cheshma* (spring) along this road,' he says, 'and the buses can't go down into the ravine, unless they fall into it. So, they have to stop here!' He is triumphant.

We return to the shopfront, where a milkman has just arrived with a container of milk. He too sits down for rest, refreshment and conversation. Next year, if the road is ready (and it is a big if, because with hill roads, you can never be sure), and if he can afford the fare (an even bigger if), the milkman will be able to use the bus. But there are some who will walk anyway, because they have always been walking. Or ride mules because they have been doing it all their lives.

Still, when the road comes, time will take on new dimensions for Megh Chand. Even in remote mountain areas, buses must keep to some sort of schedule, and Megh Chand will have to be sure that his pot is on the boil and be on the lookout for arrivals and departures. He will be better off than he is today but he is aware that prosperity has its pitfalls. He remembers a cousin, who opened a small grocery shop on a new bus route near Devprayag. One day, some young hooligans got off the bus, looted his shop and left him battered and bruised. It was the sort of thing that had never happened before...

It is time for me to be on my way. 'I hope the road will soon be ready,' I say in parting. 'I hope you will make lots of money. I hope you will be able to go to Delhi for your operation. And I hope I can come this way again.'

Hill-man or plains-man, we have only our hopes to keep us going.

# RIVERS OF INDIA

# A Song of Many Rivers

## 1

When I look down from the heights of Landour to the broad Valley of the Doon far below, I can see the little Suswa River, silver in the setting sun, meandering through fields and forests on its way to its confluence with the Ganga.

The Suswa is a river I knew well as a boy, but it has been many years since I took a dip in its quiet pools or rested in the shade of the tall spreading trees growing on its banks. Now I see it from my windows, far away, dream-like in the mist, and I keep promising myself that I will visit it again, to touch its waters, cool and clear, and feel its rounded pebbles beneath my feet.

It's a little river, flowing down from the ancient Siwaliks and running the length of the valley until, with its sister river the Song, it slips into the Ganga just above the holy city of Haridwar. I could wade across (except during the monsoon when it was in spate) and the water seldom rose above the waist except in sheltered pools, where there were shoals of small fish.

There is a little known and charming legend about the Suswa and its origins, which I have always treasured. It tells us that the Hindu sage, Kasyapa, once gave a great feast to which all the gods were invited. Now Indra, the god of rain, while on his way to the entertainment, happened to meet 60,000 'balkhils' (pygmies) of the Brahmin caste, who were trying in vain to cross a cow's footprint filled with water—to them, a vast lake!

The god could not restrain his amusement. Peals of thunderous laughter echoed across the hills. The indignant Brahmins, determined to have their revenge, at once set to work creating a second Indra, who should supplant the reigning god. This could only be clone by means of penance, fasting and self-denial, in which they persevered until the sweat flowing from their tiny bodies created the 'Suswa' or 'flowing waters' of the little river.

Indra, alarmed at the effect of these religious exercises, sought the help of Brahma, the creator, who taking on the role of a referee, interceded with the priests. Indra was able to keep his position as the rain god.

I saw no pygmies or fairies near the Suswa, but I did see many spotted deer, cheetal, coming down to the water's edge to drink. They are still plentiful in that area.

## 2
## The Nautch Girl's Curse

At the other end of the Doon, far to the west, the Yamuna comes down from the mountains and forms the boundary between the states of Himachal and Uttaranchal. Today, there's a bridge across the river, but many years ago, when I first went across, it was by means of a small cable car, and a very rickety one at that.

During the monsoon, when the river was in spate, the only way across the swollen river was by means of this swaying trolley, which was suspended by a steel rope to two shaky wooden platforms on either bank. There followed a tedious bus journey, during which some sixty-odd miles were covered in six hours. And then you were at Nahan, a small town a little over 3,000 feet above sea level, set amid hill slopes thick with sal and shisham trees. This charming old town links the subtropical Siwaliks to the first foothills of the Himalayas, a unique situation.

The road from Dagshai and Shimla runs into Nahan from the north. No matter in which direction you look, the view is a fine one. To the south stretches the grand panorama of the plains of Saharanpur and Ambala, fronted by two low ranges of thickly forested hills. In the valley below, the pretty Markanda River winds its way out of the Kadir Valley.

Nahan's main street is curved and narrow, but well-made and paved with good stone. To the left of the town is the former Raja's palace. Nahan was once the capital of the state of Sirmur, now part of Himachal Pradesh. The original palace was built some three or four hundred years ago, but has been added to from time to time, and is now a large collection of buildings mostly in the Venetian style.

I suppose Nahan qualifies as a hill station, although it can be quite hot in summer. But unlike most hill stations, which are less than two hundred years old, Nahan is steeped in legend and history.

The old capital of Sirmur was destroyed by an earthquake some seven to eight hundred years ago. It was situated some twenty-four miles from present day Nahan, on the west bank of the Giri, where the river expands into a lake. The ancient capital was totally destroyed, with all its inhabitants, and apparently no record was left of its then ruling family. Little remained of the ancient city, just a ruined temple and a few broken stone figures.

As to the cause of the tragedy, the traditional story is that a nautch girl happened to visit Sirmur, and performed some wonderful feats. The Raja challenged the girl to walk safely over the Giri on a rope, offering her half his kingdom if she was successful.

The girl accepted the challenge. A rope was stretched across the river. But before starting out, the girl promised that if she fell victim to any treachery on the part of the Raja, a curse would fall upon the city and it would be destroyed by a terrible catastrophe.

While she was on her way to successfully carrying out the feat, some of the Raja's people cut the rope. She fell into the river and was drowned. As predicted, total destruction came to the town.

The founder of the next line of the Sirmur Raja came from the Jaisalmer family in Rajasthan. He was on a pilgrimage to Haridwar with his wife when he heard of the catastrophe that had immolated every member of the state's ancient dynasty. He went at once with his wife into the territory, and established a Jaisalmer Raj. The descent from the first Rajput ruler of Jaisalmer stock, some seven hundred years ago, followed from father to son in an unbroken line. And after much intitial moving about, Nahan was fixed upon as the capital.

The territory was captured by the Gurkhas in 1803, but twelve years later they were expelled by the British after some severe fighting, to which a small English cemetery bears witness. The territory was restored to the Raja, with the exception of the Jaunsar Bawar region.

Six or seven miles north of Nahan lies the mountain of Jaitak, where the Gurkhas made their last desperate stand. The place is worth a visit, not only for seeing the remains of the

Gurkha fort, but also for the magnificent view the mountain commands.

From the northernmost of the mountain's twin peaks, the whole south face of the Himalayas may be seen. From west to north you see the rugged prominences of the Jaunsar Bawar, flanked by the Mussoorie range of hills. It is wild mountain scenery, with a few patches of cultivation and little villages nestling on the sides of the hills. Garhwal and Dehradun are to the east, and as you go downhill you can see the broad sweep of the Yamuna as it cuts its way through the western Siwaliks.

## 3
## Gently Flows the Ganga

The Bhagirathi is a beautiful river, gentle and caressing (as compared to the turbulent Alaknanda), and pilgrims and others have responded to it with love and respect. The god Shiva released the waters of Goddess Ganga from his locks, and she sped towards the plains in the tracks of Prince Bhagirath's chariot.

> He held the river on his head
> And kept her wandering, where
> Dense as Himalaya's woods were spread
> The tangles of his hair.

Revered by Hindus and loved by all, Goddess Ganga weaves her spell over all who come to her. Some assert that the true Ganga (in its upper reaches) is the Alaknanda. Geographically, this may be so. But tradition carries greater weight in the abode of the Gods, and traditionally the Bhagirathi is the Ganga. Of course, the two rivers meet at Deoprayag, in the foothills, and this marriage of the waters settles the issue.

I put the question to my friend Dr Sudhakar Misra, from whom words of wisdom sometimes flow; and true to form, he answered: 'The Alaknanda is Ganga, but the Bhagirathi is Ganga-ji.'

She issues from the very heart of the Himalayas. Visiting Gangotri in 1820, the writer and traveller Baillie Fraser noted: 'We are now in the centre of the Himalayas, the loftiest and perhaps the most rugged range of mountains in the world.'

Here, at the source of the river, we come to the realization that we are at the very centre and heart of things. One has an almost primaeval sense of belonging to these mountains and to this valley in particular. For me, and for many who have been here, the Bhagirathi is the most beautiful of the four main river valleys of Garhwal.

The Bhagirathi seems to have everything—a gentle disposition, deep glens and forests, the ultravision of an open valley graced with tiers of cultivation leading up by degrees to the peaks and glaciers at its head.

At Tehri, the big dam slows down Prince Bhagirath's chariot. But upstream, from Bhatwari to Harsil, there are extensive pine forests. They fill the ravines and plateaus, before giving way to yew and cypress, oak and chestnut. Above 9,000 feet the deodar (deodar, tree of the gods) is the principal tree. It grows to a little distance above Gangotri, and then gives way to the birch, which is found in patches to within half a mile of the glacier.

It was the valuable timber of the deodar that attracted the adventurer Frederick 'Pahari' Wilson to the valley in the 1850s. He leased the forests from the Raja of Tehri, and within a few years he had made a fortune. From his horse and depot at Harsil, he would float the logs downstream to Tehri, where they would be sawn up and despatched to buyers in the cities.

Bridge-building was another of Wilson's ventures. The most famous of these was a 350 feet suspension bridge at Bhaironghat, over 1,200 feet above the young Bhagirathi where it thunders through a deep defile. This rippling contraption was at first a source of terror to travellers, and only a few ventured across it.

To reassure people, Wilson would mount his horse and gallop to and fro across the bridge. It has since collapsed, but local people will tell you that the ghostly hoof beats of Wilson's horse can still be heard on full moon nights. The supports of the old bridge were massive deodar trunks, and they can still be seen to one side of the new road bridge built by engineers of the Northern Railway.

The old forest rest houses at Dharasu, Bhatwari and Harsil were all built by Wilson as staging posts, for the only roads were narrow tracks linking one village to another. Wilson married a local girl, Gulabi, from the village of Mukhba, and the portraits of the Wilsons (early examples of the photographer's art) still hang in these sturdy little bungalows. At any rate, I found their pictures at Bhatwari. Harsil is now out of bounds to civilians, and I believe part of the old house was destroyed in a fire a few years ago. This sturdy building withstood the earthquake which devastated the area in 1991.

Among other things, Wilson introduced the apple into this area, 'Wilson apples'—large, red and juicy—sold to travellers and pilgrims on their way to Gangotri. This fascinating man also acquired an encyclopaedic knowledge of the wildlife of the region, and his articles, which appeared in *Indian Sporting Life* in the 1860s, were later plundered by so-called wildlife writers for their own works.

He acquired properties in Dehradun and Mussoorie, and his wife lived there in some style, giving him three sons. Two died young. The third, Charlie Wilson, went through most of his father's fortune. His grave lies next to my grandfather's grave in the old Dehradun cemetery. Gulabi is buried in Mussoorie, next to her husband. I wrote this haiku for her:

> Her beauty brought her fame,
> But only the wild rose growing beside her grave
> Is there to hear her whispered name—
> Gulabi.

I remember old Mrs Wilson, Charlie's widow, when I was a boy in Dehra. She lived next door in what was the last of the Wilson properties. Her nephew, Geoffrey Davis, went to school with me in Shimla, and later joined the Indian Air Force. But luck never went the way of Wilson's descendants, and Geoffrey died when his plane crashed.

Wilson's life is fit subject for a romance; but even if one were never written, his legend would live on, as it has done for over a hundred years. There has never been any attempt to commemorate him, but people in the valley still speak of him in awe and admiration, as though he had lived only yesterday.

Some men leave a trail of legend behind them because they give their spirit to the place where they have lived, and remain forever a part of the rocks and mountain streams.

Gangotri is situated at just a little over 10,300 feet. On the right bank of the river is the Gangotri temple, a small neat building without too much ornamentation, built by Amar Singh Thapa, a Nepali General, early in the nineteenth century. It was renovated by the Maharaja of Jaipur in the 1920s. The rock on which it stands is called Bhagirath Shila and is said to be the place where Prince Bhagirath did penance in order that Ganga be brought down from her abode of eternal snow. Here the rocks are carved and polished by ice and water, so smooth that in places they look like rolls of silk. The fast flowing waters of this mountain torrent look very different from the huge sluggish river that finally empties its waters into the Bay of Bengal fifteen hundred miles away.

The river emerges from beneath a great glacier, thickly studded with enormous loose rocks and earth. The glacier is about a mile in width and extends upwards for many miles. The chasm in the glacier through which the stream rushed forth into the light of day is named Gaumukh, the cow's mouth, and is held in deepest reverence by Hindus. The regions of eternal frost in the vicinity were the scene of many of their most sacred mysteries.

The Ganga enters the world no puny stream, but bursts from its icy womb a river thirty or forty yards in breadth. At Gauri Kund (below the Gangotri temple) it falls over a rock of considerable height and continues tumbling over a succession of small cascades until it enters the Bhaironghati gorge.

A night spent beside the river, within the sound of the fall, is an eerie experience. After some time it begins to sound, not like one fall but a hundred, and this sound permeates both one's dreams and waking hours. Rising early to greet the dawn proved rather pointless at Gangotri, for the surrounding peaks did not let the sun in till after 9 a.m. Everyone rushed about to keep warm, exclaiming delightedly at what they call 'gulabi thand', literally, 'rosy cold'. Guaranteed to turn the cheeks a rosy pink! A charming expression, but I prefer a rosy sunburn, and remained beneath a heavy quilt until the sun came up to throw its golden shafts across the river.

This is mid-October, and after Diwali the shrine and the small township will close for winter, the pandits retreating to the relative warmth of Mukbha. Soon snow will cover everything, and even the hardy purple-plumaged whistling thrushes, lovers of deep shade, will move further down the valley. And down below the forest-line, the Garhwali farmers go about harvesting their terraced fields which form patterns of yellow, green and gold above the deep green of the river.

Yes, the Bhagirathi is a green river. Although deep and swift, it does not lose its serenity. At no place does it look hurried or confused—unlike the turbulent Alaknanda, fretting and frothing as it goes crashing down its boulder-strewn bed. The Alaknanda gives one a feeling of being trapped, because the river itself is trapped. The Bhagirathi is free-flowing, easy. At all times and places it seems to find its true level.

In the old days, only the staunchest of pilgrims visited the shrines at Gangotri and Jamnotri. The roads were rocky and dangerous, winding along in some places, ascending and descending the faces of deep precipices and ravines, at times leading along banks of loose earth where landslides had swept the original path away.

There are still no large towns above Uttarkashi, and this absence of large centres of population may be reason why the forests are better preserved than those in the Alaknanda valley, or further downstream. Uttarkashi, though a large and growing town, is as yet uncrowded. The seediness of towns like Rishikesh and parts of Dehradun is not yet evident here. One can take a leisurely walk through its long (and well-supplied) bazaar, without being jostled by crowds or knocked over by three-wheelers. Here, too, the river is always with you, and you must live in harmony with its sound as it goes rushing and humming along its shingly bed.

Uttarkashi is not without its own religious and historical

importance, although all traces of its ancient town of Barahat appear to have vanished. There are four important temples here, and on the occasion of Makar Sankranti, early in January a week-long fair is held when thousands from the surrounding areas throng the roads to the town. To the beating of drums and blowing of trumpets, the gods and goddesses are brought to the fair in gaily decorated palanquins. The surrounding villages wear a deserted look that day as everyone flocks to the temples and bathing ghats and to the entertainments of the fair itself.

We have to move far downstream to reach another large centre of population, the town of Tehri, and this is a very different place from Uttarkashi. Tehri has all the characteristics of a small town in the plains—crowds, noise, traffic congestion, dust and refuse, scruffy dhabas—with this difference that here it is all ephemeral, for Tehri is destined to be submerged by the water of the Bhagirathi when the Tehri dam is finally completed.

The rulers of Garhwal were often changing their capitals, and when, after the Gurkha War (of 1811–15), the former capital of Srinagar became part of British Garhwal, Raja Sudershan Shah established his new capital at Tehri. It is said that when he reached this spot, his horse refused to go any further. This was enough for the king, it seems; or so the story goes.

Perhaps Prince Bhagirath's chariot will come to a halt here too, when the dam is built. The two hundred and forty-six metre high earthen dam, with forty-two square miles of reservoir capacity, will submerge the town and about thirty villages.

But as we leave the town and cross the narrow bridge over the river, a mighty blast from above sends rocks hurtling down the defile, just to remind us that work is indeed in progress.

Unlike the Raja's horse, I have no wish to be stopped in my tracks at Tehri. There are livelier places upstream. And as for Ganga herself, that deceptively gentle river, I wonder if she will take kindly to our efforts to contain her.

## 4
## Falling for Mandakini

A great river at its confluence with another great river is, for me, a special moment in time. And so it was with the Mandakini at Rudraprayag, where its waters joined the waters of the Alaknanda, the one having come from the glacial snows above Kedarnath, the other from the Himalayan heights beyond Badrinath. Both sacred rivers, destined to become the holy Ganga further downstream.

I fell in love with the Mandakini at first sight. Or was it the valley that I fell in love with? I am not sure, and it doesn't really matter. The valley is the river.

While the Alaknanda Valley, especially in its higher reaches, is a deep and narrow gorge where precipitous outcrops of rock hang threateningly over the traveller, the Mandakini Valley is broader, gentler, the terraced fields wider, the banks of the river a green sward in many places. Somehow, one does not feel that one is at the mercy of the Mandakini whereas one is always at the mercy of the Alaknanda with its sudden floods.

Rudraprayag is hot. It is probably a pleasant spot in winter, but at the end of June, it is decidedly hot. Perhaps its chief claim to fame is that it gave its name to the dreaded man-eating leopard of Rudraprayag, who in the course of seven years (1918–25) accounted for more than 300 victims. It was finally shot by Jim Corbett, who recounted the saga of his long hunt for the killer in his fine book, *The Man-eating Leopard of Rudraprayag*.

The place at which the leopard was shot was the village of Gulabrai, two miles south of Rudraprayag. Under a large mango tree stands a memorial raised to Jim Corbett by officers and men of the Border Roads Organisation. It is a touching gesture to one who loved Garhwal and India. Unfortunately, several buffaloes are tethered close by, and one has to wade through slush and buffalo dung to get to the memorial stone. A board tacked on to the mango tree attracts the attention of motorists who might pass without noticing the memorial, which is off to one side.

The killer leopard was noted for its direct method of attack on humans; and, in spite of being poisoned, trapped in a cave, and shot at innumerable times, it did not lose its contempt for man. Two English sportsmen covering both ends to the old suspension bridge over the Alaknanda fired several times at the man-eater but to little effect.

It was not long before the leopard acquired a reputation among the hill folk for being an evil spirit. A sadhu was suspected of turning into the leopard by night, and was only saved from being lynched by the ingenuity of Philip Mason, then deputy commissioner of Garhwal. Mason kept the sadhu in custody until the leopard made his next attack, thus proving the man innocent. Years later, when Mason turned novelist and (using the pen name Philip Woodruffe) wrote *The Wild Sweet Witch,* he had as one of the characters, a beautiful young woman who apparently turns into a man-eating leopard by night.

Corbett's host at Gulabrai was one of the few who survived an encounter with the leopard. It left him with a hole in his throat. Apart from being a superb story teller, Corbett displayed great compassion for people from all walks of life and is still a legend in Garhwal and Kumaon among people who have never read his books.

In June, one does not linger long in the steamy heat of Rudraprayag. But as one travels up the river, making a gradual ascent of the Mandakini Valley, there is a cool breeze coming down from the snows, and the smell of rain is in the air.

The thriving little township of Agastmuni spreads itself along the wide river banks. Further upstream, near a little place called Chandrapuri, we cannot resist breaking our journey to sprawl on the tender green grass that slopes gently down to the swift flowing river. A small rest house is in the making. Around it, banana fronds sway and poplar leaves dance in the breeze.

This is no sluggish river of the plains, but a fast moving current, tumbling over rocks, turning and twisting in its efforts to discover the easiest way for its frothy snow-fed waters to escape the mountains. Escape is the word! For the constant complaint of many a Garliwali is that, while his hills abound in rivers, the water runs down and away, and little, if any, reaches the fields and villages above it. Cultivation must depend on the rain and not on the river.

The road climbs gradually, still keeping to the river. Just outside Guptakashi, my attention is drawn to a clump of huge trees sheltering a small but ancient temple. We stop here and enter the shade of the trees.

The temple is deserted. It is a temple dedicated to Shiva, and in the courtyard are several river-rounded stone lingams on which leaves and blossoms have fallen. No one seems to come here, which is strange, since it is on the pilgrim route. Two boys from a neighbouring field leave their yoked bullock to come and talk to me, but they cannot tell me much about the temple except to confirm that it is seldom visited. 'The buses do not stop here.' That seems explanation enough. For where the buses go, the pilgrims go; and where the pilgrims go, other pilgrims will follow. Thus far and no further.

The trees seem to be magnolias. But I have never seen magnolia trees grow to such huge proportions. Perhaps they are something else. Never mind; let them remain a mystery.

Guptakashi in the evening is all a bustle. A coachload of pilgrims (headed for Kedarnath) has just arrived and the tea shops near the bus stand are doing brisk business. Then the 'local' bus from Ukhimath, across the river, arrives and many of the passengers head for a tea shop famed for its samosas. The local bus is called the *bhook hartal*, the 'hunger-strike' bus.

'How did it get that name?' I ask one of the samosa-eaters.

'Well, it's an interesting story. For a long time we had been asking the authorities to provide a bus service for the local people and for the villagers who live off the roads. All the buses came from Srinagar or Rishikesh, and were taken up by pilgrims. The locals couldn't find room in them. But our pleas went unheard until the whole town, or most of it, decided to go on hunger-strike.'

'They nearly put me out of business too,' says the tea shop owner cheerfully. 'Nobody ate any samosas for two days!'

There is no cinema or public place of entertainment at Guptakashi, and the town goes to sleep early. And wakes early.

At six, the hillside, green from recent rain, sparkles in the morning sunshine. Snowcapped Chaukhamba (7,140 metres) is dazzling. The air is clear; no smoke or dust up here. The climate, I am told, is mild all the year round judging by the scent and shape of the flowers, and the boys call them champs, Hindi for champa blossom. Ukhimath, on the other side of the river, lies in the shadow. It gets the sun at nine. In winter, it must wait till afternoon.

Guptakashi has not yet been rendered ugly by the barrack-type architecture that has come up in some growing hill towns. The old double storeyed houses are built of stone, with gray slate roofs. They blend well with the hillside. Cobbled paths meander through the old bazaar.

One of these takes up to the famed Guptakashi temple, tucked away above the old part of the town. Here, as in Benaras, Shiva is worshipped as Vishwanath, and two underground streams representing the sacred Jamuna and Bhagirathi rivers feed the pool sacred to the God. This temple gives the town its name, Gupta-Kashi, the 'Invisible Benaras', just as Uttarkashi on the Bhagirathi is 'Upper Benaras'.

Guptakashi and its environs have so many lingams that the saying *'June kanhar utne shanhar'*—'As many stones, so many Shivas'—has become a proverb to describe its holiness.

From Guptakashi, pilgrims proceed north to Kedarnath, and the last stage of their journey—about a day's march—must be covered on foot or horseback. The temple of Kedarnath, situated at a height of 11,753 feet, is encircled by snowcapped peaks, and Atkinson has conjectured that 'the symbol of the *linga* may have arisen front the pointed peaks around his (God Shiva's) original home.'

The temple is dedicated to Sadashiva, the subterranean form of the God, who, according to Atkinson, 'fleeing from the Pandavas took refuge here in the form of a he-buffalo and finding himself hard- pressed, dived into the ground leaving the hinder parts on the surface, which continue to be the subject of adoration.'

The other portions of the God are worshipped as follows: the arms at Tungnath, at a height of 13,000 feet, the face at Rudranath (12,000 feet), the belly at Madmaheshwar, eighteen miles northeast of Guptakashi; and the hair and head at Kalpeshwar, near Joshimath. These five sacred shrines form the Punch Kedar (five Kedars).

We leave the Mandakini to visit Tungnath on the Chandrashila range. But I will return to this river. It has captured my mind and heart.

# Of Rivers and Pilgrims

It's a funny thing, but long before I arrive at a place I can usually tell whether I am going to like it or not. Thus, while I was still some twenty miles from the district town of Pauri, I felt it was not going to be my sort of place, and sure enough it wasn't. A seedy, overgrown place, with too many government offices. On the other hand, while Nandprayag was still out of sight, I knew I was going to like it. And I did.

Perhaps, it's something on the wind—emanations of an atmosphere—that carry to me well before I arrive at my destination. I can't really explain it, and of course it's silly to make judgements in advance. But it does happen.

Anyway, I felt I was nearing home as soon as the bus brought me into the cheerful roadside hamlet, a little way above the Nandakini River's confluence with the Alaknanda. A prayag is a meeting place of two rivers, hence Nandprayag, the place where these two mountain rivers meet. As there are many rivers in the Garhwal Himalayas, all linking up to join either the Ganga or the Yamuna, it follows that there are numerous prayags, in themselves places of pilgrimage as well as wayside halts en route to the higher Hindu shrines at Kedarnath and Badrinath. Nowhere else in these mountains are there so many temples, sacred streams, holy places, and holy men.

Some little way above Nandprayag's sleepy little bazaar is a tourist rest house. It has a well-kept garden surrounded by fruit trees and is a little distance from the general hubbub of the main road.

Above it is the old pilgrim path. Just over twenty years ago, if you were a pilgrim intent on seeking salvation at the abode of the gods, you travelled on foot all the way from the plains, climbing about 200 miles in a couple of months. Those pilgrims had the time, the faith, and the endurance. Illness and misadventure often dogged their footsteps, but what was a little suffering if at the end of the day they arrived at the very portals of heaven?

Today's pilgrims may not be lacking in devotion, but most of them do expect to come home again.

Along the old pilgrim path are several handsome houses, set among mango trees and the fronds of the papaya and banana. Higher up the hill the pine forests commence, but down here it is almost subtropical. Nandprayag is only about 3,000 feet above sea level—a height at which the vegetation is usually lush provided there is protection from the wind.

In one of these double-storeyed houses lives Devki Nandan, a scholar and recluse. He welcomes me into his home and plies me with food till I am close to bursting. He has a great love for this little corner of Garhwal and proudly shows me his collection of cuttings of articles about the area. One is from a travelogue by Sister Nivedita—an Englishwoman, Margaret Noble, who became an interpreter of Hinduism to the West. Visiting Nandprayag in 1928, she wrote:

> Nandprayag is a place that ought to be famous for its beauty and order. For a mile or two before reaching it we had noticed the superior character of the agriculture and even some careful gardening of fruits and vegetables.

> The peasantry also suddenly grew handsome, not unlike the Kashmiris. The town itself is new, rebuilt since the Gohna flood, and its temple stands far out across the fields on the shore of the Prayag. But in this short time a wonderful energy has been at work on architectural carvings and the little place is full of gem-like beauties. As the road crosses the river, I noticed two or three old Pathan tombs, the only traces of Mohammedanism that we had seen north of Srinagar in Garhwal.

Little has changed since Sister Nivedita's visit. There is still a small and thriving Pathan population in Nandprayag. In fact, when I called on Mr Nandan, he was in the act of sending out Eid greetings to his Muslim friends. Some of the old graves have disappeared in the debris from new road cuttings. As for the beautiful temple described by Sister Nivedita, I learned that it had been swept away by a mighty flood in 1970 when a cloudburst and subsequent landslide up-river resulted in great destruction downstream.

Mr Nandan remembers the time when he walked to the small hill station of Pauri to join the old Messmore Christian Mission School, where so many famous sons of Garhwal received their early education. It took him four days marching to get to Pauri. Now it is just four hours by bus. It was only after the Chinese invasion of 1962 that there was a sudden spurt in road building in the northern hill districts. Before that, everyone walked and thought nothing of it.

Sitting on my own that same evening in the little garden of the rest house, I heard innumerable birds break into song. I did not see them, because the light was fading and the trees were dark; but I heard the rather melancholy call of the hill dove, the ascending trill of the koel, and much shrieking, whistling, and twittering that I could not assign to any particular species.

Now, once again, while I sit on the lawn surrounded by zinnias in full bloom, I am teased by that feeling of having been here before, on this lush hillside, among the pomegranates and oleanders. Is it some childhood memory asserting itself? As far as I know, I never travelled in these parts.

It's true that Nandprayag resembles some parts of the Doon Valley (where I grew up) before the Doon was submerged by a tidal wave of humanity. But in the Doon there is no great river running past your garden. Here there are two, and they are also part of this feeling of belonging.

Presently, the room boy joins me for a chat on the lawn. He is in fact running the rest house in the absence of the manager. Wherever I go in India, the manager is usually absent; it seems to make no difference. A coachload of pilgrims is due at any moment, but until they arrive the place is empty and only the birds can be heard.

The room boy's name is Janakpal and he tells me something about his village on the next mountain, where a marauding leopard has been carrying off goats and cattle. He doesn't think much of the laws protecting leopards—nothing can be done unless the animal becomes a man-eater.

A shower of rain descends on us, and so do the pilgrims. Janakpal leaves me to attend to his duties. But I am not left alone for long. A youngster with a cup of tea is the next to interview me. He wants me to take him to Mussoorie or New Delhi. He is fed up, he says, with washing dishes here.

'You are better off here,' I tell him sincerely. 'In Mussoorie you will have twice as many dishes to wash. In Delhi, ten times as many.'

'Yes, but there are cinemas and video and TV there,' he says, leaving me without an argument. Birdsong may have charms for me, but not for the restless dishwasher in tranquil Nandprayag.

The rain stops and I go for a walk. The pilgrims keep to themselves, but the locals are always ready to talk. I remember a saying (and it may have originated in these hills), which goes: 'All men are my friends. I have only to meet them.' In Nandprayag, where life still moves at a leisurely and civilized pace, one is constantly meeting them.

# Flowers on the Ganga

Flowers floating down the river: yellow and scarlet cannas, roses, jasmine, hibiscus. They are placed in boats made of broad leaves; then consigned to the waters with a prayer. The strong current carries them swiftly downstream, and they bob about on the water for fifty, sometimes a hundred yards, before being submerged in the river. Do the prayers sink too, or do they reach the hearts of the many gods who have favoured Haridwar—'Door of Hari or Vishnu' —these several hundred years?

The river issues through a gorge in the mountains with a low booming sound. It does not break its banks until it levels out over the flat plains of Uttar Pradesh and Bihar. It is fast and muddy; but this does not deter thousands from descending the steps of the bathing ghats and plunging into the cold, snow-fed waters, for the Ganga washes away all sin.

Says the Mahabharata: 'To repeat her name brings purity, to see her secures prosperity, to bathe in or drink her waters saves seven generations of our race... There is no place of pilgrimage like the Ganga, no god like Vishnu...'

Almost every child knows the story of how the Ganga descended from heaven. For 1,000 years, King Sagara's great-grandson stood with his hands upraised, praying for water to enable him to make the funeral oblations for the ashes of his 60,000 grand-uncles. Almost all the gods were involved in the affair. Finally, when the waters of the Ganga were released from heaven and the river reached the earth, the prince mounted his chariot and drove towards the spot where the ashes of his kinsmen lay. Wherever he went, the Ganga meekly followed. Gods, nymphs, demons, giants, sages and great snakes, all joined in the procession, and as the river followed in the footsteps of the prince, the whole multitude of created beings bathed in her sacred waters and washed away their sins.

―∞―

The multitude that followed the prince could be the same multitude that throngs the riverfront today. I see no one who is not delighted at the prospect of entering the water. '*Ganga-Mai ki jai*!' The cry goes up mostly from the older people who have come here, many for the last time, to make their peace with the gods. Only their ashes will make the trip again.

It is a big crowd, although this is just an ordinary day of the week and not an occasion of special religious significance. Every day is a good day for bathing in the Ganga. But at the time of major festivals, such as Baisakhi, elaborate arrangements have to be made, including special trains and police reinforcements, to take care of the great influx of pilgrims. The number of pilgrims at the Baisakhi festival usually exceeds one lakh. During the Kumbh Mela, held every twelve years, there may be as many as five lakh present on the great bathing-day. This is ten times the normal population of Haridwar. And when one realizes that the town is bounded by the steep Siwalik Hills on one side and the river on the other, and has one main street leading to the riverfront, it is not surprising that in the past, large numbers of people were crushed to death in stampedes at the narrow entrance to the ghats.

Fortunately the main street is a broad and pleasant thoroughfare. Although Haridwar is ancient (the Chinese traveller, Hiuen Tsang, records a visit made in the seventh century), little remains of earlier settlements. There are only two or three old temples. But the present buildings—tall, balconied structures put up in the 1920s and 1930s have a certain old-world charm. Even new houses follow the same pattern. This isn't conscious planning; it is simply that Haridwar is a conservative town and clings to its traditions.

Most of the buildings along the road are *dharamshalas*. The road is shaded by tall old peepul and banyan trees. In some places the trees reach right across the street to touch the roofs of the three-storey buildings on the other side. At several places, I find small peepul saplings growing out of the walls of buildings. One young peepul has sprung up in the fork of an adult kadam tree and will probably throttle it in time. No one fells the sacred peepul. It is better that walls should crumble or kadam trees wither. At least this guarantees the survival of one species of tree in a world where forests are rapidly disappearing.

Peepuls live for hundreds of years, and Haridwar's oldest trees must have been here before the present town reached maturity. Some will be as old as the eleventh-century Maya-devi temple, which is probably the oldest temple in Haridwar. On a sultry day, there can be no pleasanter spot than the shade of a peepul tree; the leaves are perpetually in motion, even when there is no breeze, and spin around in currents of their own making. It is no wonder that the man who plants a peepul is blessed by generations of Hindus to come.

While I stand beneath one of these giant trees, a devout and elderly man approaches with a watering-can and, circling the tree, waters the soil around the base of the trunk. I move out of the way of his sprinkler watching the ritual in some surprise. It has been raining steadily for some days, and the tree should have no need of water.

'Why are you watering it?' I ask.

'Why does one water anything?' asks the old man. 'So that it may grow and flourish, of course.'

'But it's been raining almost every day.'

'Rain is something else,' he says. 'I am not responsible for the rain; this is water from the Ganga, and I have fetched it myself. That makes a lot of difference.'

I cannot argue. He waters the tree with love; and his love for the tree, as much as rainwater or river water, is what makes it flourish.

Leaving the main street, I enter the bazaar.

The Haridwar Bazaar is a long, narrow, winding street, probably the oldest part of the town, and free of all vehicular traffic. The road is no more than four yards wide. The small shops are spilling over with sweets, pickles, bead-necklaces, sacred texts, ritual designs, festival images and pictures of the gods in vibrant technicolour. There is something in these naive, gaudy prints that acts as a transformer, making the more abstract Hindu philosophies comprehensible to anxious farmer or acquisitive taxi driver.

The bazaar winds and turns back upon itself, and eventually I find myself back at the riverfront, gazing out across the river at the forested foothills. Few of the pilgrims on the bathing-steps can realize that sometimes at night a tiger stands on the opposite bank watching the bright illuminations of the temples, or that elephants listen to the rumbling of the trains bringing pilgrims to Haridwar from all parts of India.

It is evening now, and there are fewer people at the ghats. Most of the bathers are family people—farmers and small shopkeepers with their women, children and aged parents. One does not see many students or young people in Western clothes. Haridwar is old- fashioned and so are most of the people who come here.

∽

Charity, too, is old-fashioned, and Haridwar thrives on charity: donations to the temples and alms to the beggars, mendicants and itinerant ash-smeared sadhus. The beggars do not follow one about as in the larger cities. They are confident of receiving coins from the pilgrims who pass by on the steps to the river. They simply sit there, occasionally calling out, but preferring to listen to the music of small coins dropping into brass begging-bowls.

Close by are the money changers, squatting before baskets which are brimming over with small change. In the rest of the country there is a shortage of small coins, and shopkeepers often decline to provide change; but in Haridwar, you can change any number of notes for small coins. You are going to leave all the coins here anyway, when you distribute them along the riverfront.

As the pilgrims leave the ghats, the joy of having accomplished their mission bursts forth in songs of praise: 'Henceforth no more pain, no more sickness; all will be well in future; Ganga-mai ki jai.

More flowers are being sold; and now the leaf-boats are lit by diyas. The little boats are swept away, sometimes travelling a considerable distance before being upset by submerged rocks or inquisitive fish.

I, too, send an offering downstream, but my boat sails beneath the legs of a late bather, and disappears beneath the pilgrim. My boat is lost; but my rose petals still float on the Ganga.

It has been said that if the Ganga ran dry, all life in India would cease. There is no likelihood of that happening. The Ganga is overgenerous as the annual floods will testify. So long as the Himalayas stand, this river will flow to the sea and millions will come to immerse their bodies, their sins and their prayers in its sacred waters.

# Sita and the River

In the middle of the big river, the river that began in the mountains and ended in the sea, was a small island. The river swept round the island, sometimes clawing at its banks, but never going right over it. It had been over twenty years since the river had flooded the island, and at that time no one had lived there. But for the last ten years a small hut had stood there, a mud-walled hut with a sloping thatched roof. The hut had been built into a huge rock, so only three of the walls were mud, and the fourth was rock.

Goats grazed on the short grass which grew on the island, and on the prickly leaves of thorn bushes. A few hens followed them about. There was a melon patch and a vegetable patch.

In the middle of the island stood a peepul tree. It was the only tree there.

Even during the Great Flood, when the island had been under water, the tree had stood firm.

It was an old tree. A seed had been carried to the island by a strong wind some fifty years back, had found shelter between two rocks, had taken root there, and had sprung up to give shade and shelter to a small family. Indians love peepul trees, especially during the hot summer months when the heart-shaped leaves catch the least breath of air and flutter eagerly, fanning those who sit beneath.

A sacred tree, the peepul: the abode of spirits, good and bad.

'Don't yawn when you are sitting beneath the tree,' Grandmother used to warn Sita. 'And if you must yawn, always snap your fingers in front of your mouth. If you forget to do that, a spirit might jump down your throat!'

'And then what will happen?' asked Sita.

'It will probably ruin your digestion,' said Grandfather, who wasn't much of a believer in spirits.

The peepul had a beautiful leaf, and Grandmother likened it to the body of the mighty god Krishna—broad at the shoulders, then tapering down to a very slim waist.

It was an old tree, and an old man sat beneath it.

He was mending a fishing net. He had fished in the river for ten years, and he was a good fisherman. He knew where to find the slim silver Chilwa fish and the big beautiful Mahseer and the long-moustached Singhara; he knew where the river was deep and where it was shallow; he knew which baits to use—which fish liked worms and which liked gram. He had taught his son to fish, but his son had gone to work in a factory in a city, nearly a hundred miles away. He had no grandson; but he had a granddaughter, Sita, and she could do all the things a boy could do, and sometimes she could do them better. She had lost her mother when she was very small. Grandmother had taught her all the things a girl should know, and she could do these as well as most girls. But neither of her grandparents could read or write, and as a result Sita couldn't read or write either.

There was a school in one of the villages across the river, but Sita had never seen it. There was too much to do on the island.

While Grandfather mended his net, Sita was inside the hut, pressing her Grandmother's forehead, which was hot with fever. Grandmother had been ill for three days and could not eat. She had been ill before, but she had never been so bad. Grandfather had brought her some sweet oranges from the market in the nearest town, and she could suck the juice from the oranges, but she couldn't eat anything else.

She was younger than Grandfather, but because she was sick, she looked much older. She had never been very strong.

When Sita noticed that Grandmother had fallen asleep, she tiptoed out of the room on her bare feet and stood outside.

The sky was dark with monsoon clouds. It had rained all night, and in a few hours it would rain again. The monsoon rains had come early, at the end of June. Now it was the middle of July, and already the river was swollen. Its rushing sound seemed nearer and more menacing than usual.

Sita went to her grandfather and sat down beside him beneath the peepul tree.

'When you are hungry, tell me,' she said, 'and I will make the bread.'

'Is your grandmother asleep?'

'She sleeps. But she will wake soon, for she has a deep pain.'

The old man stared out across the river, at the dark green of the forest, at the grey sky, and said, 'Tomorrow, if she is not better, I will take her to the hospital at Shahganj. There they will know how to make her well. You may be on your own for a few days—but you have been on your own before…'

Sita nodded gravely; she had been alone before, even during the rainy season. Now she wanted Grandmother to get well, and she knew that only Grandfather had the skill to take the small dugout boat across the river when the current was so strong. Someone would have to stay behind to look after their few possessions.

Sita was not afraid of being alone, but she did not like the look of the river. That morning, when she had gone down to fetch water, she had noticed that the level had risen. Those rocks which were normally spattered with the droppings of snipe and curlew and other waterbirds had suddenly disappeared.

They disappeared every year—but not so soon, surely?

'Grandfather, if the river rises, what will I do?'

'You will keep to the high ground.'

'And if the water reaches the high ground?'

'Then take the hens into the hut, and stay there.'

'And if the water comes into the hut?'

'Then climb into the peepul tree. It is a strong tree. It will not fall. And the water cannot rise higher than the tree!'

'And the goats, Grandfather?'

'I will be taking them with me, Sita. I may have to sell them to pay for good food and medicines for your grandmother. As for the hens, if it becomes necessary, put them on the roof. But do not worry too much'—and he patted Sita's head—'the water will not rise as high. I will be back soon, remember that.'

'And won't Grandmother come back?'

'Yes, of course, but they may keep her in the hospital for some time.'

∞

Towards evening, it began to rain again—big pellets of rain, scarring the surface of the river. But it was warm rain, and Sita could move about in it. She was not afraid of getting wet, she rather liked it. In the previous month, when the first monsoon shower had arrived, washing the dusty leaves of the tree and bringing up the good smell of the earth, she had exulted in it, had run about shouting for joy. She was used to it now, and indeed a little tired of the rain, but she did not mind getting wet. It was steamy indoors, and her thin dress would soon dry in the heat from the kitchen fire.

She walked about barefooted, barelegged. She was very sure on her feet; her toes had grown accustomed to gripping all kinds of rocks, slippery or sharp. And though thin, she was surprisingly strong.

Black hair, streaming across her face. Black eyes. Slim brown arms. A scar on her thigh—when she was small, visiting her mother's village, a hyaena had entered the house where she was sleeping, fastened on to her leg and tried to drag her away, but her screams had roused the villagers and the hyaena had run off.

She moved about in the pouring rain, chasing the hens into a shelter behind the hut. A harmless brown snake, flooded out of its hole, was moving across the open ground. Sita picked up a stick, scooped the snake up, and dropped it between a cluster of rocks. She had no quarrel with snakes. They kept down the rats and the frogs. She wondered how the rats had first come to the island—probably in someone's boat, or in a sack of grain. Now it was a job to keep their numbers down.

When Sita finally went indoors, she was hungry. She ate some dried peas and warmed up some goat's milk.

Grandmother woke once and asked for water, and Grandfather held the brass tumbler to her lips.

It rained all night.

The roof was leaking, and a small puddle formed on the floor. They kept the kerosene lamp alight. They did not need the light, but somehow it made them feel safer.

The sound of the river had always been with them, although they were seldom aware of it; but that night they noticed a change in its sound. There was something like a moan, like a wind in the tops of tall trees and a swift hiss as the water swept round the rocks and carried away pebbles. And sometimes there was a rumble, as loose earth fell into the water.

Sita could not sleep.

She had a rag doll, made with Grandmother's help out of bits of old clothing. She kept it by her side every night. The doll was someone to talk to, when the nights were long and sleep elusive. Her grandparents were often ready to talk—and Grandmother, when she was well, was a good storyteller—but sometimes Sita wanted to have secrets, and though there were no special secrets in her life, she made up a few, because it was fun to have them. And if you have secrets, you must have a friend to share them with, a companion of one's own age. Since there were no other children on the island, Sita shared her secrets with the rag doll whose name was Mumta.

Grandfather and Grandmother were asleep, though the sound of Grandmother's laboured breathing was almost as persistent as the sound of the river.

'Mumta,' whispered Sita in the dark, starting one of her private conversations. 'Do you think Grandmother will get well again?'

Mumta always answered Sita's questions, even though the answers could only be heard by Sita.

'She is very old,' said Mumta.

'Do you think the river will reach the hut?' asked Sita.

'If it keeps raining like this, and the river keeps rising, it will reach the hut.'

'I am a little afraid of the river, Mumta. Aren't you afraid?'

'Don't be afraid. The river has always been good to us.'

'What will we do if it comes into the hut?'

'We will climb onto the roof.'

'And if it reaches the roof?'

'We will climb the peepul tree. The river has never gone higher than the peepul tree.'

As soon as the first light showed through the little skylight, Sita got up and went outside. It wasn't raining hard, it was drizzling, but it was the sort of drizzle that could continue for days, and it probably meant that heavy rain was falling in the hills where the river originated.

Sita went down to the water's edge. She couldn't find her favourite rock, the one on which she often sat dangling her feet in the water, watching the little Chilwa fish swim by. It was still there, no doubt, but the river had gone over it.

She stood on the sand, and she could feel the water oozing and bubbling beneath her feet.

The river was no longer green and blue and flecked with white, but a muddy colour.

She went back to the hut. Grandfather was up now. He was getting his boat ready.

Sita milked the goat. Perhaps it was the last time she would milk it.

༺༻

The sun was just coming up when Grandfather prepared to push off in the boat. Grandmother lay in the prow. She was staring hard at Sita, trying to speak, but the words would not come. She raised her hand in a blessing.

Sita bent and touched her grandmother's feet, and then Grandfather pushed off. The little boat—with its two old people and three goats—riding swiftly on the river, moved slowly, very slowly, towards the opposite bank. The current was so swift now that Sita realized the boat would be carried about half a mile downstream before Grandfather could get it to dry land.

It bobbed about on the water, getting smaller and smaller, until it was just a speck on the broad river.

And suddenly Sita was alone.

There was a wind, whipping the raindrops against her face; and there was the water, rushing past the island; and there was the distant shore, blurred by rain; and there was the small hut; and there was the tree.

Sita got busy. The hens had to be fed. They weren't bothered about anything except food. Sita threw them handfuls of coarse grain and potato peelings and peanut shells.

Then she took the broom and swept out the hut, lit the charcoal burner, warmed some milk and thought, 'Tomorrow there will be no milk…' She began peeling onions. Soon her eyes started smarting and, pausing for a few moments and glancing round the quiet room, she became aware again that she was alone. Grandfather's hookah pipe stood by itself in one corner. It was a beautiful old hookah, which had belonged to Sita's great-grandfather. The bowl was made out of a coconut encased in silver. The long winding stem was at least four feet in length. It was their most valuable possession. Grandmother's sturdy shisham-wood walking stick stood in another corner.

Sita looked around for Mumta, found the doll beneath the cot, and placed her within sight and hearing.

Thunder rolled down from the hills. BOOM—BOOM—BOOM…

'The gods of the mountains are angry,' said Sita. 'Do you think they are angry with me?'

'Why should they be angry with you?' asked Mumta.

'They don't have to have a reason for being angry. They are

angry with everything, and we are in the middle of everything. We are so small—do you think they know we are here?'

'Who knows what the gods think?'

'But I made you,' said Sita, 'and I know you are here.'

'And will you save me if the river rises?'

'Yes, of course. I won't go anywhere without you, Mumta.'

Sita couldn't stay indoors for long. She went out, taking Mumta with her, and stared out across the river, to the safe land on the other side. But was it safe there? The river looked much wider now. Yes, it had crept over its banks and spread far across the flat plain. Far away, people were driving their cattle through waterlogged, flooded fields, carrying their belongings in bundles on their heads or shoulders, leaving their homes, making for the high land. It wasn't safe anywhere.

She wondered what had happened to Grandfather and Grandmother. If they had reached the shore safely, Grandfather would have to engage a bullock cart, or a pony-drawn carriage, to get Grandmother to the district town, five or six miles away, where there was a market, a court, a jail, a cinema and a hospital.

She wondered if she would ever see Grandmother again. She had done her best to look after the old lady, remembering the times when Grandmother had looked after her, had gently touched her fevered brow and had told her stories—stories about the gods: about the young Krishna, friend of birds and animals, so full of mischief, always causing confusion among the other gods; and Indra, who made the thunder and lightning; and Vishnu, the preserver of all good things, whose steed was a great white bird; and Ganesh, with the elephant's head; and Hanuman, the monkey-god, who helped the young Prince Rama in his war with the King of Ceylon. Would Grandmother return to tell her more about them, or would she have to find out for herself?

The island looked much smaller now. In parts, the mud banks had dissolved quickly, sinking into the river. But in the middle of the island there was rocky ground, and the rocks would never crumble, they could only be submerged. In a space in the middle of the rocks grew the tree.

Sita climbed into the tree to get a better view. She had climbed the tree many times and it took her only a few seconds to reach the higher branches. She put her hand to her eyes to shield them from the rain, and gazed upstream.

There was water everywhere. The world had become one vast river. Even the trees on the forested side of the river looked as though they had grown from the water, like mangroves. The sky was banked with massive, moisture-laden clouds. Thunder rolled down from the hills and the river seemed to take it up with a hollow booming sound.

Something was floating down with the current, something big and bloated. It was closer now, and Sita could make out the bulky object—a drowned buffalo, being carried rapidly downstream.

So the water had already inundated the villages further upstream. Or perhaps the buffalo had been grazing too close to the rising river.

Sita's worst fears were confirmed when, a little later, she saw planks of wood, small trees and bushes, and then a wooden bedstead, floating past the island.

How long would it take for the river to reach her own small hut?

As she climbed down from the tree, it began to rain more heavily. She ran indoors, shooing the hens before her. They flew into the hut and huddled under Grandmother's cot. Sita thought it would be best to keep them together now. And having them with her took away some of the loneliness.

There were three hens and a cock bird. The river did not bother them. They were interested only in food, and Sita kept them happy by throwing them a handful of onion skins.

She would have liked to close the door and shut out the swish of the rain and the boom of the river, but then she would have no way of knowing how fast the water was rising.

She took Mumta in her arms, and began praying for the rain to stop and the river to fall. She prayed to the god Indra, and, just in case he was busy elsewhere, she prayed to other gods too. She prayed for the safety of her grandparents and for her own safety. She put herself last but only with great difficulty.

She would have to make herself a meal. So she chopped up some onions, fried them, then added turmeric and red chilli powder and stirred until she had everything sizzling; then she added a tumbler of water, some salt, and a cup of one of the cheaper lentils. She covered the pot and allowed the mixture to simmer.

Doing this took Sita about ten minutes. It would take at least half an hour for the dish to be ready.

When she looked outside, she saw pools of water among the rocks and near the tree. She couldn't tell if it was rain water or overflow from the river.

She had an idea.

A big tin trunk stood in a corner of the room. It had belonged to Sita's mother. There was nothing in it except a cotton-filled quilt, for use during the cold weather. She would stuff the trunk with everything useful or valuable, and weigh it down so that it wouldn't be carried away, just in case the river came over the island.

Grandfather's hookah went into the trunk. Grandmother's walking stick went in too. So did a number of small tins containing the spices used in cooking—nutmeg, caraway seed, cinnamon, coriander and pepper—a bigger tin of flour and a tin of raw sugar. Even if Sita had to spend several hours in the tree, there would be something to eat when she came down again.

A clean white cotton shirt of Grandfather's, and Grandmother's only spare sari also went into the trunk. Never mind if they got stained with yellow curry powder! Never mind if they got to smell of salted fish, some of that went in too.

Sita was so busy packing the trunk that she paid no attention to the lick of cold water at her heels. She locked the trunk, placed the key high on the rock wall, and turned to give her attention to the lentils. It was only then that she discovered that she was walking about on a watery floor.

She stood still, horrified by what she saw. The water was oozing over the threshold, pushing its way into the room.

Sita was filled with panic. She forgot about her meal and everything else. Darting out of the hut, she ran splashing through ankle-deep water towards the safety of the peepul tree. If the tree hadn't been there, such a well-known landmark, she might have floundered into deep water, into the river.

She climbed swiftly into the strong arms of the tree, made herself secure on a familiar branch, and thrust the wet hair away from her eyes.

∽∞∽

She was glad she had hurried. The hut was now surrounded by water. Only the higher parts of the island could still be seen—a few rocks, the big rock on which the hut was built, a hillock on which some thorny bilberry bushes grew.

The hens hadn't bothered to leave the hut. They were probably perched on the cot now.

Would the river rise still higher? Sita had never seen it like this before. It swirled around her, stretching in all directions.

More drowned cattle came floating down. The most unusual things went by on the water—an aluminium kettle, a cane chair, a tin of tooth powder, an empty cigarette packet, a wooden slipper, a plastic doll…

A doll!

With a sinking feeling, Sita remembered Mumta.

Poor Mumta! She had been left behind in the hut. Sita, in her hurry, had forgotten her only companion.

*Well*, thought Sita, *if I can be careless with someone I've made, how can I expect the gods to notice me, alone in the middle of the river?*

The waters were higher now, the island fast disappearing.

Something came floating out of the hut.

It was an empty kerosene tin, with one of the hens perched on top. The tin came bobbing along on the water, not far from the tree, and was then caught by the current and swept into the river. The hen still managed to keep its perch.

A little later, the water must have reached the cot because the remaining hens flew up to the rock ledge and sat huddled there in the small recess.

The water was rising rapidly now, and all that remained of the island was the big rock that supported the hut, the top of the hut itself and the peepul tree.

It was a tall tree with many branches and it seemed unlikely that the water could ever go right over it. But how long would Sita have to remain there? She climbed a little higher, and as she did so, a jet-black jungle crow settled in the upper branches, and Sita saw that there was a nest in them—a crow's nest, an untidy platform of twigs wedged in the fork of a branch.

In the nest were four blue-green, speckled eggs. The crow sat on them and cawed disconsolately. But though the crow was miserable, its presence brought some cheer to Sita. At least she was not alone. Better to have a crow for company than no one at all.

Other things came floating out of the hut—a large pumpkin; a red turban belonging to Grandfather, unwinding in the water like a long snake; and then—Mumta!

The doll, being filled with straw and wood-shavings, moved quite swiftly on the water and passed close to the peepul tree. Sita saw it and wanted to call out, to urge her friend to make for the tree, but she knew that Mumta could not swim—the doll could only float, travel with the river, and perhaps be washed ashore many miles downstream.

The tree shook in the wind and the rain. The crow cawed and flew up, circled the tree a few times and returned to the nest. Sita clung to her branch.

The tree trembled throughout its tall frame. To Sita it felt like an earthquake tremor; she felt the shudder of the tree in her own bones.

The river swirled all around her now. It was almost up to the roof of the hut. Soon the mud walls would crumble and vanish. Except for the big rock and some trees far, far away, there was only water to be seen.

For a moment or two Sita glimpsed a boat with several people in it moving sluggishly away from the ruins of a flooded village, and she thought she saw someone pointing towards her, but the river swept them on and the boat was lost to view.

The river was very angry; it was like a wild beast, a dragon on the rampage, thundering down from the hills and sweeping across the plain, bringing with it dead animals, uprooted trees, household goods and huge fish choked to death by the swirling mud.

The tall old peepul tree groaned. Its long, winding roots clung tenaciously to the earth from which the tree had sprung many, many years ago. But the earth was softening, the stones were being washed away. The roots of the tree were rapidly losing their hold.

The crow must have known that something was wrong, because it kept flying up and circling the tree, reluctant to settle in it and reluctant to fly away. As long as the nest was there, the crow would remain, flapping about and cawing in alarm.

Sita's wet cotton dress clung to her thin body. The rain ran down from her long black hair. It poured from every leaf of the tree. The crow, too, was drenched and groggy.

The tree groaned and moved again. It had seen many monsoons. Once before, it had stood firm while the river had swirled around its massive trunk. But it had been young then.

Now, old in years and tired of standing still, the tree was ready to join the river.

With a flurry of its beautiful leaves, and a surge of mud from below, the tree left its place in the earth, and, tilting, moved slowly forward, turning a little from side to side, dragging its roots along the ground. To Sita, it seemed as though the river was rising to meet the sky. Then the tree moved into the main current of the river, and went a little faster, swinging Sita from side to side. Her feet were in the water but she clung tenaciously to her branch.

---

The branches swayed, but Sita did not lose her grip. The water was very close now. Sita was frightened. She could not see the extent of the flood or the width of the river. She could only see the immediate danger—the water surrounding the tree.

The crow kept flying around the tree. The bird was in a terrible rage. The nest was still in the branches, but not for long... The tree lurched and twisted slightly to one side, and the nest fell into the water. Sita saw the eggs go one by one.

The crow swooped low over the water, but there was nothing it could do. In a few moments, the nest had disappeared.

The bird followed the tree for about fifty yards, as though hoping that something still remained in the tree. Then, flapping its wings, it rose high into the air and flew across the river until it was out of sight.

Sita was alone once more. But there was no time for feeling lonely. Everything was in motion—up and down and sideways and forwards. *Any moment*, thought Sita, *the tree will turn right over and I'll be in the water!*

She saw a turtle swimming past—a great river turtle, the kind that feeds on decaying flesh. Sita turned her face away. In the distance, she saw a flooded village and people in flat-bottomed boats but they were very far away.

Because of its great size, the tree did not move very swiftly on the river. Sometimes, when it passed into shallow water, it stopped, its roots catching in the rocks; but not for long—the river's momentum soon swept it on.

At one place, where there was a bend in the river, the tree struck a sandbank and was still.

Sita felt very tired. Her arms were aching and she was no longer upright. With the tree almost on its side, she had to cling tightly to her branch to avoid falling off. The grey weeping sky was like a great shifting dome.

## Sita and the River

She knew she could not remain much longer in that position. It might be better to try swimming to some distant rooftop or tree. Then she heard someone calling. Craning her neck to look upriver, she was able to make out a small boat coming directly towards her.

The boat approached the tree. There was a boy in the boat who held on to one of the branches to steady himself, giving his free hand to Sita.

She grasped it, and slipped into the boat beside him.

The boy placed his bare foot against the tree trunk and pushed away.

The little boat moved swiftly down the river. The big tree was left far behind. Sita would never see it again.

---

She lay stretched out in the boat, too frightened to talk. The boy looked at her, but he did not say anything, he did not even smile. He lay on his two small oars, stroking smoothly, rhythmically, trying to keep from going into the middle of the river. He wasn't strong enough to get the boat right out of the swift current, but he kept trying.

A small boat on a big river—a river that had no boundaries but which reached across the plains in all directions. The boat moved swiftly on the wild waters, and Sita's home was left far behind.

The boy wore only a loincloth. A sheathed knife was knotted into his waistband. He was a slim, wiry boy, with a hard flat belly; he had high cheekbones, strong white teeth. He was a little darker than Sita.

'You live on the island,' he said at last, resting on his oars and allowing the boat to drift a little, for he had reached a broader, more placid stretch of the river. 'I have seen you sometimes. But where are the others?'

'My grandmother was sick,' said Sita, 'so Grandfather took her to the hospital in Shahganj.'

'When did they leave?'

'Early this morning.'

Only that morning—and yet it seemed to Sita as though it had been many mornings ago.

'Where have you come from?' she asked. She had never seen the boy before.

'I come from...' he hesitated, '...near the foothills. I was in my boat, trying to get across the river with the news that one of the villages was badly flooded, but the current was too strong. I was swept down past your island. We cannot fight the river, we must go wherever it takes us.'

'You must be tired. Give me the oars.'

'No. There is not much to do now, except keep the boat steady.'

He brought in one oar, and with his free hand he felt under the seat where there was a small basket. He produced two mangoes, and gave one to Sita.

They bit deep into the ripe fleshy mangoes, using their teeth to tear the skin away. The sweet juice trickled down their chins. The flavour of the fruit was heavenly—truly this was the nectar of the gods! Sita hadn't tasted a mango for over a year. For a few moments she forgot about the flood—all that mattered was the mango!

The boat drifted, but not so swiftly now, for as they went further away across the plains, the river lost much of its tremendous force.

'My name is Krishan,' said the boy. 'My father has many

cows and buffaloes, but several have been lost in the flood.'

'I suppose you go to school,' said Sita.

'Yes, I am supposed to go to school. There is one not far from our village. Do you have to go to school?'

'No—there is too much work at home.'

It was no use wishing she was at home—home wouldn't be there any more—but she wished, at that moment, that she had another mango.

Towards evening, the river changed colour. The sun, low in the sky, emerged from behind the clouds, and the river changed slowly from grey to gold, from gold to a deep orange, and then, as the sun went down, all these colours were drowned in the river, and the river took on the colour of the night.

The moon was almost full and Sita could see across the river, to where the trees grew on its banks.

'I will try to reach the trees,' said the boy, Krishan. 'We do not want to spend the night on the water, do we?'

And so he pulled for the trees. After ten minutes of strenuous rowing, he reached a turn in the river and was able to escape the pull of the main current.

Soon they were in a forest, rowing between tall evergreens.

⁂

They moved slowly now, paddling between the trees, and the moon lighted their way, making a crooked silver path over the water.

'We will tie the boat to one of these trees,' said Krishan. 'Then we can rest. Tomorrow we will have to find our way out of the forest.'

He produced a length of rope from the bottom of the boat, tied one end to the boat's stern and threw the other end over a stout branch which hung only a few feet above the water. The boat came to rest against the trunk of the tree.

It was a tall, sturdy toon tree—the Indian mahogany—and it was quite safe, for there was no rush of water here; besides, the trees grew close together, making the earth firm and unyielding.

But the denizens of the forest were on the move. The animals had been flooded out of their holes, caves and lairs, and were looking for shelter and dry ground.

Sita and Krishan had barely finished tying the boat to the tree when they saw a huge python gliding over the water towards them. Sita was afraid that it might try to get into the boat; but it went past them, its head above water, its great awesome length trailing behind, until it was lost in the shadows.

Krishan had more mangoes in the basket, and he and Sita sucked hungrily on them while they sat in the boat.

A big sambur stag came thrashing through the water. He did not have to swim; he was so tall that his head and shoulders remained well above the water. His antlers were big and beautiful.

'There will be other animals,' said Sita. 'Should we climb into the tree?'

'We are quite safe in the boat,' said Krishan. 'The animals are interested only in reaching dry land. They will not even hunt each other. Tonight, the deer are safe from the panther and the tiger. So lie down and sleep, and I will keep watch.'

Sita stretched herself out in the boat and closed her eyes, and the sound of the water lapping against the sides of the boat soon lulled her to sleep. She woke once, when a strange bird called overhead. She raised herself on one elbow, but Krishan was awake, sitting in the prow, and he smiled reassuringly at her. He looked blue in the moonlight, the colour of the young god Krishna, and for a few moments Sita was confused and wondered if the boy was indeed Krishna; but when she thought about it, she decided that it wasn't possible. He was just a village boy and she had seen hundreds like him—well, not exactly like him; he was different, in a way she couldn't explain to herself...

And when she slept again, she dreamt that the boy and Krishna were one, and that she was sitting beside him on a great white bird which flew over mountains, over the snow peaks of the Himalayas, into the cloud-land of the gods. There was a great rumbling sound, as though the gods were angry about the whole thing, and she woke up to this terrible sound and looked about her, and there in the moonlit glade, up to his belly in water, stood a young elephant, his trunk raised as he trumpeted his predicament to the forest—for he was a young elephant, and he was lost, and he was looking for his mother.

He trumpeted again, and then lowered his head and listened. And presently, from far away, came the shrill trumpeting of another elephant. It must have been the young one's mother, because he gave several excited trumpet calls, and then went stamping and churning through the flood water towards a gap in the trees. The boat rocked in the waves made by his passing.

'It's all right now,' said Krishan. 'You can go to sleep again.'

'I don't think I will sleep now,' said Sita.

'Then I will play my flute for you,' said the boy, 'and the time will pass more quickly.'

From the bottom of the boat he took a flute, and putting it to his lips, he began to play. The sweetest music that Sita had ever heard came pouring from the little flute, and it seemed to fill the forest with its beautiful sound. And the music carried her away again, into the land of dreams, and they were riding on the bird once more, Sita and the Blue God, and they were passing through clouds and mist, until suddenly the sun shot out through the clouds. And at the same moment, Sita opened her eyes and saw the sun streaming through the branches of the toon tree, its bright green leaves making a dark pattern against the blinding blue of the sky.

Sita sat up with a start, rocking the boat. There were hardly any clouds left. The trees were drenched with sunshine.

The boy Krishan was fast asleep in the bottom of the boat. His flute lay in the palm of his half-open hand. The sun came slanting across his bare brown legs. A leaf had fallen on his upturned face, but it had not woken him, it lay on his cheek as though it had grown there.

Sita did not move again. She did not want to wake the boy. It didn't look as though the water had gone down, but it hadn't risen, and that meant the flood had spent itself.

The warmth of the sun, as it crept up Krishan's body, woke him at last. He yawned, stretched his limbs, and sat up beside Sita.

'I'm hungry,' he said with a smile.

'So am I,' said Sita.

'The last mangoes,' he said, and emptied the basket of its last two mangoes.

After they had finished the fruit, they sucked the big seeds until these were quite dry. The discarded seeds floated well on the water. Sita had always preferred them to paper boats.

'We had better move on,' said Krishan.

He rowed the boat through the trees, and then for about an hour they were passing through the flooded forest, under the dripping branches of rain-washed trees. Sometimes they had to use the oars to push away vines and creepers. Sometimes drowned bushes hampered them. But they were out of the forest before noon.

Now the water was not very deep and they were gliding over flooded fields. In the distance, they saw a village. It was on high ground. In the old days, people had built their villages on hilltops, which gave them a better defence against bandits and invading armies. This was an old village, and though its inhabitants had long ago exchanged their swords for pruning forks, the hill on which it stood now protected it from the flood.

The people of the village—long-limbed, sturdy Jats—were generous, and gave the stranded children food and shelter. Sita was anxious to find her grandparents, and an old farmer who had business in Shahganj offered to take her there. She was hoping that Krishan would accompany her, but he said he would wait in the village, where he knew others would soon be arriving, his own people among them.

'You will be all right now,' said Krishan. 'Your grandfather will be anxious for you, so it is best that you go to him as soon as you can. And in two or three days, the water will go down and you will be able to return to the island.'

'Perhaps the island is gone forever,' said Sita.

As she climbed into the farmer's bullock cart, Krishan handed her his flute.

'Please keep it for me,' he said. 'I will come for it one day.' And when he saw her hesitate, he added, his eyes twinkling, 'It is a good flute!'

It was slow going in the bullock cart. The road was awash, the wheels got stuck in the mud, and the farmer, his grown son and Sita had to keep getting down to heave and push in order to free the big wooden wheels. They were still in a foot or two of water. The bullocks were bespattered with mud, and Sita's legs were caked with it.

They were a day and a night in the bullock cart before they reached Shahganj; by that time, Sita, walking down the narrow bazaar of the busy market town, was hardly recognizable.

Grandfather did not recognize her. He was walking stiffly down the road, looking straight ahead of him, and would have walked right past the dusty, dishevelled girl if she had not charged straight at his thin, shaky legs and clasped him around the waist.

'Sita!' he cried, when he had recovered his wind and his balance. 'But how are you here? How did you get off the island? I was so worried—it has been very bad these last two days…'

'Is Grandmother all right?' asked Sita.

But even as she spoke, she knew that Grandmother was no longer with them. The dazed look in the old man's eyes told her as much. She wanted to cry, not for Grandmother, who could suffer no more, but for Grandfather, who looked so helpless and bewildered; she did not want him to be unhappy. She forced back her tears, took his gnarled and trembling hand, and led him down the crowded street. And she knew, then, that it would be on her shoulder that Grandfather would have to lean in the years to come.

They returned to the island after a few days, when the river was no longer in spate. There was more rain, but the worst was over. Grandfather still had two of the goats; it had not been necessary to sell more than one.

He could hardly believe his eyes when he saw that the tree had disappeared from the island—the tree that had seemed as permanent as the island, as much a part of his life as the river itself. He marvelled at Sita's escape. 'It was the tree that saved you,' he said.

'And the boy,' said Sita.

'Yes, and the boy.'

She thought about the boy, and wondered if she would ever see him again. But she did not think too much, because there was so much to do.

For three nights they slept under a crude shelter made out of jute bags. During the day, she helped Grandfather rebuild the mud hut. Once again, they used the big rock as a support.

The trunk which Sita had packed so carefully had not been swept off the island, but the water had got into it, and the food and clothing had been spoilt. But Grandfather's hookah had been saved, and, in the evenings, after their work was done and they had eaten the light meal which Sita prepared, he would smoke with a little of his old contentment, and tell Sita about other floods and storms which he had experienced as a boy.

Sita planted a mango seed in the same spot where the peepul tree had stood. It would be many years before it grew into a big tree, but Sita liked to imagine sitting in its branches one day, picking the mangoes straight from the tree, and feasting on them all day. Grandfather was more particular about making a vegetable garden and putting down peas, carrots, gram and mustard.

One day, when most of the hard work had been done and the new hut was almost ready, Sita took the flute which had been given to her by the boy, and walked down to the water's edge and tried to play it. But all she could produce were a few broken notes, and even the goats paid no attention to her music.

Sometimes, Sita thought she saw a boat coming down the river and she would run to meet it; but usually there was no boat, or if there was, it belonged to a stranger or to another fisherman. And so she stopped looking out for boats. Sometimes she thought she heard the music of a flute, but it seemed very distant and she could never tell where the music came from.

Slowly, the rains came to an end. The flood waters had receded, and in the villages people began to till the land again and sow crops for the winter months. There were cattle fairs and wrestling matches. The days were warm and sultry. The water in the river was no longer muddy, and one evening Grandfather brought home a huge Mahseer fish and Sita made it into a delicious curry.

---

Grandfather sat outside the hut, smoking his hookah. Sita was at the far end of the island, spreading clothes on the rocks to dry. One of the goats had followed her. It was the friendlier of the two, and often followed Sita about the island. She had made it a necklace of coloured beads.

She sat down on a smooth rock, and, as she did so, she noticed a small bright object in the sand near her feet. She stooped and picked it up. It was a little wooden toy—a coloured peacock—that must have come down on the river and been swept ashore on the island. Some of the paint had rubbed off, but for Sita, who had no toys, it was a great find. Perhaps it would speak to her, as Mumta had spoken to her.

As she held the toy peacock in the palm of her hand, she thought she heard the flute music again, but she did not look up. She had heard it before, and she was sure that it was all in her mind.

But this time the music sounded nearer, much nearer. There was a soft footfall in the sand. And, looking up, she saw the boy, Krishan, standing over her.

'I thought you would never come,' said Sita.

'I had to wait until the rains were over. Now that I am free, I will come more often. Did you keep my flute?'

'Yes, but I cannot play it properly. Sometimes it plays by itself, I think, but it will not play for me!'

'I will teach you how to play it,' said Krishan.

He sat down beside her, and they cooled their feet in the water, which was clear now, reflecting the blue of the sky. You could see the sand and the pebbles of the riverbed.

'Sometimes the river is angry, and sometimes it is kind,' said Sita.

'We are part of the river,' said the boy. 'We cannot live without it.'

It was a good river, deep and strong, beginning in the mountains and ending in the sea. Along its banks, for hundreds of miles, lived millions of people, and Sita was only one small girl among them, and no one had ever heard of her, no one knew her—except for the old man, the boy, and the river.

# TREES OF INDIA

# My Trees in Himalayas

Living in a cottage at 7,000 feet in the Garhwal Himalayas, I am fortunate to have a big window that opens out on the forest so that the trees are almost within my reach. If I jumped, I could land quite neatly in the arms of an oak or horse chestnut. I have never made that leap, but the big langurs—silver-gray monkeys with long, swishing tails—often spring from the trees onto my corrugated tin roof, making enough noise to frighten all the birds away.

Standing on its own outside my window is a walnut tree, and truly this is a tree for all seasons. In winter the branches are bare, but beautifully smooth and rounded. In spring each limb produces a bright green spear of new growth, and by midsummer the entire tree is in leaf. Toward the end of the monsoon the walnuts, encased in their green jackets, have reached maturity. When the jackets begin to split, you can see the hard brown shells of the nuts, and inside each shell is the delicious meat itself.

Every year this tree gives me a basket of walnuts. But last year the nuts were disappearing one by one, and I was at a loss as to who had been taking them. Could it have been the milkman's small son? He was an inveterate tree climber, but he was usually to be found on the oak trees, gathering fodder for his herd. He admitted that his cows had enjoyed my dahlias, which they had eaten the previous week, but he stoutly denied having fed them walnuts.

It wasn't the woodpecker either. He was out there every day, knocking furiously against the bark of the tree, trying to pry an insect out of a narrow crack, but he was strictly non-vegetarian. As for the langurs, they ate my geraniums but did not care for the walnuts.

The nuts seemed to disappear early in the morning while I was still in bed, so one day I surprised everyone, including myself by getting up before sunrise. I was just in time to catch the culprit climbing out of the walnut tree. She was an old woman who sometimes came to cut grass on the hillside. Her face was as wrinkled as the walnuts she so fancied, but her arms and legs were very sturdy.

'And how many walnuts did you gather today, Grandmother?' I asked.

'Just two,' she said with a giggle, offering them to me on her open palm. I accepted one, and thus encouraged, she climbed higher into the tree and helped herself to the remaining nuts. It was impossible for me to object. I was taken with admiration for her agility. She must have been twice my age, but I knew I could never get up that tree. To the victor, the spoils!

Unlike the prized walnuts, the horse chestnuts are inedible. Even the rhesus monkeys throw them away in disgust. But the tree itself is a friendly one, especially in summer when it is in full leaf. The lightest breeze makes the leaves break into conversation, and their rustle is a cheerful sound. The spring flowers of the horse chestnut look like candelabra, and when the blossoms fall, they carpet the hillside with their pale pink petals.

It stands erect and dignified and does not bend with the wind. In spring the new leaves, or needles, are a tender green, while during the monsoon the tiny young cones spread like blossoms in the dark green folds of the branches. The deodar enjoys the company of its own kind: where one deodar grows, there will be others. A walk in a deodar forest is awe-inspiring—surrounded on all sides by these great sentinels of the mountains, you feel as though the trees themselves are on the march.

I walk among the trees outside my window often, acknowledging their presence with a touch of my hand against their trunks. The oak has been there the longest, and the wind has bent its upper branches and twisted a few so that it looks shaggy and undistinguished. But it is a good tree for the privacy of birds. Sometimes it seems completely uninhabited until there is a whining sound, as of a helicopter approaching, and a party of long-tailed blue magpies flies across the forest glade.

Most of the pines near my home are on the next hillside. But there is a small Himalayan blue one a little way below the cottage, and sometimes I sit beneath it to listen to the wind playing softly in its branches.

When I open the window at night, there is almost always something to listen to—the mellow whistle of a pygmy owlet, or the sharp cry of a barking deer. Sometimes, if I am lucky, I will see the moon coming up over the next mountain, and two distant deodars in perfect silhouette.

Some night sounds outside my window remain strange and mysterious. Perhaps they are the sounds of the trees themselves, stretching their limbs in the dark, shifting a little, flexing their fingers, whispering to one another. These great trees of the mountains, I feel they know me well, as I watch them and listen to their secrets, happy to rest my head beneath their outstretched arms.

# Gentle Shade by Day

Those who have spent time in non-air-conditioned parts of India will remember with gratitude those gracious trees that provide shade and shelter during the summer months—the banyan, peepul, mango, neem and others. Coastal dwellers are not so fortunate for there is not much shade to be had from a palm tree unless you keep moving in its long but insubstantial shadow.

I am not surprised that the sages of old were given to sitting beneath the peepul tree. They might have had various religious reasons for calling it sacred but I am sure there was a good practical reason as well. Few trees provide a cooler shade than it does. Even on the stillest of days, the peepul leaves are forever twirling and with thousands of leaves spinning like tops, there is quite a breeze for anyone sitting below.

However, there are warnings about peepul trees—'Gentle shade by day and terror by night!' During the night the tree is said to be alive with various spirits, most of them inimical to man. One is advised not to sleep beneath it for this is construed by a ghost as an invitation to jump down your throat and take possession of you, or at the very least ruin your digestion.

It is also said to be unlucky to sleep beneath a tamarind, but I have often reclined in the pleasant shade of this noble tree and have come to no harm. A famous tamarind stands over the tomb of Tansen, the great musician and singer of Akbar's court at Gwalior. Its leaves, though bitter, are eaten by singers to improve their voices.

A mango grove is a wonderful place for an afternoon siesta. But if the mangoes are ripening, there is usually a great deal of activity going on with parrots, crows, monkeys and small boys, all attempting to evade the watchman who uses an empty kerosene tin as a drum to try and frighten them away. So it's not the ideal place for a nap then, but the shade under a mango grove is dark, deep and very soothing.

The banyan tree with its aerial roots represents the matted hair of Lord Shiva. There is always shade and space beneath a venerable old banyan. It is still a popular community centre in our Indian villages but is becoming a rarity in cities simply because it covers so large an area. And if you cut its aerial roots the tree topples over. Other handsome trees related to the banyan are the pilkhan and the chilkhan, large spreading evergreens, both quite noticeable on some of New Delhi's wider avenues.

The neem is a tall tree, but its numerous branches give it a shady head. One of my greatest pleasures is to walk beneath an avenue of neem trees after a shower of rain. As the fallen berries are crushed underfoot they give out a sharp heady fragrance, which I find exhilarating. Apart from its medicinal uses, the tree is connected in legends with the Sun God as in the story of Neembarak. 'The Sun in a Neem Tree' who invited to dinner a Bairagi tribal whose rules forbade him to eat anything except by daylight. When dinner was delayed after sundown, Suraj Narayan, the Sun God, obligingly descended from a neem tree and continued shining till dinner was over.

On this pleasant note I end this tribute, only adding that shade-giving trees symbolize the harmony between man and nature and that our ancestors in their devotion to trees and reverence for them, clearly showed that they knew what was good for them.

# Music in the Trees

In India, the monsoon is the season when our insect orchestra is at its best. It is true that the shrill music of the cicada is heard throughout the hot weather; but theirs is a prelude to the great concert that comes into full play once the rainy season begins. When the monsoon with its magic touch brings life and greenness to rock and earth and tree, the whole air seems to come alive with the music of insects. Grasshoppers shrill in the bushes, crickets chirp from under stones, and in the water-laden fields there are hundreds of minor artists providing a medley of sounds.

Among our more vocal and better-known insect musicians are those that dwell in trees, the cicadas and the crickets. As musicians, the cicadas are in a class by themselves. Most of the species in India are forest dwellers, but there are some who inhabit the open country in the plains. All through the hot weather their chorus rings through the jungle, while a shower of rain, far from damping their spirits, only rouses them to a deafening, combined effort. The ancient Greeks knew the cicada well. They appreciated his music so much that they kept him captive in a cage to sing. Only the males were chosen, for the females, like most insect musicians, were completely dumb. This moved one of the Greek poets to exclaim, 'Happy are the cicadas, for they have voiceless wives.'

The cicada's sound-producing organs are among the most remarkable in the animal kingdom. The underside of his body carries a pair of flaps, each of which covers an oval membrane, which looks like the head of a drum. These are set into motion by a great pair of muscles attached to them from within the body, and the sound is produced by their vibration. The whole abdomen, which is practically hollow, helps to increase or diminish the sound.

Simple, isn't it? To be truthful, I find it extremely complicated, and am able to describe the process only by consulting the notes of S.H. Prater, one-time curator of the Bombay Natural History Society.

Let it be added that the female carries these structures in a modified form, but as she has no muscles to bring them into play, she is unable to use them. This is why she must remain silent while her spouse shrieks away. I would change the line from that Greek poet (Xenarchos, I think) and say instead: 'Pity the female cicadas, for they have singing husbands!'

The object of the cicadas' mirthful music is a mystery. It may attract the opposite sex, or it may be just a diversion of the male. Or perhaps he sings because he is happy.

The tree crickets are a band of willing artists who commence their performance as soon as it is dusk. Their sounds are familiar, but the crickets are seldom seen. If one of them enters the house and treats us to a solo, the sound is so surprisingly loud that we can hardly believe it is being produced by so small a creature.

The common Indian tree cricket is a delicate pale-green little creature with hazy, transparent green wings. In full song he holds his wings outspread over his back. They vibrate so rapidly that they are but a blurred outline. A tap on the bush or leaf on which he sits will put an immediate stop to his performance.

His music ceases, and he lowers his wings and folds them flat on his back. The grasshopper makes his music by rubbing his legs against his forewing.

I won't go into detail over how the cricket produces its music, except to say that its louder notes are produced by a rapid vibration of the wings, the right wing usually working over the left, and the edge of one acting on the file of the other to produce a shrill, long-sustained note.

One of the best-known crickets is a large black fellow who lives underground and rarely comes out by day, except when the rains flood him out of his burrow. But when night falls, he sits on his doorstep and pours out his soul in a strident song. This cricket's name is as impressive as his sound—*Brachytrypes portentosus.*

The mole cricket is a genius by itself. Mole crickets are tillers of the soil. They use their powerful forelimbs for shovelling up the earth and their hard heads for butting into it. Notwithstanding its earthy occupations, the mole cricket is sometimes moved to creating music. But as he repeats his note—a solemn deep-toned chirp, about a hundred times a minute—the performance can be monotonous.

In India, the cone-headed katydids are probably the most notable performers. Katydids are trim, slender grasshopper-like insects, much in evidence in the fresh green grass of the monsoon. In the fields, the loud, shrill notes of the males may be heard both by day and by night. Sometimes one of them comes into a house and treats its occupants to a sudden outburst of high-pitched fiddling. His song rises in pitch as the performer warms to his work. In a room it can be quite deafening, and the sound is always difficult to locate—it seems to come from everywhere.

Finally we come to the tree crickets, a band of willing artistes who commence their performance at dusk. Their sounds are familiar, but it is difficult to see the musicians. Presumably the males sing in order to attract their more silent females. The music advertises the presence of the male; just as in other creatures, it is the colour or smell that does the job. And if music be the food of love, play on, cicada!

Why are grasshoppers and crickets such persistent little singers? Do they really sing to charm and attract the females, or is their song the voice of mirth? A curious habit has been noticed among certain tree crickets, which may offer a clue to the mystery. Sometimes, as a male sings, a female steals up to him from behind. The male ceases his music. He sits quite still with his wings uplifted. The female noses about his back and soon discovers the object of her search—a deep cavity situated just behind the base of his wings. This cavity contains a clear liquid which she eagerly laps up. Well, even the human male seeks to please his sweetheart with the offer of chocolates.

It is supposed that in this instance, the lady is attracted rather by the sweets the male has to offer than by his music. But the music advertises his whereabouts. She hears his sound and knows that he has a sweet nectar to offer her and comes after it. If the artful luring of the male sometimes results in mating, we see the real reason for the male possessing his musical instruments, and understand his urge to play them so continuously. After all, the luring of the female with music and sweets is even practised by human beings. It may not always succeed in its purpose. Sometimes, as with the crickets, the female accepts the gifts so generously offered—and then takes her leave!

# The Cherry Tree

One day, when Rakesh was six, he walked home from the Mussoorie Bazaar eating cherries. They were a little sweet, a little sour; small, bright red cherries, which had come all the way from the Kashmir Valley.

Here in the Himalayan foothills where Rakesh lived, there were not many fruit trees. The soil was stony and the dry cold winds stunted the growth of most plants. But on the more sheltered slopes there were forests of oak and deodar.

Rakesh lived with his grandfather on the outskirts of Mussoorie, just where the forest began. His father and mother lived in a small village fifty miles away, where they grew maize and rice and barley in narrow terraced fields on the lower slopes of the mountain. But there were no schools in the village and Rakesh's parents were keen that he should go to school. As soon as he was of school-going age, they sent him to stay with his grandfather in Mussoorie.

Grandfather was a retired forest ranger. He had a little cottage outside the town.

Rakesh was on his way home from school when he bought the cherries. He paid fifty paise for the bunch. It took him about half an hour to walk home, and by the time he reached the cottage, there were only three cherries left.

'Have a cherry, Grandfather,' he said, as soon as he saw his grandfather in the garden.

Grandfather took one cherry and Rakesh promptly ate the other two. He kept the last seed in his mouth for some time, rolling it round and round on his tongue until all the tang had gone. Then he placed the seed on the palm of his hand and studied it.

'Are cherry seeds lucky?' asked Rakesh.

'Of course.'

'Then I'll keep it.'

'Nothing is lucky if you put it away. If you want luck, you must put it to some use.'

'What can I do with a seed?'

'Plant it.'

So Rakesh found a small space and began to dig up a flower bed.

'Hey, not there,' said Grandfather, 'I've sown mustard in that bed. Plant it in that shady corner, where it won't be disturbed.'

Rakesh went to a corner of the garden where the earth was soft and yielding. He did not have to dig. He pressed the seed into the soil with his thumb and it went right in.

Then he had his lunch and ran off to play cricket with his friends, and forgot all about the cherry seed.

When it was winter in the hills, a cold wind blew down from the snows and went whoo-whoo-whoo in the deodar trees and the garden was dry and bare. In the evenings Grandfather and Rakesh sat around a charcoal fire and Grandfather told Rakesh stories—stories about people who turned into animals and ghosts who lived in trees and beans that jumped and stones that wept—and in turn Rakesh would read to him from the newspaper, Grandfather's eyesight being rather weak. Rakesh found the newspaper very dull—especially after the stories—but Grandfather wanted all the news...

They knew it was spring when the wild duck flew north

again, to Siberia. Early in the morning, when he got up to chop wood and light a fire, Rakesh saw the V-shaped formation streaming northward, the calls of the birds carrying clearly through the thin mountain air.

One morning in the garden he bent to pick up what he thought was a small twig and found to his surprise that it was well rooted. He stared at it for a moment, then ran to fetch Grandfather, calling, 'Dada, come and look, the cherry tree has come up!'

'What cherry tree?' asked Grandfather, who had forgotten about it. 'The seed we planted last year—look, it's come up!'

Rakesh went down on his haunches, while Grandfather bent almost double and peered down at the tiny tree. It was about four inches high.

'Yes, it's a cherry tree,' said Grandfather. 'You should water it now and then.'

Rakesh ran indoors and came back with a bucket of water.

'Don't drown it!' said Grandfather.

Rakesh gave it a sprinkling and circled it with pebbles.

'What are the pebbles for?' asked Grandfather.

'For privacy,' said Rakesh.

He looked at the tree every morning but it did not seem to be growing very fast, so he stopped looking at it except quickly, out of the corner of his eye. And, after a week or two, when he allowed himself to look at it properly, he found that it had grown—at least an inch!

That year the monsoon rains came early and Rakesh plodded to and from school in raincoat and gumboots. Ferns sprang from the trunks of trees, strange-looking lilies came up in the long grass and even when it wasn't raining the trees dripped and mist came curling up the valley. The cherry tree grew quickly in this season.

It was about two feet high when a goat entered the garden and ate all the leaves. Only the main stem and two thin branches remained.

'Never mind,' said Grandfather, seeing that Rakesh was upset. 'It will grow again, cherry trees are tough.'

Towards the end of the rainy season new leaves appeared on the tree. Then a woman cutting grass scrambled down the hillside, her scythe swishing through the heavy monsoon foliage. She did not try to avoid the tree: one sweep, and the cherry tree was cut in two.

When Grandfather saw what had happened, he went after the woman and scolded her; but the damage could not be repaired.

'Maybe it will die now,' said Rakesh.

'Maybe,' said Grandfather.

But the cherry tree had no intention of dying.

By the time summer came round again, it had sent out several new shoots with tender green leaves. Rakesh had grown taller too. He was eight now, a sturdy boy with curly black hair and deep black eyes. 'Blackberry eyes,' Grandfather called them.

That monsoon Rakesh went home to his village, to help his father and mother with the planting and ploughing and sowing. He was thinner but stronger when he came back to Grandfather's house at the end of the rains to find that the cherry tree had grown another foot. It was now up to his chest.

Even when there was rain, Rakesh would sometimes water the tree. He wanted it to know that he was there.

One day he found a bright green praying mantis perched on a branch, peering at him with bulging eyes. Rakesh let it remain there; it was the cherry tree's first visitor.

The next visitor was a hairy caterpillar, who started making a meal of the leaves. Rakesh removed it quickly and dropped it on a heap of dry leaves.

'Come back when you're a butterfly,' he said.

Winter came early. The cherry tree bent low with the weight of snow. Field mice sought shelter in the roof of the cottage. The road from the valley was blocked and for several days there was no newspaper and this made Grandfather quite grumpy. His stories began to have unhappy endings.

In February it was Rakesh's birthday. He was nine—and the tree was four, but almost as tall as Rakesh.

One morning, when the sun came out, Grandfather came into the garden, 'to let some warmth get into my bones,' as he put it. He stopped in front of the cherry tree, stared at it for a few moments and then called out, 'Rakesh! Come and look! Come quickly before it falls!'

Rakesh and Grandfather gazed at the tree as though it had performed a miracle. There was a pale pink blossom at the end of a branch.

The following year there were more blossoms. And suddenly the tree was taller than Rakesh, even though it was less than half his age. And then it was taller than Grandfather, who was older than some of the oak trees.

But Rakesh had grown too. He could run and jump and climb trees as well as most boys, and he read a lot of books, although he still liked listening to Grandfather's tales.

In the cherry tree, bees came to feed on the nectar in the blossoms and tiny birds pecked at the blossoms and broke them off. But the tree kept blossoming right through the spring and there were always more blossoms than birds.

That summer there were small cherries on the tree. Rakesh tasted one and spat it out.

'It's too sour,' he said.

'They'll be better next year,' said Grandfather.

But the birds liked them—especially the bigger birds, such as the bulbuls and scarlet minivets—and they flitted in and out of the foliage, feasting on the cherries.

On a warm sunny afternoon, when even the bees looked sleepy, Rakesh was looking for Grandfather without finding him in any of his favourite places around the house. Then he looked out of the bedroom window and saw Grandfather reclining on a cane chair under the cherry tree.

'There's just the right amount of shade here,' said Grandfather. 'And I like looking at the leaves.'

'They're pretty leaves,' said Rakesh. 'And they are always ready to dance if there's a breeze.'

After Grandfather had come indoors, Rakesh went into the garden and lay down on the grass beneath the tree. He gazed up through the leaves at the great blue sky; and turning on his side, he could see the mountains striding away into the clouds. He was still lying beneath the tree when the evening shadows crept across the garden. Grandfather came back and sat down beside Rakesh, and they waited in silence until the stars came out and the nightjar began to call. In the forest below, the crickets and cicadas began tuning up; and suddenly the trees were full of the sound of insects.

'There are so many trees in the forest,' said Rakesh, 'What's so special about this tree? Why do we like it so much?'

'We planted it ourselves,' said Grandfather. 'That's why it's special.'

'Just one small seed,' said Rakesh, and he touched the smooth bark of the tree that he had grown. He ran his hand along the trunk of the tree and put his finger to the tip of a leaf. 'I wonder,' he whispered. 'Is this what it feels to be God?'

# Death of the Trees

The peace and quiet of the Maplewood hillside disappeared forever one winter. The powers that be decided to build another new road into the mountains, and the PWD saw fit to take it right past the cottage, about six feet from the large window which had overlooked the forest.

In my journal I wrote:

Already they have felled most of the trees. The walnut was one of the first to go. A tree I had lived with for over ten years, watching it grow just as I had watched Prem's little son, Rakesh, grow up... Looking forward to its new leafbuds, the broad, green leaves of summer turning to spears of gold in September when the walnuts were ripe and ready to fall. I knew this tree better than the others. It was just below the window, where a buttress for the road is going up.

Another tree I'll miss is the young deodar, the only one growing in this stretch of the woods. Some years back it was stunted from lack of sunlight. The oaks covered it with their shaggy branches. So I cut away some of the overhanging branches and after that the deodar grew much faster. It was just coming into its own this year; now cut down in its prime like my young brother on the road to Delhi last month: both victims of the roads; the tree killed by the PWD, my brother by a truck.

Twenty oaks have been felled. Just in this small stretch

near the cottage. By the time this bypass reaches Jabarkhet, about six miles from here, over a thousand oaks will have been slaughtered, besides many other fine trees—maples, deodars and pines—most of them unnecessarily, as they grow some fifty to sixty yards from the roadside.

The trouble is, hardly anyone (with the exception of the contractor who buys the felled trees) really believes that trees and shrubs are necessary. They get in the way so much, don't they? According to my milkman, the only useful tree is one which can be picked clean of its leaves for fodder! And a young man remarked to me: 'You should come to Pauri. The view is terrific, there are no trees in the way!'

Well, he can stay here now, and enjoy the view of the ravaged hillside. But as the oaks have gone, the milkman will have to look further afield for his fodder.

Rakesh calls the maples the butterfly trees because when the winged seeds fall they flutter like butterflies in the breeze. No maples now. No bright red leaves to flame against the sky. No birds!

That is to say, no birds near the house. No longer will it be possible for me to open the window and watch the scarlet minivets flitting through the dark green foliage of the oaks; the long-tailed magpies gliding through the trees; the barbet calling insistently from his perch on top of the deodar. Forest birds, all of them, they will now be in search of some other stretch of surviving forest. The only visitors will be the crows, who have learnt to live with, and off, humans and seem to multiply along with roads, houses and people. And even when all the people have gone, the crows will still be around.

Other things to look forward to: trucks thundering past in the night; perhaps a tea and pakora shop round the corner; the grinding of gears, the music of motor horns. Will the whistling thrush be heard above them? The explosions that continually shatter the silence of the mountains—as thousand-year-old rocks are dynamited—have frightened away all but the most intrepid of birds and animals. Even the bold langurs haven't shown their faces for over a fortnight.

Somehow, I don't think we shall wait for the tea shop to arrive. There must be some other quiet corner, possibly on the next mountain, where new roads have yet to come into being. No doubt this is a negative attitude, and if I had any sense I'd open my own tea shop. To retreat is to be a loser. But the trees are losers too; and when they fall, they do so with a certain dignity. Never mind. Men come and go; the mountains remain.